My Darling Detective

BOOKS BY HOWARD NORMAN

The Northern Lights

The Chauffeur

The Bird Artist

The Museum Guard

The Haunting of L.

My Famous Evening

In Fond Remembrance of Me

Devotion

What Is Left the Daughter

I Hate to Leave This Beautiful Place

Next Life Might Be Kinder

My Darling Detective

My Darling Detective

HOWARD NORMAN

HOUGHTON MIFFLIN HARCOURT
Boston   New York   2017

Library of Congress Cataloging-in-Publication Data is available.
ISBN 978-0-544-23610-3

Book design by Kelly Dubeau Smydra

Printed in the United States of America
DOC 10 9 8 7 6 5 4 3 2 1

To Emma

Things keep their secrets.

— HERACLITUS

My Darling Detective

Interlocutrix

THE AUCTION WAS HELD AT 5 P.M. IN THE STREET-LEVEL drawing room of the Lord Nelson Hotel, here in Halifax. *Death on a Leipzig Balcony,* by Robert Capa, was the first item on the docket. The auctioneer had just said, "... taken on April 18, 1945," when my mother, Nora Ives — married name, Nora Ives Rigolet — walked almost casually up the center aisle and flung an open jar of black ink at the photograph. I heard, "No, it can't be you!" But it was my own voice, already trying to refute the incident. My mother was tackled to the floor by the auctioneer's assistant. An octopus of ink sent tentacles down the glass. My mother was lifted roughly to her feet by two security guards and escorted from the room. And here I thought she was safely tucked away in Nova Scotia Rest Hospital, across the harbor in Dartmouth, room 340.

I had been at the hotel to bid on *Forest of Fontainbleau,* an 1863 landscape by Eugène Cuvelier, the tenth photograph on the docket. Of course I lost out on that. Because immediately I went to the police station on Gottingen Street. There, through the one-way window, I witnessed my mother's interrogation at the hands of my fiancée, Martha Crauchet. "We get the *Chronicle-Herald* in the common room, interlocutrix," my mother said to Martha. I saw Martha jot down a word on her legal pad; I assumed it was "interlocutrix." "Last week, Tuesday's edition, maybe it was Wednesday's, there was a notice of the auction. Right then I put my thinking cap on." My mother fit on an invisible cap, like screwing in a lightbulb. "I decided it was best to leave during tea. You must understand, interlocutrix, that the hospital staff is always distracted during tea. I filched money from the attendant's station. A little tin box they keep there. Then I slipped out the food service door. Free as a bird."

"Then what — you made your way down to the wharf, right?" Martha said.

"I had on my good overcoat," my mother said. "Not to worry I'd catch a cold."

"And of course you now had pocket money for the ferry."

"Once I arrived Halifax-side, I made my way to the Lord Nelson and sat down in the room where the auction was held. Have you ever been to the Lord Nelson, interlocutrix?"

"I have. Yes."

"A very nice hotel, don't you think? I sat there just as I pleased. Just like that. It was all quite exciting. I had my little jar of ink in my coat pocket. From Arts and Crafts."

— TRANSCRIPT, MARCH 19, 1977, HALIFAX REGIONAL POLICE

The interrogation ended around 7 p.m. Before a police officer accompanied her on the return ferry to Dartmouth and then to Nova Scotia Rest Hospital, I watched my mother, still in the interrogation room, make a drawing of Halifax Harbor for Martha. She drew it on a napkin. My mother had been given cups of coffee and a scone to tide her over. She signed the drawing, and in addition wrote, "Thank you for the warmest conversation I've had in possibly three years. Let's please stay in touch."

I lived in the cottage out back of 112 Spring Garden Road, a big Victorian house owned by Mrs. Esther Hamelin, my employer. The other person who lived on the property was a Mrs. Brevittmore (whose position was referred to as the "all-purpose"), who occupied a large, sunny room toward the rear of the house, overlooking the spacious, manicured lawn and garden. Mrs. Hamelin had turned seventy on March first. As she put it, "I was born into money. It was from the fisheries."

Mrs. Hamelin's photographic collection was mostly on the walls of the master bedroom, down the hall from the library, and two guest rooms on the third floor had some photographs on their walls. Also, there were fifteen late-nineteenth-century French photographs in the library. In my time working for Mrs. Hamelin, I knew her to have plenty of people in for tea. Plenty of professors of art from far-flung places. Plenty of dinner parties, but no overnight guests. Depends, of course, on what one means by overnight guest. Because one morning at about 4:30 I did notice Mrs. Brevittmore leave Mrs. Hamelin's bedroom, carrying a tray with teacups and saucers and a teapot on it. I had been an insomniac in the library, studying up on *Avignon Pont St. Bénezet,* 1861, by Édouard Baldus, which I was to bid on in London a week later. (I lost out on it seconds before the final gavel.) It depicted wooden boats along a riverbank, an unfinished stone bridge, quiet waters. Anyway, I heard a rustle in the hallway, looked up, and saw Mrs. Brevittmore closing Mrs. Hamelin's bedroom door. When I mentioned this to Martha, she said, "Well, either they'd just had a rendezvous or they didn't. Either/or, it's none of your business. Love is difficult enough to find in the world, isn't it, and judgments don't have a place here. You're either happy for someone or you're not. I'm happy for them. If you aren't, then I'm not happy with you. Like my mother put it, 'Some things say a lot, even if you can't pronounce all the words.' Then again, my mother read a lot of Victorian novels."

"Okay, fine, but by 'rendezvous' you mean —"

"Use your imagination, Jacob. It's the one thing left you when someone's door is closed. I want to meet those two. Please introduce me to them soon. It's just not right that I haven't met them yet."

"Mrs. Hamelin wants to meet you too," I said. "She told me she's looking at her calendar for when."

"She's been looking at it a long time," Martha said. "But I refuse to get grumpy about it. I just won't. Things happen when they're meant to, mostly. But you have told her we're serious, haven't you?"

"Yes, I have," I said. "I most definitely have."

My employment had originally been listed in the *Chronicle-Herald:* "Wanted: Live-in assistant. Must have special interest in travel. Interviews by appointment." During my interview, Mrs. Hamelin asked how much education I'd had. I told her one year at Dalhousie University. She asked why I had dropped out. I told her I couldn't afford the tuition. "Oh, I see," she said, adding, "even though I've heard it's modest for residents of Nova Scotia." She asked my age. I told her I was twenty-nine. She asked how I'd been supporting myself, and I said, "Receiving and sorting stock at John W. Doull, Bookseller. Also, weekends I worked in the Halifax Free Library. My mother formerly was head librarian there." She asked if I read a lot. I dissembled by replying with a question, hoping there was just enough irony in my voice to imply that the answer should be obvious. "Well, I am around books seven days a week, aren't I?" She laughed hesitantly and asked if I'd done particularly well in any subject during my one year at university. I said, "That would have been a course called Introduction to Psychology." She asked, "Why do you suppose you did well?" I said, "Because as I understood it, it was all about taking notice of people's behavior and having strong opinions about it." She said, "Good, good. Taking notice of people's behavior at auction is very useful. You have to be competitive, especially at the opportune moment. You have to keep your wits about you. Do you think you're up to that, Jacob?" "Yes," I said truthfully, "and I also need the work. I'm helping support my mother." She listed what would be my other responsibilities and then I was hired. "We'll give it a try, then, you and I," she said. Five weeks later in Amsterdam, I bid for and brought home *Rock-Tombs and Pyramid,* 1857, by Francis Frith, for three hundred dollars below what Mrs. Hamelin instructed was to be my ceiling bid. And that was exactly my bonus, three hundred dollars. A small fortune to me at the time, and still would be.

What were those other responsibilities? Daily shopping — list provided by Mrs. Brevittmore. Calla lilies to be picked up every Monday at the Flower Shop on Granville Street, a standing order. Purchase of new books, titles provided by Mrs. Hamelin. Carpentry as needed; I was good at that. Chauffeuring, though not often, because Mrs. Hamelin, as she put it, was "something of a homebody." I drove her American car, a 1956 black Buick four-door sedan, with the word *Dynaflow* gliding across the glove compartment in silver metal cursive. Every other Sunday I would drive her to Mount Olive Holiness Church for the 9 a.m. service; I would sit in the back pew. Once I escorted her to a play by Harold Pinter, *No Man's Land.* On rare occasions I would drive Mrs. Hamelin and Mrs. Brevittmore to the movies. They preferred matinees, tea afterward in the lobby of the Lord Nelson. In the lobby I would sit on a sofa in the corner and watch the comings and goings.

I was originally hired in March 1975, the fifteenth to be exact. All of that July I painted the exterior of Mrs. Hamelin's house. In the first twenty-two months of my employment, my passport was stamped by customs officials in Amsterdam, London, Paris, and Copenhagen. In Paris and London I lost out on the bidding. I have already mentioned my success in Amsterdam. And I was successful in Copenhagen too, with *Château de Bagatelle,* c. 1860, by Charles Marville.

I often slept at Martha's three-room apartment at 406 Cunard Street. That's how I knew what my mother wrote on the napkin. Martha had put it in a transparent evidence bag and stuck it to the door of her refrigerator with a magnet. Late on the night of the auction I got up from Martha's bed, walked to the refrigerator to pour a glass of ice water, and there it was, in plain sight. I studied the drawing a moment. Its one seagull wasn't just the letter *V* floating in the sky; it had feathery definition and a keen eye. Clouds were filled-in black. Rain in the offing. In my mother's depiction of a tugboat, I could make out the pilot in the wheelhouse. Life preservers. Mops. A fire ax and an accordion of hose behind glass. Old tire fenders along the rail. The drawing was altogether not bad.

I set the water glass on the bedside table and got under the bedclothes. Martha stretched her legs along mine and pressed against me. "I couldn't get enough of you before," she said. She breathed gently at my ear for a full minute at least. "Does your mouth hurt? Mine does. You don't realize you're kissing that hard until later. Maybe I'm feeling guilty, how I had to speak to Nora earlier."

"Well, that's what I call putting your guilt to good use," I said.

"I know it's my job, but after all, it was your own mother I was questioning. I'm sorry you had to watch me do it."

"Martha, I asked to watch. I wanted to try and figure out what happened. Same as you tried. Besides, you weren't exactly putting the screws to her."

"No, but there's protocol and conniving strategies and psychological tricks of the trade they teach us. None of that I much mind when the person's a creep. I get mostly lowlife creeps, I've told you. But your mother, she seemed, I don't know. Mainly she seemed disoriented, and I'd say kind of excited. Obviously a very intelligent woman, Nora. All those librarian awards and citations. She's read, what, maybe five thousand books, you said. A very intelligent woman to talk with."

"Anyway, you put her at ease. She was so shaky at first. And I haven't seen her smoke a cigarette in ages."

"The thing is, I'd have liked to have met your mother for the first time under different circumstances, for God's sake. I mean, you proposed marriage October second, last year."

"Same day you accepted."

"Strange, don't you think, how she kept calling me interlocutrix? I had to look the word up."

"I looked it up too. Technically speaking, you do fit the definition, but it sounds so medieval torture chamber or something."

"Interlocutrix, that's me."

"I'm confused. She was doing so well, my mother. The hospital said no episodes for eleven months. And then that photograph set her off. I have no earthly idea why."

"You and me both."

"Say the glass shattered. Say the photograph got splinters of glass. Say it was damaged. I'm talking thousands of dollars, maybe."

"Luckily, it's just ink on glass. Still and all, darling, a crime was committed. But factoring in that your mother's been living in a hospital like she has, it's unlikely she'll go to jail. You'll have to face the music tomorrow with Mrs. Hamelin, right?"

"First thing in the morning, I'll go back to the house. She won't have read about it in the papers probably till lunch. If it even makes the papers."

"Want me to go with? To Mrs. Hamelin's."

"Sweet of you, but no. I'm just going to tell the truth and say why I lost out on the French photograph."

"How do you think she's going to take it?"

"Esther? Oh, probably get into a foul mood. She suffers from a kind of acquisition fever — her words. Of course, I've come back empty-handed before. Just because she's rich as Croesus doesn't mean I always get to outbid everyone. This one time in London, I bid higher than she'd instructed I should — it was reckless, way above my assigned ceiling bid. And I still got trounced. Esther brooded for a month, very aggressively."

"I've noticed, to me she's Esther, to everyone else she's Mrs. Hamelin. What do you call her day to day?"

"Mrs. Hamelin. But I'm always thinking Esther. Two years of working for her, I allow myself that secret informality."

"If you want, give me a call after you speak with her."

"Want to sleep?"

"Definitely not. I haven't shared this bed with you four nights in a row this week."

Halifax Isn't Mentioned
in the Old Testament

THE NEXT MORNING, I WATCHED MARTHA SLIP FROM BED, holding her auburn hair up behind her head, sleep creases along her shoulders. She took such good care of herself — she bicycled ten miles every Saturday morning, unless weather or some urgency at work prohibited. She had slim hips and an ever so slightly noticeable, and to me endearing, oddly syncopated walk, from a childhood injury. She only had a bathtub, no shower, and took quick morning baths, but in the evening could linger in the tub a long time, adding hot water, listening to the radio. There was nothing she liked more than to have a glass of wine delivered to her in the bathtub, to step from the bath, slip on her robe, and have dinner waiting on the kitchen table.

This morning she teased me by pulling back the bedclothes and lying down atop me, breasts pressed to my back. She kissed both of my ears, then said, "Oops, time to go." She put on her street clothes and left the apartment. I got up from bed and turned off the radio. Martha had left a cup of coffee with a book set over it, to keep the coffee warm. The book was *The Journals of Susanna Moodie*, a collection of poems by Margaret Atwood. At John W. Doull, Bookseller, on Barrington Street, she had said to me at the cash register, "That's right, I'm a detective who reads poetry. By the way, thanks for the employee discount. Every little bit helps."

Setting the book on the table, I drank the coffee and thought back to my mother's interrogation. When I'd asked Martha if I could watch and listen through the one-way glass, she'd said, "Against policy, but sure. Just don't let the two other detectives give you any grief. If they snap at you, snap right back. Just, if they ask, say Detective Crauchet said it was okay to be there."

During the interrogation, Martha couldn't help but glance at the window now and then. I stood in the viewing room with Detective Tides and Detective Hodgdon. Naturally, Martha had mentioned their names, but I hadn't met them before. I would guess that they were both in their early fifties. Tides was trim, about five feet nine, with short, entirely white hair, and wore glasses with owl-eyed black frames. He had an indoor pallor, a tight-lipped smile. Then there was Detective Hodgdon. He had thinning black hair, slicked back; you could see the comb tracks. He was an inch or so taller than Tides and far more wound up. Fidgety and impatient, he habitually snapped his fingers as if time itself wasn't passing at an acceptable rate. He was out of shape, had an insomniac's eyes, and, within one minute, exhibited ten different expressions of glumness. Tides wore a pinstripe suit, like he had a formal engagement later and was already dressed for it. Hodgdon's suit was off the rack, and his white shirt was a size too small, at least around the stomach. Once, when he unbuttoned his jacket as if to let air circulate, I noticed a small Rorschach test of coffee splattered on his shirt, just above the pocket. "In the interrogation room," Martha told me, "they like to alternate between bad cop and worse cop. That's why I was glad I was the one in there with your mother. Tides and Hodgdon don't know a thing about auctions anyway — believe me, they couldn't care less. They just think, Hoity-toity folks with too much money, just for things to put on their walls." Martha had also informed me that Hodgdon and Tides had worked together for fourteen years. She had been their colleague for five.

Ten or so minutes into the interrogation, Hodgdon said, "Detective Crauchet's using some gentle tactics, you ask me. Maybe it's a woman-to-woman thing. Me? I'd just say, 'Hey, dipshit, why'd you want to go and attack those American war heroes in that photograph like you did?'"

"Look how gussied up the loon is," Tides said, of course referring to my mother. "Hair all neatly coiffed, that silk scarf. Japanese- or Chinese-looking, that scarf, don't you think, going by the pattern, that scarf? Slacks, blouse, shoes, all not cheap. Nicely turned out. She's got to be what, maybe fifty-five, sixty? The point is, she got dressed for the occasion. I'd have to call that premeditated."

"Probably been some time since she'd had a night on the town, eh?" Hodgdon said. "Can't blame her for wanting to escape the loony bin for a few hours."

"Rest hospital," I said.

Hodgdon turned to me and said, "And you're who again? I forget."

"Name's Jacob Rigolet," Tides said. "That's his mother in there, Nora Rigolet."

"Rest hospital. Loony bin. Call it what you want, Jake," Hodgdon said. "Hope you don't mind me using the familiar — Jake. I'm a familiar sort of fellow."

"Sssshhhh, hear that?" Tides said. "Just now she called it 'my despised photograph.' Now that's personal. That's very personal. What's the story with that, do you suppose?"

"The story?" Hodgdon said. "What is this, English literature class? The story? Leave that to the shrinks. Willful destruction of private property is what we're looking at here."

"Attempted to destroy what she despised," Tides said. "That behavior's been around since the Old Testament."

"However, considering Halifax isn't mentioned in the Old Testament — following that logic, what you said doesn't fall into our purview."

"It was just a figure of speech," Tides said.

"Oh, right, professor, a figure of speech," Hodgdon said.

I cleared my throat loudly and said, "My mother was a librarian at the Halifax Free Library for thirty-eight years. She was a highly respected librarian."

"No kidding, the Halifax Free Library," Hodgdon said. "I got called out there last year. Turns out some dangerous criminal had moved the A volume of the *Encyclopaedia Britannica* over between the E and the F. I thought, What's the big deal? But the head librarian thought it had gone missing. She actually referred to it as a 'book kidnapping.' Needed some drama in her life, or what? I had to include that phrase in my report. Librarians are control freaks."

Tides and Hodgdon broke up laughing.

"That would have been Mrs. Rebecca Savernor," I said. I had my temper up a little by this time. "She took my mother's place when my mother — retired. Mrs. Savernor's a respected librarian herself. Just so you know."

Through the window, I saw Martha pour my mother a second cup of coffee from a thermos. Detective Tides and Detective Hodgdon suddenly left the room, like they'd been telepathically called away. At the door Tides threw me a glance of annoyed pity. At least now I could concentrate on the interrogation. "Nora, tell me, why this particular photograph?" Martha said. "You went to considerable effort, sneaking out of the hospital, terribly cold, windy afternoon like it was. Lovely coat, by the way. I admire it." Martha ran her hand over the collar of my mother's cashmere coat, which was draped over a separate chair. "But getting back to the auction in the Lord Nelson Hotel. You were, how to say it, very determined, Nora. A very determined woman. So, what is it about this particular photograph? Please tell me."

"I demur," my mother said. "But let me ask you something. It's Detective Martha Crauchet, isn't it?"

"Yes," Martha said.

"Martha, let me ask you something. Would you ever consider participating in Arts and Crafts where I live? It's every morning at eleven. You could stay for lunch after."

So You're Telling Me That I Was Born in the Halifax Free Library and the Man I Thought Was My Father Was Not Really My Father

IN THE LIBRARY, LATE ON THE MORNING AFTER THE AUCTION, I gave Mrs. Hamelin all the details, except about the interrogation. "Your own mother, how sad," she said. She was slowly shaking her head in pity, and maybe a touch of condescension spicing her sympathetic tone. "As I think about it, Jacob, there's so little I really know about you. The sort of family you come from. But that wasn't part of the initial interview, was it? I suppose I didn't think it necessary."

"Do you now?" I said.

"A little late for that, I'm afraid. Besides, you've been a splendid employee for the most part. I've no complaints."

"When you've had complaints —"

"Yes, I've directly complained, haven't I."

"My mother was an excellent librarian. She's just in a difficult stretch."

"How long has this difficult stretch been so far?" Mrs. Hamelin said. "If you don't mind my asking."

"At least three years. She had a breakdown. She went into the hospital a little over three years ago."

"Oh, my. I see."

"I'm sorry I lost out on the French photograph. But everyone lost out on everything. The auction was shut down right away."

Mrs. Hamelin left the library. From my room in the cottage, I telephoned Martha at work. "It went badly," I said.

"I thought it might," she said.

"What are you doing?"

"Getting a real education."

"Tell me at dinner, okay?"

"Philomene's at eight o'clock. Is that all right?"

"See you."

It was one of our longer telephone conversations. Neither of us much liked talking on the phone. We didn't much like watching television, either. We were radio people. More specifically, we loved the old-time radio shows that were broadcast almost nightly on the series *When Radio Was Radio*, out of Montreal. Martha had a short-wave and taught me how to use it.

Movies, now that was a different story. In a five-month period, we had seen *Chinatown, The Conversation, The Parallax View, The Odessa File, Alice Doesn't Live Here Anymore, The Man with the Golden Gun, Lenny,* and *A Woman Under the Influence.* We always sat about three-quarters back from the screen, and Martha had to have an aisle seat. "It guarantees only you are next to me," she said. "Half the same for you, right?"

Martha had all sorts of platitudes. One was, "A person has to run on a very personal kind of logic, or you end up feeling like any other sort of jerk. You just feel interchangeable." She preferred platitudes that had a practical application. "If the kissing goes well, the rest has a good chance. If the kissing goes badly, best to just have a coffee together and call it a night." The latter she said on our first date, actually, before any kissing had occurred.

15

Philomene's was on the corner of Cogswell and Lower Water Streets. We had a partial view of the harbor from our table. Once the waiter left with our orders, I said, "On the phone you said you were getting quite the education."

"An education having a lot to do with your mother, Jake. I've been studying her case file. Which is part of my job, case files are. As you know."

"I never thought I'd hear those words: 'her case file.' What's in it, though?"

"I've got to look right at you when I say all of this," Martha said. "Because if I don't, you'll notice. And then you might think I'm keeping something from you. Because I'm not. It's very important stuff. And it's likely to get importanter. Is that even a word? Or, more important. The more time that passes, the more important it's going to get."

"They wouldn't let me visit her today, my mother. I went over to the hospital and they said I should wait a week or so. Isn't that something? My own mother. My librarian mother. I have to wait at least a week."

"The thing is, right in my handbag I've got Nora's case file."

"Martha, I realize she's committed a crime. I know there's got to be a case file on her."

"Yes, but there's some real surprises in hers. She's got what we call a history."

"Surprises like what?"

"See, a case file doesn't just include a description of whatever crime. It includes all sorts of background information. Modern archiving of all sorts of stuff, Jake. So, your mother's file has a lot of her personal information. You know, dates and places and names, like who she was married to."

"What do you mean, who she was married to? She was married to my father. Bernard Rigolet. What are you talking about?"

"Yes. Right. Nora and Bernard were married. But there's other information."

Martha reached into her handbag and took out the case file. She set it over her plate, opened it, put the third page on top, and traced her finger down a couple of paragraphs. "See, right here," she said, tapping the page. "Right here it says: Nora Ives. Married on December 19, 1943, to an American named Bernard Rigolet. A son, Jacob Rigolet, born April 18, 1945. Place of birth: Halifax Free Library. Emergency situation. Baby born in good health."

"This document says I was born in the library?"

"A copy of your birth certificate's also in the file here, Jacob. But yes. Yes, Nora actually gave birth to you in the library. It was assisted by a female police officer."

"How could that have happened? My mother never told me that. Why didn't she ever tell me that?"

The waiter arrived with our salads. But Martha said to him, "We're not going to eat, sorry. We've decided against eating. But I'm going to pay for the meal, all right? And we're just going to sit for a while and talk." She took out her wallet and displayed her detective's ID.

The waiter nodded solemnly, which was actually kind of comical, though I wasn't laughing, for obvious reasons, and he said, "I get it. Just consider you're paying for your time at the table. Tonight's not crowded anyway. Wave me over when you want the check. I'll go and tell the kitchen to hold off on the entrées."

"Thanks a lot," Martha said.

The waiter took away the salads. Martha sipped some water and said, "I like our waiter for not sacrificing his tip."

"Stick to the file, please," I said.

"All right. According to Nora's file, your father — I mean, the man you think of as your father —"

"What did you just say?"

"Please hear me out, darling, please. The file states: Bernard Rigolet completed his basic training at Fort Ord, California, on March 9, 1944. He was shipped overseas on March 28, 1944. He was in the U.S. First Army and fought for a year in France before he was shipped to Germany, where he was killed near the town of Leipzig on —"

"He died two days after I was born," I said.

"Yes, on April 20, 1945."

"My mother did tell me that. She did once tell me, 'Your father was killed two days after you were born.' I remember her saying that. Otherwise, I didn't know much. She told me that Bernard was an American soldier in Germany while she was pregnant with me. That's about it, really. I have some photographs of him, of course. I have photographs of them together, before he went overseas. And my mother has dozens of photographs of them together."

Martha had her eyes fixed on me, encouraging me to concentrate, waiting for certain facts to sink in. But I was slow on the uptake.

Martha turned the page toward me. "Look at the dates in your mother's file here," she said. "If you look at the dates, you'll see that Bernard Rigolet was sent overseas on March 28, 1944, like I said — which was more than a year before you were born, Jake."

"So you're saying —"

"I'm saying that Bernard was not your father."

Martha placed her hands over mine on the table and said, "It's all here in the file, Jacob."

"So you're telling me that I was born in the Halifax Free Library and the man I thought was my father was not really my father."

"That's right," Martha said. "And because I love you, I'm not going to keep anything from you. And there's something else. It has to do with the photograph that Nora . . . violated. Threw the ink against."

"The photograph that was taken on the day I was born, you mean."

"Bernard Rigolet is in the photograph."

Martha took out a photocopy of *Death on a Leipzig Balcony* and set it in front of me. There was a soldier half in shadow, on all fours, looking at another soldier, who had been shot by a sniper and whose blood was darkly pooling near his body. The soldier half in shadow was circled in black Magic Marker. Martha lightly touched the circled man's body. "That's Bernard Rigolet," she said. "The same Bernard Rigolet that all this time you thought was your father, but he wasn't your father. That's him. And by the end of the day, April 20, 1945, he was dead. Right near Leipzig. He was killed in another skirmish, after the First Army took Leipzig."

You Detectives Stopped By
Quite Early

THREE NIGHTS AFTER THE CALAMITOUS AUCTION, WE HAD dinner in Martha's apartment (I made kale-and-sausage soup, a recipe given me by Mrs. Brevittmore), and afterward Martha and I relaxed in bed, atop the bedclothes, listening to her favorite show, *Detective Levy Detects*, at its regular time, ten o'clock. *Detective Levy Detects* was set in a fictional Toronto "just after the war," as the introductory narration to each episode informed the radio audience.

"Every episode is like American noir, except in Canada," Martha once said when she was in a philosophical mood about *Detective Levy Detects*. "But noir is noir, and it's the atmosphere that counts, in my opinion. I mean, it could be set in Tokyo or Mexico City or on the moon, for all I care, as long as the language is right and you can picture the sleazeballs and crooked cops and slinky dames and righteous but cynical gumshoes and innocent just-got-to-town types, all moving in and out of the shadows. The radio has to let you *see* all of this, right?"

The concept—if that's the right word—of *Detective Levy Detects* has to do with time travel. The main setting is a kind of fleabag hotel (in fact, the first episode was titled "Say, What Kind of Hotel Is This, Anyway?"), the Devonshire, where a woman named Leah Diamond keeps a room. She is Detective Levy's love interest. He is crazy about her. On the day the Toronto newspapers are filled with how Detective Levy screwed up a case involving a kidnapped child, he goes to the bar of the Devonshire Hotel to drown his sorrows. And that's where he first meets Leah Diamond. One thing leads to the next, and they take the electric lift up to her room. The narrator said, "Their clothes fell away like they preferred the floor. The clothes, that is." Pillow talk; then the telephone rings, and to Detective Levy's great surprise, Leah Diamond not only answers the phone, but says, "Yeah, sure, come on up." Soon three tough guys and their lady friends, all of whom talk like they are right out of 1940s Gangster Central Casting, walk right in without knocking. Leah Diamond introduces everyone all around.

Here is where the time travel comes in. By the end of the first episode, Detective Levy understands that every time he enters the hotel, he steps out of current-day Toronto and into the forties. And there it is: time-travel noir.

At the end of the first episode, Detective Levy and Leah Diamond get married in the hotel room. ("Why rush things?" he says. She replies, "So we can get to the honeymoon part, where we won't rush things.") What happens is, episode after episode, Leah Diamond, the hoodlums, and their wisecracking lady friends help Detective Levy solve his cases. "Bring us your little problems, Freddy," a gangster named Slog Carmichael says to Detective Frederik Levy, "and we'll work wonders orchestrating our various street smarts, and we'll make beautiful music together, and you don't even have to tell nobody we're the ones upped your crime-fighting IQ. That way we get to help eliminate some of the competition — see, a life of crime is very competitive — and you get all the credit. Life works out fine sometimes, don't it?"

But back to three nights after the auction. As I have mentioned, Martha and I were lying on top of the bedclothes. The second I turned on the radio, we heard a tough, bristling woman's voice say, "Okay, gumshoe, I suppose you wanna know what happened here in my lousy hotel room, right?"

Detective Levy replies, "Well, I'm looking at a man lying here on the floor, and his face perfectly matches the face in this photograph, and this mug's wife hired me to find him."

"So now you found him," the woman says.

"So did a bullet, by the looks of it."

"He never mentioned the word 'wife.'"

"Maybe he couldn't pronounce it."

"What happened was this," the woman says. "He insisted we right away get horizontal. But I say I want to stay vertical. He says, 'Aw, come on, sugar.' I say no. He gets a certain look. So I shot him. So he got his wish. He's horizontal."

Martha lifted her sweater off over her head and tossed it onto the overstuffed chair near the bed. "You have to admit," she said, "that woman's got a way with words."

The woman on the radio then says to Detective Levy, "See that room with the bed in it? It's called a bedroom. Whattaya think about adding to my sins?"

"I'm of two minds about that," Detective Levy says.

"I'm of two minds about it too," she says, "but they're both thinking the same thing."

Martha and I got undressed and under the bedclothes. We made love through the rest of the episode, listened to repeat episodes, and then fell asleep. But at about 6:30 in the morning, we found ourselves making love again. It just happened. I had turned one way, she turned the same way. "I'm not quite awake," she said, but she had reached down and slipped me inside her; we were both facing the east window.

"I can come this way so easily," she said, "but I don't want to yet."

And at that moment Detective Tides called up rudely from the street. Then, equally disregarding the time and the neighbors, Detective Hodgdon pounded on Martha's door, saying loudly, "Detective Crauchet, it's your colleagues! Wake up. We're on official business here. You alone? Come on, Martha, get up!" *Knock knock knock.*

Martha made me leave her, if you know what I mean. "Sorry, darling," she said. "As much for me as for you, believe me." She threw on a bathrobe and walked to the door. I heard her open it and say demurely, "You detectives stopped by quite early," as if she'd forgotten she had invited them for tea or something. Then, with crankiness, "This better be something. I was getting my beauty sleep."

"Got any coffee?" Detective Hodgdon said. "I take it black. Course, you know that from the office."

Dressed now, I walked into the kitchen. "Oh, oh, oh, look who was invited to the slumber party," Detective Tides said, pointing me out to Hodgdon. "Son of the librarian who went loony at the auction."

"Oh, the pieces are all falling into place," Hodgdon said archly. "This is just too much for me. I have to sit down."

I saw that both detectives were unshaven, their suits rumpled, and it seemed that Hodgdon was already caffeine-wired.

"What pieces, pray tell?" Martha said. "That I have a private life and you don't? Does your wife know that? Probably she does."

"What what what? Is she always this off-tilt first thing in the morning?" Tides said to me. "It's Jake, isn't it?"

"What couldn't wait that you had to barge in like this?" Martha said.

While I served coffee all around, Tides and Hodgdon got down to business. "Look, sorry for the ungodly hour," Tides said. "You know as well as me, 'off duty' and 'on duty' are just figures of speech. Anyway, we've been up all night on a stakeout that didn't amount to shit. We were in the neighborhood. And besides, we wanted to let you know something. Being your devoted colleagues."

"What something?" Martha said.

Hodgdon sighed deeply, looked at Tides, who nodded and said, "As senior detectives, we're obligated to review your notes on file — just routine stuff. And we noticed in the file of Nora Ives Rigolet that your research surfaced a fellow named Robert Emil."

Martha looked at me and gestured for me to leave the room, but I refused, and she shot me a look.

"Oh, yeah, Robert Emil," Martha said. "Sounds vaguely familiar — maybe a footnote in Nora's life or something."

"Well, maybe so, maybe a footnote," Hodgdon said. "But we were wondering if you intended to follow up on this Robert Emil or not. You know, to see if he stays just a footnote or, lo and behold, becomes something else. Possibly something other than a footnote, say."

"If that's your suggestion, sure," Martha said. She was so obviously uncomfortable with the direction this conversation was taking that she took it out on me. "Jacob, darling, this is police business, you know. Maybe you want to get some more sleep or something."

"Yeah, but it's about my mother's file," I said.

"Yeah, but your mother's police business," Martha said.

"Let me cut to the chase here, Martha," Tides said. "You, me, and Detective Hodgdon caught a cold case."

"How cold?" Martha said.

I stood against the counter; Martha, Hodgdon, and Tides were sitting at the small kitchen table. "How cold?" Martha said again.

"It's from 1945," Hodgdon said. He placed a file folder on the table. "The one we caught is very complicated. It was sensational in the city when it happened. It was really one for the books. Had centrally — *centrally* — to do with this fellow named Robert Emil. That's why a warning flag went up when we read the Nora Rigolet file. You see, life is strange, isn't it, but back in 1945 Nora Rigolet had been under surveillance in connection with an event involving Robert Emil. Some coincidence, eh?"

"Yes, some coincidence," Martha said, almost in a whisper.

"Actually, it was *Officer* Robert Emil," Tides said. "He was Halifax police."

"Oh, goody," Martha said cynically. "We get to investigate one of our own. Could a day start out with any worse news? Is this Robert Emil still with us?"

"There's no death notice, at least nothing official," Tides said. "In 1945 Officer Emil was thirty-two years old. Which, if he's alive, would make him sixty-five."

Martha poured herself a second cup of coffee. "What'd Officer Emil do," Martha said, "that warrants such high priority over thirty years after the fact?"

"Apparently," Hodgdon said, "near the end of the war, this goddamn idiot Emil started up a personal Jewish hate thing toward a man named Max Berall. Now, this Max Berall played the piano at all sorts of events at Baron de Hirsch Synagogue — you'll find a photograph of him in the file. The whys and wherefores had a lot to do with a flare-up of anti-Semitic incidents at the time, spring of 1945. The end of the war, there were a lot of those. Some sick stuff, if you study up on it. Officer Robert Emil's part in one of these incidents — a murder. Possibly two. His involvement could never be proven. But according to his file, it was pretty obvious he was responsible."

"A Jew-hating police officer," Detective Tides said. "He was forced into retirement. But get this: he kept his pension."

"Max Berall, he was an important man in his community," Hodgdon said.

"Found him in an alley," Tides went on, "not too far from Baron de Hirsch. Shot with two bullets. Wallet intact. Expensive watch on his person. What's more, an eyewitness identified Officer Robert Emil running from the alley. This witness, a Mrs. Yablon, gave her description to a sketch artist. The likeness to Emil was considerable. More than considerable."

Hodgdon slid the artist's sketch from the file onto the table and set next to it a photograph of Officer Robert Emil. He looked at me and said, "This was all in the newspapers at the time, Jake — that's why you're allowed to see this evidence. Otherwise, we'd send you out for some breakfast, eh?"

"But guess what?" Tides said. "On her way home from the sketch artist, Mrs. Yablon disappears. She doesn't show up for Sabbath services on Saturday at Baron de Hirsch, which she never once missed in twenty years. It's all in the file."

"What'd Officer Emil have against Jews?" Martha asked.

Tides said, "It's in the Robert Emil cold-case file."

"I'll study up on it," Martha said.

"Three musketeers, us three," Hodgdon said.

"All for one, one for all," Tides said, sipping his coffee.

"Yeah, well, the thing is, Martha," Hodgdon said, "I think with a closer look we're all going to find out that Robert Emil maybe wasn't —"

"— merely a footnote in 1945," Tides said.

Arts and Crafts

EARLY ON THE MORNING OF APRIL 10, THREE WEEKS AFTER my mother had attempted to destroy *Death on a Leipzig Balcony,* Martha and I sat with cups of coffee at her kitchen table. Martha said, "Remember from the interrogation room? How your mother wrote on the napkin, 'Thank you for the warmest conversation I've had in possibly three years'?"

"I read it every time I open your refrigerator," I said.

"Well, sitting at my desk, I got to thinking about it. And it broke my heart. Really it did. I mean, look: if sitting in a room getting interrogated provided the warmest conversation she'd had in three years — that's way past irony, Jacob. Way past irony. That really said something about what Nora's life's been like in that hospital over in Dartmouth."

"Even though we're not married, you're already a good daughter-in-law, is how I see it."

"I can start practicing, at least."

"You're going to visit her, aren't you? Isn't that what you're saying?"

"No, I'm saying I already did visit her."

"When was that?"

"Yours truly participated in Arts and Crafts yesterday. I waited to see you in person to tell you."

"What do they do in Arts and Crafts?"

"That question proves you've never participated, right? Why haven't you?"

"I just haven't got around to it."

"You haven't seen your mother since the auction. You used to visit her once a week. You should give that some thought. We could do it together, the two of us."

"I don't know."

"Anyway, I must admit, Arts and Crafts is very well organized. You know, it's not remotely like that movie we saw, *One Flew over the Cuckoo's Nest*. The one with Jack Nicholson. Nova Scotia Rest Hospital is advanced civilization compared to that nuthouse. Well, there's one lady, Evelyn what's-her-name. Evelyn Accord — unusual last name. She's quite bonkers. Always on suicide watch, an attendant told me. I flash my detective badge and people talk to me. That's just how it works."

"Look, I'm grateful you went to see my mother. I think it's nice."

"Jacob, it's not that I'm such a quick study, but you know, don't you, that Nora has no business being there. No goddamn business whatsoever. I mean, just during Arts and Crafts — we were making something called Chinese finger traps, those woven things you stick a finger in either side and can't get them out. Of course you eventually can. Though Evelyn Accord asked your mother to cut her finger trap with a scissors, which Nora did. She cut the finger trap in half and Evelyn wore the halves like extended witch fingers the rest of Arts and Crafts time. Six of us sitting at a table making Chinese finger traps. Big sunny day right out the window."

"Now you know how to make Chinese finger traps."

"Anyway, during the Chinese finger traps, Nora provided me her complete history as a librarian. From her childhood inclinations toward reading to her nervous breakdown in the library — what, nearly three years ago. I mean *complete* history. And talk about reading books — I counted eighty, more or less, in her room."

"She's got access to interlibrary loan, Martha. Special dispensation for my mother there. She's become —"

"Yes. She's become the librarian of Nova Scotia Rest Hospital."

"No surprise there."

Martha poured us each another cup of coffee. She was dressed for work; I was wearing pajama bottoms and a T-shirt. "Can you please call in sick, at least a half-day?"

"So you yourself have no work to do for Mrs. Hamelin?"

"Later, she's starting me in on research for an auction in three weeks."

"Where?"

"London."

"I don't have enough vacation time left."

"That's the only reason I didn't ask you to come with me."

"My question is, how'd Nora end up in the hospital in the first place? She's saner than I'll ever be. What happened, Jacob? I don't understand. I want to know. I feel I should know."

"I shouldn't have waited for you to ask. Sorry. I should've told you already."

"Jake, the thing is, I've resigned myself to the idea that our courtship, as it pertains to Nora, is unconventional. First, look how things have been so far. How they actually are. Not necessarily how I'd have preferred it, but life provides. I meet your mother for the first time because I'm interrogating her as part of my job. Clearly you haven't yet told her we're engaged to be married. That's okay, Jacob, I'm not reproaching you. So I'm in the interrogation room strafing her with questions, but all the while, in the back of my mind, I'm thinking: This is my future mother-in-law, this is Nora, Jake's own mother. That very tug-of-war was almost enough to have me committed to Nova Scotia Rest Hospital myself! Taking up Arts and Crafts.

"As far as I know, your mother thinks I'm just some nice woman detective in need of human company who's come to visit her. She actually said, 'Now, dear, don't feel bad about the things you asked me at the police station. I understand.'

"Second, I realize I can get to know Nora on my own. And maybe while doing that, I can find out what you and I both need to know, Jacob. Because I very much think we both need to know what's up with that photograph. What's with *Death on a Leipzig Balcony*? Where the hell is Leipzig, and what's so personal about it, and what's with Robert Capa, and who's your father, anyway? When I marry someone, I want to know something about his family. So I won't be worried about what I don't know about his family."

"You and me both. What we *both* don't know."

"So my question to you is, how'd she end up there in the first place? What really happened?"

"Interlocutrix of your fiancé in your own kitchen, him in pajama bottoms and a T-shirt."

"Don't be that way."

"Three years ago, my mother had a series of nervous breakdowns — they called it 'nervous shock' — and each time it happened in the Halifax Free Library. Finally, the Province of Nova Scotia legally stepped in, or something like that. Next thing I know, I'm visiting my mother in Nova Scotia Rest Hospital."

"But *why* did the nervous breakdowns happen in the first place, is what I'm asking."

"That's what her doctors are supposed to find out, right? To my knowledge, so far they haven't. Or not completely they haven't."

"My sense is that Nora needs to get out of there."

"Aren't you late for work?"

"I'll trade night shift with Tides. No problem there. He's always up for that."

"So I'll stay at Mrs. Hamelin's house tonight, then."

"Up to you."

"I could stay here and have breakfast waiting in the morning."

"What I wonder is, what happened to Nora in the first place, darling? Maybe she'll tell me. Through a hundred more Chinese finger traps. Then again, maybe she won't."

Delinquent Notices

AT AGE FIFTY-FIVE, MY MOTHER HAD BEEN APPOINTED HEAD librarian at the Halifax Free Library, after working in the library system since she was thirty. At the time, I was sitting in on Introduction to Art History at Dalhousie; there weren't many art history courses, but the professors were considered excellent. One professor was from Copenhagen, another from Florence. When I looked at the art history students, I considered them worldly. I met my first real girlfriend, Alexis Boyce, in that class. One day when a bunch of hipster students from the Nova Scotia School of Art came into the Wired Monk Café on Morris Street, my own favorite café, Alexis and I struck up a conversation with them. They told us that Allen Ginsberg had recently visited their school; walking up to the podium, Ginsberg suddenly kissed the man who'd introduced him, a painter named Theodore Bowler — whose wife was also on the faculty and in the audience — on the lips. Then Ginsberg read his poems, and later hung out with students till all hours. Ginsberg declared he had always wanted to give a reading in Halifax because Oscar Wilde had lectured here. Ginsberg's presence was all the talk of the bohemian students. People might not commonly think of Halifax as having a bohemian scene, but it does.

That evening at the Wired Monk, once the NSSA students left, Alexis and I talked for a couple of hours, during which time I embarrassed myself by asking if Allen Ginsberg had been friends with Oscar Wilde. Alexis tapped me gently on the shoulder and, with a look of astonished pity, said, "There, there." Coffee after coffee. But for the one waiter and the woman making the drinks, who were themselves holding hands and smooching at a corner table, the café was empty.

Between Alexis and me there weren't necessarily sparks, but a kind of slow burn. She was fidgety, her nails bitten to the quick, had a ring on each of her fingers, and when she saw me glance, as young men will do, along her body, then look quickly away, hoping not to have been caught out, she said, "I have a dancer's figure, but I'm really too tall and gangly, and if you saw me try" — at which point she stood up, got into a ballet position, and then wobbled sideways, catching herself at the last moment before flailing onto our table — "you'd know I can't do ballet shit to save my soul." Alexis fell into such wonderful laughter that I think right there I was, in a preliminary way, smitten. Alexis was in fact five feet ten inches tall, two inches taller than I am.

"If I ate exclusively crème brûlées by the dozen, three meals a day, I'd probably not gain an ounce. I'd like to gain some ounces, actually. Food-wise, I don't have a mental problem, by the way. Probably I'll one day wake up at three hundred pounds. It's just that I've always had this kind of woodstove in my stomach, or something, that burns up calories. Anyway, what you see is what you get."

We made a date to meet at the Wired Monk the next evening at eight o'clock, and both of us showed up on time. "All that talk about my drawings I laid on you, Jacob. You were sweet to listen. I can get carried away. I must sound like a typical art student to you, right?"

"I don't know any typical art students," I said. "I don't know any atypical ones either."

"Oh, I'm your first?"

"You could put it that way. Yes."

"Anyway, I only make drawings. This one day, I made a drawing of a birch tree in the small park near Historic Properties. I just looked at it in a kind of anthropomorphic way, I guess."

"Anthropomorphic?"

"Something not human that you give human characteristics to. To me, the tree looked like a ballet dancer. And after that first drawing, I made my life-altering decision. To draw only birch trees. I want to be a kind of birch tree savant. So far I've made four hundred sixteen drawings of the same birch tree. I will continue to make drawings only of the one birch tree, unless it's blown down by a hurricane, and even then I can draw it from memory. And I intend eventually to rent an apartment with a window looking down on the park, and I'll set up my easel and look at the birch tree through the window and draw it. I'll live in that apartment hopefully for decades, until I die. I'll have by that time made a very stalwart attempt to draw the birch tree into infinity, and hopefully I'll fall over dead in the process, age one hundred five, my face wrinkled as a fingerprint."

Despite thinking her analogy between a birch tree and a ballet dancer unoriginal, still, I was so impressed, so taken aback at how someone her age could already know what she wanted to do in life, that it didn't yet occur to me that she was a solar system beyond pretentious, and maybe a little nuts. She just sounded all passionate intent. It was really something, to be so prescient about one's own life.

"My father always told me, 'Make a road map for life and follow it,'" she said, "and mine leads me to an apartment near Historic Properties, in Halifax, Nova Scotia, overlooking a birch tree."

"I hope you sell a lot of drawings. I really do," I said.

"Well, Jacob, that's beside the point, really. It's all about art."

"I'm always thinking about how to pay my bills, I guess. Sorry."

"When my father first saw my drawings — of people; this was before I started exclusively drawing the birch tree — when I showed him my portraits, he got me an interview at the police station. He found out they were advertising for a police artist. How it works is, the police call in witnesses to a crime, and those witnesses try the best they can to give a physical description of the criminal to the police sketch artist, and the sketch artist is supposed to come up with a close enough likeness to put on a Wanted poster."

"Would you ever consider doing that?"

"Jacob, no."

"It sounds like steady employment to me, is why I asked."

"I'm drawing my birch tree. I wouldn't have time for that shit."

"You couldn't fit it in somehow? It probably would pay pretty well. If you got the job."

"You and my father would get along well."

Outside of university, I worked all day Monday and Friday evenings, after store hours, in the stock room at John W. Doull, Bookseller. Also, thanks to my mother, I worked weekend days at the Halifax Free Library. In that capacity I oversaw the Delinquent Borrowers File. During the average Saturday and Sunday, I'd process anywhere between a hundred and a hundred fifty book delinquencies. "You're the truant officer of the library," my mother would say. On average, books were two to three weeks overdue, sometimes a month. I'd tuck overdue notices into envelopes with the library's return address on them and drop a stack of the notices into the nearest mailbox. On occasion the library would receive letters in return. One read:

Dear Halifax Free Library,

I received notice that the book *A Moveable Feast,* by Ernest Hemingway, is three months overdue. However, please consider the fact that I have a very busy life. I do not have time to read every evening as some people do. Don't you think that the Halifax Free Library should take into account actual real daily lives of their patrons in this regard? *A Moveable Feast,* in case you don't know, is about the author's life in Paris when he was a young and mostly unknown writer. I still have two chapters to go. What is more, I have been to Paris twice and very little of what the author writes squares with my own experience. My disappointment in this is endless. Ernest Hemingway and I are not in touch, so I could not relay this to him. In addition, given the fact that my husband, Gerald, is pretty much confined to the living room sofa — by choice — I cannot ask him to return *A Moveable Feast.* Let's strike a compromise. I will return the book as soon as I am finished with it and the Halifax Free Library can keep the advice I have given about how to better take into consideration the lives of your patrons free of charge.

Best regards,
Mrs. Peter Irby

I had been seeing Alexis regularly for six months when the incident with the stolen book occurred. Between my work commitments and her academic courses, plus her obsessive drawing of the birch tree, we decided to meet a maximum of twice a week, for dinner, a movie, or just to sit in the Wired Monk Café. When one of us had a little extra money, we'd take a room at the Lord Nelson Hotel. The best way I can describe our relationship is that it didn't seem to get any deeper, and yet it didn't get any shallower either. Which must've meant we were treading water. Early on, she had indeed rented a one-room apartment overlooking the park near Historic Properties (one year's rent paid in advance by her father), and the only thing on the walls were her drawings of the birch tree, held up by thumbtacks. There was a cot, one chair, and a ratty sofa. No refrigerator. Bathroom down the hall. I didn't much like visiting her there. Some evenings I'd go over as planned and would find that Alexis had set out folding chairs for eight or ten of her art student friends. They'd listen to music, mainly John Coltrane and Thelonious Monk, and then they'd play the same goddamn rock songs over and over — "Rikki Don't Lose That Number," "Nothing from Nothing," "Whatever Gets You Through the Night," "Bungle in the Jungle," "I Shot the Sheriff," and "Haven't Got Time for the Pain" — which would drive me crazy, the way they sang along with sanctimonious devotion, though Alexis did point out that everyone thought I was a pill and didn't know how to have fun, and "in this miserable world, if you can't have fun, you're really lost." But I suppose I wasn't capable of seeing, given that her rent was paid and she could do exactly what she wanted all day and night, every day and night, and that she ate at restaurants four or five nights a week, just how miserable life was for her. "People have inner lives, Jake," she'd say, "not just outer lives." Her friends liked to discuss all manner of esoteric theories about painting. I heard one fellow say to Alexis, "Your trees are definitely in the same lineage of genius as Mondrian's early drawings, before he went all geometrical." On a number of occasions, when there were new friends in the apartment, Alexis would often not even introduce me, and when I'd mention this, she'd say, "It's not what a person is named but what he or she thinks that matters."

"I must not matter much, then," I said, "at least to your friends. Since I don't tell them what I think about anything. Neither do they ask." To me, Alexis was unusual.

One Saturday afternoon I was going through delinquent notices and discovered that one Alexis Boyce (address: Nova Scotia School of Art) had failed to return the two volumes of *Henri Matisse*, by Louis Aragon, for nearly two months. Not only was I surprised to see the name Alexis Boyce, but I immediately recalled registering in the inventory at John W. Doull those very same volumes. To give Alexis the benefit of the doubt, I privately dissembled on her behalf: thousands of copies of the two-volume set had been published. They were elegant books, and Denise Carle, the buyer of used books at John W. Doull, would no doubt have paid anyone a decent amount for them. Still, I started to get a stomach cramp and walked over to the bookstore. I lied and said that I was worried about a mistake I might've made in the inventory ledger. My immediate boss at the time was a man named Mordechai (Morty) Shaloom, who had worked in antiquarian books for twenty years. He said, "Go ahead, Jake. Good of you to be so conscientious." I went into the storeroom, checked the ledger, and, sure enough, listed there were the two volumes on Matisse. Next I went to the art section of the store and found the books on a low shelf. I examined the inside back covers and could detect the faint outline of the library's pocket in which the borrower's card would be stamped and dated. Someone had taken great pains in removing those pockets. My heart sank.

When I reported all of this to my mother, she said, "I never liked that Alexis. And I certainly can't like her now, can I? But you have to figure this out for yourself."

Over the next few days my mother went through the delinquent notices for the past year and found that Alexis had borrowed no fewer than sixteen art books listed as Outstanding Delinquencies. The library was always way behind in its paperwork, so a six-month or even a year's delinquency wasn't all that unusual. However, now that my mother had been specially alerted, and with the authority and responsibilities of being head librarian, she felt the need to address the issue with her board of directors, which she did. The board insisted on taking immediate legal action against Alexis. One evening at our dining room table, my mother said, "Jacob, there's something I want you to do, please. I'm going to give you the delinquent notices that pertain to Alexis Boyce, and I'd like you to check them against the inventory at John W. Doull. You can, of course, say no to this. Because what I'm asking, in part, is for you to help investigate Miss Boyce, and she being your present girlfriend, that cannot be a pleasant task, not pleasant for me or for you, and potentially quite seriously unpleasant for Miss Boyce herself. But she may be in real trouble, and you may want to discuss it with her. I have not told the board of your relationship, and I never will. It's none of their business. You're my son, and I'll trust you to handle this for yourself."

The next day, I checked the bookstore's inventory against the library's delinquent notices. Every single book in question had been taken from the Halifax Free Library and sold by Alexis to John W. Doull — every one. In turn, more than half had already been sold to bookstore customers. I hurried over to Alexis's apartment, but she wasn't home. She never locked the door, so I went in and described at length, on three pieces of drawing paper, what the situation was. I asked her to telephone me.

The following day, I learned that my mother had Alexis arrested. By the time I got to the police station, Alexis's father had posted bail for her, and I never saw her again. I contacted a number of her friends at Nova Scotia School of Art, each of whom said something to the effect that she had been "sent to Europe." They didn't seem to be hiding anything; no, I think it was all they knew. A month later, I was near Alexis's former apartment and saw her landlord, Mrs. Templeton, stepping from the building. I asked her what happened to all the drawings in Alexis's apartment. "Oh, right," she said. "Well, before her arrest, she slipped an envelope under my door. Inside was a request that I gather up all the drawings and send them to the Museum of Modern Art in New York City. She'd left enough funds in the envelope to cover the cost, dear girl. And so I followed her wishes to the last drawing. There were hundreds, you see. I've had no word yet from the Museum of Modern Art. But I imagine these things take time."

"Did Alexis leave a forwarding address?"

"Her father dropped by saying he would do that, but never did," Mrs. Templeton said. "Alexis is living in Europe somewhere, I believe."

"Well, thank you anyway," I said.

"Would you be Jacob, by any chance?"

"I am — Jacob Rigolet."

"Oh, Lord, well, wait right here. I'll go fetch what she left you."

I waited in front of the building for a few minutes, and when Mrs. Templeton returned, she handed me a rolled-up drawing, held fast by a rubber band. "This one she left for you, Jacob," she said. "You can see your name printed in pencil there on the back. Along with the title."

I saw that the title, in quotation marks, was "Birch Tree #344."

"Thank you," I said.

"There, that's properly done. Goodbye, then."

The End of the War Café

TO FURTHER CONSIDER MARTHA'S QUESTION CONCERNING Nora: "What really happened, Jacob?"

A year before I was employed by Mrs. Hamelin, my mother began to put up family photographs on the walls of our house at 78 Robie Street, across from the Common. Ours was more a bungalow than a house. It had two bedrooms: mine was at the back, my mother's directly off the dining room. There was a modest-sized kitchen, a small study, a front porch, and a backyard. The house was painted white, with black shutters and flower boxes. "The flower boxes will always be the fullest extent of my gardening," my mother said.

My mother worked long hours, especially after she became head librarian. She would be at work by 7 a.m., though the library opened at 10 a.m. She held weekly staff meetings and attended intra-provincial library conferences and, once a year, the national library conference in Ottawa, at which time she'd be away for three nights. She visited elementary and high schools to talk about the Halifax Free Library, was occasionally quoted in the *Chronicle-Herald* about civic issues, and once even spoke on the radio, when she commented on the ten most frequently borrowed books of that year. I thought she did brilliantly. I was very proud.

But when my mother arrived home from her stint on the radio, she seemed quite despondent. She slumped into the Morris chair in the study (which also had a pull-out sofa, and would have served as a guest room, had we had any guests) and said, "Would you bring me a whiskey, please, Jacob. And I fully realize it's only five o'clock on a Tuesday afternoon." Sipping the whiskey, she said, "I listened to the playback and felt I sounded like a fuddy-duddy spinster librarian. I just hated it. I hated my voice. I hated what I said."

"Well, I listened carefully, and I thought you did a very good job," I said.

My mother took another sip. "Is that how you think of me, Jacob? Be honest with your mother now. Do you think of me as a spinster librarian?"

"Whatever that is, I don't think of you that way."

"'Whatever that is'?" I could see her hesitate, to summon up a little courage. She finished off the glass and held it out for me to pour her another, which I did. She took several sips from the second glass, then said, "It's a woman — in my case a widow — who is *dried up*. Here" — she moved her hands over her body, from neck to knees, then clutched at her heart — "and *here*." She threw back the rest of the whiskey. "Oh, have I embarrassed my son? I don't mean to embarrass you, Jacob."

"Mother, nothing you could do, absolutely nothing, would embarrass me."

"You know, several men have found me quite beautiful over the course of my lifetime. And I think lately Mr. Hebersall in children's books might have certain designs . . ."

"Bernard Rigolet must have," I said.

"Must have what?"

"Thought you were beautiful."

"Oh, Bernard, well. Well, Bernard." She was slurring her words slightly. "Bernard Rigolet found me ravishing. You see, I have very nice features, if I may put it that way myself. Put it that way myself to my grown son. Very nice features under the silk pajamas, as they used to say. Oh, I see you're blushing. But I am only telling you something of my early marriage. Before the war. Before my husband went off to die in Germany. The German city of Leipzig."

This was the first time I'd ever heard her utter the name Leipzig.

"The love of my life, Bernard. Such a handsome man. I might even elevate that to *dashing*. He said I was like a figure in an Edwardian painting."

"So, my father knew Edwardian paintings?"

"Well, I'd brought home a book of Edwardian portraiture. To put on the table."

That same night, I heard my mother banging around in the dining room. When I went out to investigate, I saw that she had dragged three boxes of old photographs into the room and was hanging them on the wall. She was dressed in her pajamas and robe and bedroom slippers.

"Need some help here, Mom?" I said.

"No, I have to curate this room myself. But you can sit and keep me company if you want to."

"What are you doing, exactly?"

"Portrait gallery of happy days. Hand me that picture there on top, that box nearest to the table."

I lifted the black-and-white photograph in its frame and looked at it. It showed my mother and father — that is, the man I believed at the time was my father, Bernard — standing in front of the very same bungalow Mother and I still lived in. The words "Nora looks quite fetching here," in what I figured was Bernard's cursive, were written along the bottom. It was a winter scene; my mother was wearing an overcoat and high boots. Her dark hair fell loosely, and she wore a stocking cap. She had a worried smile. Bernard was wearing a U.S. Army–issue coat and his hair was cut short. He had his right arm around my mother's shoulders and was looking directly at her, so his face was in profile. "It's the day before Bernard left for Europe," my mother said. "To join ranks with the U.S. First Army."

It wasn't until 4 a.m. that she had hung the last photograph of the night. Now the dining room walls and the walls of her bedroom were covered, and I mean covered, from near the ceiling to eye level. I broke down the empty boxes and put them in the trash. When I went back inside, my mother was asleep on the sofa.

Within a month, the walls of every room in our house, including my bedroom, including the bathroom and the pantry, were full of photographs. The one time Alexis came to my house, my mother cooked dinner for the three of us. She had made chicken and rice — bland, considering what an inventive, excellent cook she otherwise was, and I have always thought she did it on purpose. What's more, it was the first and only occasion on which I had seen Alexis almost speechless. Usually she was quite the live-wire chatterbox. And I loved that, because she could hold the conversations while I listened in, which was my preference most of the time. But that evening at dinner, Alexis mainly gazed silently at the walls. Just before dessert and coffee, she excused herself to use the bathroom, and when she came back, she looked almost pale. She could not have missed the hundreds of photographs everywhere. My mother and Alexis had said no more than ten words to each other. The long silences were deafening. When I had cleared the dishes and was standing in the kitchen, I heard my mother finally say, "If I thought you were going to be part of this family, Alexis, I would take you through the pictures one by one and tell you the full story. It would probably give you, healthy as you appear to be, a heart attack, the full story would."

Alexis shot right back, "I draw the same birch tree every single day. I don't need to be part of your family."

"Oh, well," my mother said, seeming to ignore Alexis's response,

"I'm afraid I'm off to bed. An early meeting tomorrow. Lovely to meet you."

On our walk back to her apartment, Alexis said, "I now identify with the survivors of the *Titanic*."

For the time being, since I had to keep living at home, I became a kind of scholar of my mother's photographs — to me, time well spent. Because when I'd overheard my mother say to Alexis, "If I thought you were going to be part of this family," I thought, Well, I *am* part of this family, and I myself don't know half a thing about what's in these photographs. At the time I didn't recognize it as such, but now I realize that studying these photographs was an engagement with the first phase of my mother's fall from grace. Her obsession, her becoming derailed. Still, on the evenings I was home, I'd sit with her and discuss a given photograph. I'd take it down from the wall, and she'd give me its bona fides.

There's a Russian proverb: To taste the ocean, all you need is one gulp. So here I'll describe what happened with just one photograph, and say that the experience was, over a six-month period, repeated a total of 416 times, which was the number of photographs on the walls, and I mean right up to the day my mother was taken away to Nova Scotia Rest Hospital, on March 18, 1974. From the sheer number of photographs, I wondered if my mother had somehow sensed that Bernard would not be returning. Some days she had taken as many as thirty photographs of him.

All the photographs were taken between the day of their marriage, December 19, 1943, and the day before Bernard Rigolet left for the war, March 28, 1944. Going by what was written on the front or back of a given photograph, I knew that some had been taken by my mother, some by Bernard, but most by people unnamed. But it is the one taken on my mother and Bernard's wedding day that I want to tell about. "This was taken by a court stenographer. Her name was Gabrielle Deitzel," my mother said, sipping tea and cleaning the glass of the photograph with a cloth.

45

"Why do I remember that name? Well, I suppose you remember everything of your wedding day. Miss Deitzel worked at the courthouse, and she was asked by the justice of the peace who married us to be the legal witness. Gabrielle had the poise and wherewithal to suggest a wedding photograph. I'm not sure Bernard and I would've even thought of it. We were in such a tizzy. I'd almost forgotten that I had my Brownie box camera in my handbag. And look here — right behind us, you see that building? That's City Hall on Argyle Street. That's where we got married. The justice of the peace's name was Gustav Selig. See, I remember that too. Our legal witness was Gabrielle Deitzel, whom Gustav Selig just grabbed out of the hallway.

"Let's skip our wedding night, shall we?" my mother said to me. "For propriety's sake. We bought this house a week later. All four of our parents had already died, and so we were orphans setting up house. Bernard had a brother, Zeke, who also died in the war, and Zeke came to visit for a week and helped us pay for furniture. Zeke liked to say he bought a sofa so he would have a place to sleep, which was true. I got a job at the library, and Bernard went off to die near Leipzig."

My mother closed her eyes for a few moments and said, "I've just now remembered when I received news of Bernard's being killed. I was working at the library. An official-looking man in a suit and tie walked in and said something to the head librarian, Mrs. Doughretty. Mrs. Doughretty — God, I remember this like it was yesterday — she didn't even have to point me out. She just looked across the room at me. I was putting books on a wheeled cart. She looked at me, and the fellow in the suit looked at me, and I knew. I folded like an accordion right down to the floor.

"You see, Bernard was sent quite late to the war. Oh, he was already in the service nearly a year. But he was held up, because of his needing surgery. He had his appendix removed. He'd had an appendicitis attack and had to recover from that. He'd already had his combat training. Had his appendix only waited to burst until he'd got to Germany, he might have been alive today. They'd have taken him right out of combat, maybe to some peaceful little village hospital somewhere. Nice clean sheets on the bed. Flowers in the room. It was only about a month after he joined the First Army in Germany that he was killed.

"Bernard's body was shipped home to Vermont, where he was born and raised. And I've told you he's buried in Montpelier, which is the state capital. And a few days after the funeral, I got a ten-dollar-per-month raise. I hadn't even asked for it. That small gesture. I knew the library was the place for me."

I later learned that it was during her first year as head librarian, in 1973, that things at the Halifax Free Library really began to unravel for my mother. The basic reality, let alone how close she was to a complete breakdown, was unknown to me at the time. At first her staff thought the discord was the result of all the stresses and strains of her new position. Her temper flared at nothing of importance. After such an incident, she would call a librarian or librarian's assistant into her office, where her apology extended into an opportunity to chastise and admonish. In the first two months, one librarian gave her notice, and a librarian's assistant gave my mother an old-fashioned dunce cap she'd found in an antique store — the cap was the sort an elementary school teacher would force a student to wear as the student sat on a stool in the corner, facing the wall — and said, "Nora, maybe you want one of us to wear this when you get upset about things." To show she was not without humor, my mother wore the dunce cap all the rest of that working day. But then she began to wear it around our house too. At breakfast, at dinner.

The last weekend in August, I was working at John W. Doull, Bookseller, taking inventory, when I noticed a box marked SAVE FOR NORA RIGOLET — HALIFAX FREE LIBRARY. There was a purchase order taped to the box as well. Inside I discovered ten books

47

of World War II photographs. Among them was a book that had a section dedicated to the work of Robert Capa. I didn't know then how estimable a figure Robert Capa was, nor that he had taken *Death on a Leipzig Balcony,* which almost certainly was represented in the book I paged through, as it had been prominently featured in the May 14, 1945, issue of *Life* magazine. I decided to drive the box home in our Ford station wagon, placing it in clear view on the dining room table.

It was that box of books, I think, that finally triggered my mother's fall from grace. Things at the library went from bad to worse. By November 1973 my mother had requested, one by one, the resignation of every member of her staff, all of whom refused. When she called a staff meeting, nobody attended. At home one evening she said, "My staff is preparing a coup d'état." My mother suffered insomnia; I'd hear her at all hours in the kitchen, listening to the radio, and often I had to ask her to turn the volume down so I could sleep.

"Mother, what's the matter?" I asked. We were out having dinner at Halloran's restaurant, on Water Street.

"It's not one thing," she said. "It's many things."

But her tone was dismissive and I dropped the subject.

I was nervous as a sparrow about my mother. It seemed like I was getting an ulcer or something. I often had stomach cramps. I drank a lot of Pepto-Bismol. I had a pink tongue for days on end. Everything to do with my mother's comportment had become deeply worrisome and perniciously mysterious, in the sense that I felt I was being poisoned by what I could not comprehend.

Then, on March 18, 1974, I stopped by the Halifax Free Library fifteen minutes before closing time, at 4:45 p.m., to see if my mother would come out for coffee or an early dinner. I was going to finally insist we talk about, for starters, her wearing that dunce cap at home. But nothing could have prepared me for what I encountered next.

The library had a dramatic display of the war photographs of Robert Capa, which my mother, I learned later, had browbeat the staff into agreeing to mount. Enormous reproductions, hanging by wires, filled all three of the street-side windows of the library. I especially remember the photographs of the Spanish Civil War, and photographs of French women, heads shaved, holding their babies, being harassed by French citizens because their children had been fathered by German occupiers. A book of Capa's photographs, which was part of a series on famous photographers, was featured prominently in the center front window.

That display would've been quite enough to, literally and figuratively, put my mother's obsession, her fragility, on high exhibit. But when I stepped into the library, none of the staff would look at me, let alone greet me, in their usual friendly and familiar fashion. My mother's closest friend, a wonderful woman and senior librarian named Jinx Faltenbourg, walked up, took me by the hand, and marched me into the recently staged room, originally designed as a reading room. "Nora hired some people, and they came in last night and spent the night setting all this up," Jinx said. "Did you know anything about this, Jacob?"

"I was dead to the world last night," I said. "I thought Mom was asleep in her bedroom."

The reading room, still smelling slightly of sawdust and paint, was festooned with ribbons as if for a birthday party. There was a jukebox in one corner. The song "Ac-cent-tchu-ate the Positive," by the Andrews Sisters, was playing. Stretching almost the entire length of the back wall was a banner that read, in large block lettering, THE END OF THE WAR CAFÉ. There were three round tables with checkered tablecloths, and candles in wine bottles. There were cakes on another table, plastic spoons and forks, and paper plates. There were paper cups and pitchers of cider. Prices were marked for each food item. My mother was dancing by herself near the jukebox, facing away from us.

"We aren't licensed for this," Jinx said, "so we're going to have to lock the front door. And I'm worried that Nora advertised a party in the newspaper. I'm going to send the rest of the staff home, Jacob. It has to be done."

When the song ended, my mother pressed more buttons and on came "Shoo Shoo Baby," again by the Andrews Sisters. Still, my mother did not turn toward Jinx and me. She leaned heavily against the curved glass of the jukebox and sang along, quite loudly, and my mother did not have an especially good voice. Jinx got the rest of the staff and the last lingering patrons out the front door, locked it, and joined me back in the former reading room. Through the glass front door I could see a dozen or so people looking puzzled, unhappy to be turned away. On came a jitterbug song, the title of which I didn't know, though my mother often played the Andrews Sisters at home, and she began to jitterbug toward me. She grabbed my hands and yanked me out on what now served as the dance floor. As I stood stiffly, probably with a sour expression, my mother let go of my hands and began tossing herself about wildly, and finally stumbled backward, slamming into the jukebox. She slid to the floor. I ran over and said, "Mom, are you okay?" and she said, "How could I not be okay? The war's over. Bernie's coming home. I won't have to deal with Robert Emil anymore."

"Who?" I said. I looked at Jinx, and she just shrugged her shoulders.

"The hideous policeman Robert Emil," my mother said.

I had no earthly idea whom she was referring to.

"Okay, it's okay, let me help you up," I said. But she pushed me violently away, stood, walked to a table, took up her handbag, walked back to the jukebox, reached into her handbag, and began to jam coins in the slot, and many of them were spilling to the floor. She must've put in five dollars' worth of coins. "Bernie will be here any minute. I mean, this whole welcome party is for him, right?"

By this time Jinx had called the police and explained the situation, and in no more than twenty minutes an ambulance arrived at the library. Two attendants got my mother into a straitjacket, the type I'd seen only in the movies. It tore me up to see this. Jinx kept close to my mother, telling the attendants to take it easy, take it easy, please.

Before they led her out of the library, I had a moment to embrace my mother, and said, "Mom, what is happening to you?"

"It's going to be fine, Jacob. Life will provide. It's okay, it's all right. I'm experiencing a fall from grace," she said. "I hope I'm not embarrassing my son. But I'm experiencing a fall from grace."

Jinx unplugged the jukebox.

My mother said to the attendants, "Okay, boys, we're off to the paddy wagon."

Over the next six months or so, I attended weekly meetings with the staff psychiatrists at Nova Scotia Rest Hospital. Sometimes my mother was present, sometimes not. My mother's main attending psychiatrist was Peter Murdoch. I liked Dr. Murdoch, and he spoke to me with directness. I often talked to him in his private office. One day, about a year after my mother had been admitted, he said, "I had hoped not to have to be telling you this, Jacob, but the things that we determined were so radically obsessing Nora not only continue to do so, but in some ways have worsened. What do I mean by that? Well, take Arts and Crafts as an example. In Arts and Crafts Nora produces work — whether drawings, paintings, or other forms — more often than not about World War II. Not just about the war in general, but a particular battle. Now, we know that her husband, Bernard, died in the battle for Leipzig —"

"I knew that," I said. "She told me that."

"Yes, the battle for Leipzig, Germany. A number of American soldiers died there, and Bernard was one of them."

"And so in Arts and Crafts, what? She's re-creating the battle over and over again?"

"Basically, yes. We call it 'retraumatizing.' Except the original, actual physical trauma, of course, was inflicted on Bernard, killed as he was by a German soldier. But your mother is not only reenacting, in all these hundreds of Arts and Crafts compositions, *Bernard's* death. In one sense Nora's mentally stalled in the past."

"Generally, I get what you're saying. But why is this happening now? Why, after thirty years? It's horrible."

"One thing I can suggest is, this has been building very slowly for a long time. The mind holds subtle auditions, you might call them. *Shall this be the right time to loose my demons? No, but how about now?* She has been repressing things for years and years. Also, I've discussed with my staff the possibility of there being an intensifying element — something persistently haunting to Nora — that hasn't revealed itself yet but definitely is a factor. Our hope is that it will be revealed in our weekly conversations."

"'Persistently haunting'? What can that possibly mean?"

"Something we can't see yet. Perhaps the best way for me to describe it, or at least what I suspect it is: We think that there is some awful guilt attached to Bernard's death in Leipzig. Something Nora cannot yet speak about. And she may never be able to. These things are deeply repressed. Our job is to draw it out if possible. We're a little like detectives that way, if you'll forgive the analogy."

"What do you recommend, though?"

"At this point, I recommend electroshock therapy. To, if nothing else, relieve the pain of repression she is so powerfully experiencing. This may contradict our hope to get to the bottom of things, as it were."

"How do you mean?"

"Electroshock therapy can cause memory loss."

"What?"

"It has proven very successful, Jacob. As a treatment for trauma reenactment. But we would need you to sign a form of approval."

I then told him about the photographs lining the walls of our house.

"Yes, that makes perfect sense to me," Dr. Murdoch said. "Because Nora is attempting to reinstate a time before the trauma of Bernard's death."

"My mother calls it her portrait gallery of happy days."

"I see."

"Tell me more about this electroshock treatment. It sounds painful. I don't want my mother in any pain."

When he described the process, I stomped out of his office. I won't repeat the language I used, calling back over my shoulder.

The Auction in London

IN MID-AUGUST 1977, ABOUT FIVE MONTHS AFTER MY
mother had assaulted *Death on a Leipzig Balcony,* Mrs. Hamelin insisted that I judiciously prepare for my next auction. "You've been
distracted lately, what with Martha Crauchet and your mother and
whatnot. Did you even realize that you forgot to drive me and Mrs.
Brevittmore for our antiquing out to Peggy's Cove last Sunday?"

"I did forget and I'm very sorry."

"You should know that it took every ounce of strength not to ask
you to travel to Copenhagen this past May."

"I take it there was an auction there."

"Precisely. It was a sacrifice. But I felt I had to give you time, what
with all of your distractions. But let me be direct. In Copenhagen, a
photograph was on auction that I have very much desired for thirty
years: *Tombeau des Rois de Juda.*" One of the few from Auguste Salzmann's journey to the Holy Land in 1854. Salzmann was French
born, his years were 1824 to 1872."

"I've fallen behind in my obligations. I'll do better."

"Well, Jacob, I'm about to trust you, not just to do better, but to do your best. Because the family who purchased *Tombeau des Rois* has fallen on hard times. The photograph is up for auction in three weeks in London."

"I would imagine you have the research waiting in the library."

"I do indeed."

"What's the highest I can bid?"

"Twelve thousand, not a penny more. But if need be, Jacob, not a penny less. And that is twelve thousand English pounds, by the way."

"Of course."

From Mrs. Hamelin's library I telephoned Martha at the police station. "I've just been told I'm going to London in two weeks."

"What about our weekend in Montreal?"

"It's an important auction. I'm sorry."

"Disappointing. There was going to be that restaurant. There was going to be that hotel."

"Worse yet, I've got to start my research tonight — now, in fact. Esther read me the riot act a few minutes ago. Not happy with me. Not happy at all. My being so distracted lately. Stuff like that."

"Tell Esther — uh, Mrs. Hamelin. Tell her you've been very *attentive* to me. Use the term 'under the bedclothes.'"

"I'm afraid that wouldn't help my situation much, but I'm glad you feel the way you feel."

"I don't mind practicing for marriage for another year. But after that, if we don't set a date, I'm going to propose to both Hodgdon and Tides, possibly within the same hour."

"They're both already married."

"True, but I know many secrets about them — their so-called work habits. I could easily blackmail them into it. Once I spoke to their wives, they'd serve me tea and start packing their suitcases. They'd be appreciative. It would all get done very quickly."

"What time is *Detective Levy Detects* on tonight?"

"Ten o'clock, as usual. You'd better be here by then, Jake. We have to listen together. Want me to save you some dinner?"

"Mrs. Brevittmore will give me something, I'm sure. I'm in Esther's library now, and believe me, there's a stack of books and academic papers and all sorts of other things I've got to start in on."

"Just so you know, tonight's episode? Detective Levy and Leah Diamond get caught up in the murder of the little bald guy who sells newspapers and cigars and candy in the hotel lobby. I mean, who'd want to do that? He always had a kind word. But who knows? Maybe he was crooked."

"I'll give all this some thought when I'm walking over tonight. I've got to hit these books now, Martha."

"Me, I've got to move one report over to the other side of my desk. Then I've got to replace it with another report."

"See you around nine-thirty, okay?"

"If you're later than ten, you know I won't talk to you until the episode's over."

"If I know anything, I know that."

Auguste Salzmann: The Jerusalem Photographs, the translation of a book written in the mid-nineteenth century, was very informative, especially about Salzmann's life. He'd begun his artistic career as a painter, studying under his brother, Henri-Gustave. Then he got interested in photography. In 1854 he went to the Holy Land on a mission sponsored by the French Ministry of Public Interest, but his journey was cut short by illness — it may have been acute dysentery. Still, he managed to make 150 calotypes of historical monuments in Egypt and Jerusalem. He worked in technically refined "salt prints," as they were called. Mrs. Hamelin had also provided me with a book called *The Art of the French Calotype* and fifty or so articles about Salzmann from various journals, including four whose translation from the French she'd commissioned.

I read more than a hundred pages, took notes, then packed my shaving kit and a change of clothes and walked to Martha's apartment. I arrived at the very start of *Detective Levy Detects*. Martha had set the radio on the kitchen table and gestured, with a finger upright across her mouth, for me to stay quiet, so I sat at the kitchen table too, and she slid a cup of hot tea over to me. Of late she'd been trying to get me to drink tea at night instead of coffee.

"In tonight's episode," the announcer said, "Detective Frederik Levy and the love of his life and partner in sleuthing, Leah Diamond, have been called in to investigate the murder of Fanwell Birch, who worked the newspaper stand in the lobby of the Hotel Devonshire. Always one with a firm handshake and a hale and hearty good morning, and a good old Canadian work ethic, at work by six in the a.m. and never left the lobby before eight in the p.m., Fanwell Birch, age fifty-eight, five feet five inches tall, not a hair on his head, who owned two suits, two ties, two white shirts, and two pairs of shoes and socks, was found with a bullet in the heart, slumped over a stack of newspapers, in the hotel lobby where he spent half a lifetime. Apparently, nobody heard the shot. Well, then again, Fanwell Birch probably heard it."

Right after this, Martha took my hand and led me into her bedroom, and we lay down on top of the bedclothes. "There, that's better," she said. She loved listening to the radio a room away like this. But whether the radio was on the bedside or the kitchen table, it was almost as if *Detective Levy Detects* intensified Martha's comprehension of the powers of seduction.

"You know, darling, even when I'm here alone, I usually listen to *Detective Levy Detects* in bed. And it's not that I actually want to be Leah Diamond — well, all right, maybe for a night."

Frankly, I don't remember much of the plot, but I do remember some of the lines that made Martha laugh and say, pretty much like she always said, "Boy, those people really know how to talk, don't they?"

See my derringer, here, pointing at you? A derringer is the minia-
ture poodle of guns — with rabies.

So what you know my name, so what? Just because you know my
name don't mean you know my game.

I sized you up in two minutes, sonny. I'm a student of people. They
don't give out diplomas for that. There's no diploma for how I size peo-
ple up.

You're actually asking, is this gun loaded? Sure it's loaded, else it
wouldn't have any bullets in it.

Woke with your clothes on, eh? That don't mean at some point in
the evening you didn't have them off, now, does it? If you can't remem-
ber, why should I tell you?

Smooching, necking, kissing, none of them suffice. See, I want to do
something with our lips there ain't no dictionary word for it. Some-
thing in the dark, way beyond the dictionary.

In my experience, at heightened moments of bidding at auction, it
little matters what I know about the photographer or the photograph in question. How to say this? You aren't bidding against other
bidders' knowledge, but against their incentive. Sitting in my assigned seat, I am all nerves. I unbutton the collar of my white shirt,
loosen the knot of my tie. (Mrs. Hamelin expects me to be properly
dressed, an auction being a "formal occasion of attentiveness and
possibility," as she put it.) And being all nerves, my alertness isn't
drawn from books, articles, treatises, or my one course in art history. No, I'm merely an emissary on assignment, in a fugue state of
intuition, who can lift his right hand in a sharp little wave, or shoot
it up like a schoolboy anxious to answer the teacher's question, or
casually hoist an open palm as if gesturing to a waiter to bring the
check. Or raise the bidding paddle, if one is provided. It all depends
on the moment.

Bidding at auction is complicated for me. On the one hand, I
want to please Mrs. Hamelin and come home with the goods. On

the other hand, I am acutely aware of the systems of class, privilege, and imperiousness that, at any time, might intervene in, and violate the purported etiquette and order of, the auction room. This, in fact, occurred in London during the bidding for *Tombeau des Rois*.

I traveled to London on September 9, 1977. The auction was held in a spacious private home on George Street, a block west of Durrants Hotel, where I'd taken a room. In London I always stayed at Durrants, no matter the location of the auction. By always, I mean this was my third visit to London. Arriving jet-lagged at six o'clock in the morning, I was pleased that Mrs. Hamelin had thought to secure my room for the previous night, so I could check right in and get some much-needed sleep. Waking at about three, I found a fish and chips shop nearby, then returned to my room to brush up on my reading about *Tombeau des Rois* and telephone Martha.

"How are you?" she said. "The auction is in three hours. I sent my suit down immediately to be pressed," I said. "Esther Hamelin trained you well, Jake. Kidding aside, good luck. I hope it goes well and you get the photograph for her. What's it called again? My mind is fuzzy." *"Tombeau des Rois de Juda,"* I said. "Oooh, a man who can speak French so fluently really makes me want to —" "I wish you were here too, my darling detective. Sometime maybe you can travel with me to an auction." "I'll save my pennies. Let me know how it goes, please. Bye-bye."

I had a bowl of soup, some bread, and a salad in the hotel dining room. Then I went back up to my room and got dressed in my suit, tie, and polished shoes. I walked to the private home where the auction was to be held. I produced my credentials and was shown into what looked to me like a ballroom. Folding chairs were set out in rows. The easel and podium were up front. It was all done in good taste. By the time the first item was put on exhibit, every seat was filled. No one was standing in the back or along the sides of the room. Invitation only.

The auctioneer stepped to the podium, adjusted the micro-phone, and said, in a British accent, "Good evening, ladies and gentlemen." His name, as listed on the elegantly printed program, was Everett Gray. When he first appeared from the back room, I almost burst into laughter: he so fully met the description, on *Detective Levy Detects,* of the murdered newspaper seller, Fanwell Birch. If I wanted to end my employment with Mrs. Hamelin, I could've done so, right then and there, by standing up and shouting, "You're not Everett Gray. No, sir, you are in fact one Fanwell Birch, who sold newspapers and cigars in the lobby of the Devonshire Hotel in downtown Toronto, Canada. Because you see, sir, I am not Jacob Rigolet, as my name tag professes me to be. No, I am Detective Frederik Levy." Plus which, telling Martha what I'd done would've made her laugh. That is often, of an evening, my one ambition, to make her laugh.

Instead, I sat out the bidding for a photograph titled *Cadillac Showroom,* by Robert Frank, from the auction house's twentieth-century collection, in uninterested silence.

It was over an hour before the bidding for the twentieth-century collection was completed. Between heated rounds of bidding, the man seated next to me, Hans Frisch, an Austrian representing a private client, would lean over and provide a witty and insightful comment. I liked this fellow and arranged to have a drink with him at Durrants Hotel after the auction. When, perhaps against my better judgment, I'd told him that I was there to bid only on *Tombeau des Rois,* his whole countenance soured. He resituated himself, groaning, as if it were an arduous journey, rather than a matter of inches, to the far edge of his chair. Staring at the podium, he said, "I'll have to pass on that drink, I'm afraid, Mr. Rigolet. With professional apologies, naturally." It was then I realized he was there to bid on the same photograph.

As it turned out, he bid on all three nineteenth-century photographs on offer ahead of *Tombeau des Rois* and was successful twice. When the Salzmann was brought to the easel, its bona fides given, and the bidding begun at five thousand pounds, Hans Frisch turned to me and said, "My constitution does not allow me a subjunctive mood, always so prevalent in these auctions." (Later, I had to look up "subjunctive" in the dictionary in Durrants' library.) The bidding had upped only to six thousand five hundred when Frisch raised the paddle with his seat number on it and called out, "Twenty-two thousand pounds!" He turned to me and sniffed, then turned back to the podium, where Mr. Gray cleared his throat and said, in a tensely restrained voice, "The gentleman bids twenty-two thousand pounds. Do I hear twenty-two thousand five hundred?" But the bidding for *Tombeau des Rois* was over. The gavel came down. Hisses were heard in protest. Hans Frisch rose from his chair and walked down the aisle and out the back door. My work being over and done with, I followed him out, not close behind.

I immediately made all sorts of harsh judgments concerning Frisch, but I hadn't yet had time to sort them out. Because of Frisch's ambush, I had lost out on *Tombeau des Rois de Juda,* though I may not have won it anyway. That part was unpredictable: someone other than Frisch may have been willing to bid higher than my allotted twelve thousand. Still, Frisch had made certain to end the bidding in such an arrogant and abrupt manner, not subscribing to the received or expected notions of fairness, not allowing for the auction to build in tension, not allowing for the traditional repertoire of feints, hesitations, grandstanding, subtleties, and resignations, though Frisch's outlandish bid certainly did deliver a dramatic performance, and of course he won the Salzmann. It was Frisch's sheer crudeness that would not be forgiven. All of that. All of that. And now I dreaded telephoning Mrs. Hamelin, which she always insisted I do right after an auction ended. I'd go directly to my room and pick up the phone and ask to be connected to her number in Halifax. I would have to report that *Tombeau des Rois* was the second photograph in a row I'd failed to win for her. Next, I would telephone Martha.

I found myself following Frisch on the street. He was carrying a leather valise. He turned once to look back. When he reached Durrants Hotel, he stopped and waited for me. He held out his hand, but I refused to shake it. "I understand," he said. "But life is more complicated than what first it might appear. Allow me to stand you that drink. Please."

In the dark bar of the hotel, with its black leather couches and chairs, its small round tables, its bartender dressed in white shirt and black vest and trousers, there were three Japanese women and, at a corner table, two men speaking in low tones. Later, the bartender said one of the men was the poet Ted Hughes. He told me, "Right around the corner is Francis Edwards, Antiquarian Books. Mr. Hughes has a number of his books there. Just a suggestion, mate."

Anyway, when the waiter called out for our choices, I ordered a vodka straight up, and Frisch a White Russian; he looked apologetically at me and said, "Weak stomach — the cream helps." Frisch brought our drinks back to the table. Holding his glass in the air, he said, "To displeasing our employers." Hesitatingly, I clinked my glass against his. It seemed a peculiar toast to make, and to ask me to make.

"Look, Mr. Rigolet — may I call you Jacob?" I nodded. "Jacob, look. I've got a nervous condition. Let me explain. How you saw me behave at the auction, that is how I always behave at auctions. I work for an extremely wealthy man who lives in Zurich. Part of an old banking family. He is — how do you say it? My bread and butter. He does not give me limits on what I can bid. I proceed at my own discretion. He only expects me to bring a photograph or photographs back for his collection, you see. To not have a limit, and my nervous condition — which is that I am claustrophobic to a terrible degree, and so, in an auction room, I am often almost ready to black out. To faint dead away. So therefore I — what is the American expression? Cut in line? It almost always works, my bid being twice, three times, even more than what anyone else has bid to that point."

"But you didn't do that with the first three photographs you bid on," I said.

"Yes, but there was little bidding on those. The end came swiftly, and you might have noticed that I stepped out into the hallway between each item. To get some air."

"I did notice that."

"Yet with *Tombeau des Rois,* once I knew you were there to bid on that one photograph, I knew the bidding for it might take some time."

"So you cut in line."

"I'm afraid so."

"Better than to faint dead away."

"Still, I looked at you, my friend. I studied your face. And I said to myself: No doubt a good man. A man working for an employer of means. In that sense, a man just like myself. And by my actions I may have made life difficult for this good man. And I felt . . . I felt *artificial.* I felt artificial, here —" He held his open palm against his heart. "And now we are here, together, having a drink. And I will confess to you that I have reached a low point. I am, as the French say, experiencing the black butterfly. The depression. I can find no way to put it in reverse. My wife has left me. My children no longer acknowledge my existence. I anger everyone at the auctions — I have actually been struck in the face, in a Rotterdam auction house this occurred — and yet the auctions are my only employment."

He finished his drink and waved his glass in the air, indicating to the bartender that he wanted another of the same. The bartender delivered it himself this time.

"*Salud!*" Frisch said, and drank the second White Russian in three gulps. "Now here is what I propose. This is a way to make your visit to London a success and to reprieve me of my miserable guilt, at how shamelessly I have comported myself.

"Nine o'clock, the bank where is my employer's account will open. I will withdraw the twenty-two thousand pounds, as I am authorized to do. The bank knows me and knows whom I represent, you understand. I will then go to the auction house and complete the transaction with them. I will next meet you at this very same table. You did mention you'd taken a room here in Durrants Hotel? I will then hand to you *Tombeau des Rois*. You will then board a plane for Canada, where you will deliver the photograph to your employer. *Voilà!* You are a success in your employer's eyes. I have what is called power of attorney, and I will have provided you with a formal letter declaring *Tombeau des Rois* is a gift. It will be entirely legal. There would in my opinion be no need to provide any more details to your employer. You can simply say that life is unpredictable and the photograph is his."

"This would mean you, Mr. Frisch, will return to Zurich empty-handed. Won't you be fired? Sacked? Whatever you wish to call it."

"But you see, Jacob, that is precisely the purpose I want served. I want to leave this employment. I can no longer bear my condition, as it applies to auctions and auction houses. Because each time, I experience a thousand black butterflies."

"But wouldn't Mrs. Hamelin — that's who I work for — wouldn't she be part of an underhanded situation? Wouldn't I be putting her in that position?"

"Ah, you are worrying about what? The *situational ethics*. Oh, poor fellow."

"Not sure what that means."

"Look, I am using you, Jacob. Let me be honest. I am using you to be able to leave my ghastly employment. I do not wish even to go back to Zurich. Zurich is for me full of black butterflies, you understand."

"I think I understand."

"However selfish, it is a wonderful opportunity for me. I will have done the good deed for you, a good man. I will have no reason to return to Zurich."

He ordered a third drink and I ordered a second. He held his glass in the air and said, "To your success at auction." We clinked glasses.

I wanted to go through with Frisch's plan, but I didn't fully recognize myself in it.

"The most fortunate thing has happened," Frisch said. "I've met a good man."

We drank ourselves to near oblivion, as I remember it, which, now that I have said it, sounds like a contradiction, the *remembering* part. Still, I definitely made it to my room, and definitely telephoned Martha. Somehow I managed to relate to her the details of the auction, the conversation in the bar, the pact I had made with Frisch. ("Yes, I think I agreed to everything he asked.")

"Listen to me, Jacob," she said, her very tone of voice sobering me faster than ten pots of black coffee. "Here is what you do. You walk downstairs to the lobby. You check out of your hotel. You find another hotel. It's London — there's got to be a decent one nearby. You leave no forwarding address. You try and sleep. The next day, when you are clearheaded, you go to Heathrow and fly home. Then you come directly to my apartment. You will not — not not not — have this photograph with you, Jacob. You cannot have it with you. It is just wrong."

"This Mr. Frisch is desperate, Martha. He needs help. I can help him."

"Jacob, there's every possibility that this Mr. Frisch will wake up and remember none of this. That doesn't matter one bit. What matters is that the moment we ring off, you march down to the lobby. Jacob!"

In the morning, I woke up on the floor. I washed, dressed, and went down to the lobby. The desk clerk said, "An envelope for you, Mr. Rigolet." I took the envelope, sat in the nearest chair, opened the envelope, and read the note inside: "My dear Jacob, How foolish of me. In my own hotel I recognized two things. First, I was correct in assessing you as a good man. Second, that being a good man, you would finally not be able to accept my proposal. And yet I hold out a little hope. I wish you all great fortunes. In friendship, Hans Frisch."

The note was written on the stationery of Brown's Hotel. I stepped out to George Street, told the doorman I needed a cab, and he flagged one down in a matter of seconds. I took the cab to Brown's Hotel, at 33 Albemarle Street. "Sorry, guv'nor," the cabbie said, "looks like I'll have to drop you off a quarter block from the hotel. Look up ahead there. The bobbies are out in full." He pulled to the curb, I paid the fare, and when I stood on the sidewalk, I saw that several police cars and an ambulance were parked in front of Brown's. There was a police cordon and a dozen or so curious on-lookers. "What's happened?" I asked a doorman. "Sadly, sir, one of our dear regulars has done himself in." How could I not realize right away that it was Hans Frisch?

I was not about to stand there gawking, so I decided to walk. And walk I did, wandering the streets in a daze, I don't remember for how long. Anyway, I ended up back at Durrants. Stepping into the lobby, the concierge said, "Delivery for you, sir. You only have to sign for it." He went into the storeroom behind his podium and brought out a square package, neatly wrapped in brown paper, with the words MR. JACOB RIGOLET in black lettering. "From the auction house, I think," Mr. Bernier said. "I take it congratulations are in order."

I took the package up to my room, which was already reserved for one more night. I set the package upright on a chair and stared at it a long time. Finally, I carefully opened the package. There was *Tombeau des Rois*. There also was a manila envelope. Just as Frisch had promised, the envelope contained a copy of a typed letter stating that he had power of attorney for Mr. Peter Zellistar (his employer) and was "giving, as a gift, the photograph titled *Tombeau des Rois* to Mr. Jacob Rigolet of Halifax, Nova Scotia, Canada." Paperclipped to the letter was Hans Frisch's business card.

The consequences of my delivering *Tombeau des Rois de Juda* to Mrs. Hamelin — that is, of not sending the photograph on to Frisch's employer in Zurich — became clear relatively soon. My London-to-Montreal flight arrived at 5:30 p.m., and the connecting flight to Halifax arrived at 7:15, and I took a cab to Martha's apartment. She had put on a pot of coffee and was still wearing her "professional attire," as she called her pantsuit and white blouse. We embraced and kissed and she said, "You must be exhausted." "Not too bad, really," I said. But we were both staring at the package I had set against the kitchen wall.

"Jacob, tell me that isn't what I think it is," Martha said.

"*Tombeau des Rois,*" I said. "Want to look at it?"

"Jacob, this is a real test of our marriage, even though we aren't married."

I sat down and she poured me a cup of coffee, then one for herself. She sat across from me. "I have a real problem with what you did, Jake. You better try and talk me through this, because I'm very, very angry with you just now. I haven't seen you for nearly five days, and I love you, but I'm very angry. I don't understand how you could do what you did with this photograph. And no, I don't want to look at it."

"It's really beautiful."

"Good."

"May I ask one favor, though, Martha? Would you get out of your interlocutrix clothes, please?"

Martha gave me a tight smile, got up, went into her bedroom, and emerged wearing blue jeans and a sweatshirt and thick, dark blue socks.

"There," she said. "Now, what the hell happened, Jacob? What were you thinking?"

"All right. Let me try to explain. The fellow I mentioned, who'd bid so high on the photograph, he killed himself."

"What?"

"Hans Frisch committed suicide at Brown's Hotel. Have you ever heard the term 'black butterflies'?" Martha shook her head solemnly back and forth. "Well, he said that in French it means you're badly depressed. You have black butterflies. I didn't know the term either, but he explained it to me. He said he wasn't going back to Zurich, where he worked for some wealthy patron. A Mr. Zellistar. He told me his life was a train wreck."

"Really took you into his confidence, didn't he?"

"You had to be there."

"I'm not so sure about that, but go ahead."

"Basically, he wanted me to have the photograph. That's the long and the short of it. But I had no idea he would do what he did. How could I know that this deal with the photograph was his last act on earth. How could I know that?"

"But that's not the point, is it, Jacob? The *point* is that once you had the photograph, the right thing to do was —"

"Have the auction house send it on to Frisch's employer in Zurich."

"Correct."

"Guess what, though. The photograph is right here in your kitchen."

"Which means you can still do the ethical thing. Tomorrow you can go and send it overseas. Have you told Esther Hamelin that you have the photograph?"

"I did telephone her."

"And from the look on your face, I take it you lied to her."

"Yes. By what I didn't say. Lied to her by what I didn't say. I only said I had the photograph."

"So she thought, Well, Jacob's been successful. How nice. He's come back to me. He's my reliable employee again. Let's think about a bonus."

"Probably right."

"What are you going to do now?"

"Sleep on it."

"Not here, you aren't. You aren't going to sleep on it here."

I reached to take her hands in mine, but Martha stood, walked to the door, opened it, and stared at the floor, waiting for me to leave. She slammed the door behind me.

It was after midnight when I arrived at Mrs. Hamelin's house. I'd carried my suitcase and the photograph all those blocks. I unlocked the front door and walked to the kitchen and saw Mrs. Hamelin and Mrs. Brevittmore sitting at the table. They were dressed in the clothes they would wear on any given day. They had obviously just finished having dinner: they were eating sorbet and berries, and they both had a demitasse of espresso in front of them. Two candles had burned down to an inch high. "Jacob," Mrs. Hamelin called out, "please come in and join us. As you can see, we've had a late dinner. Coffee?"

I shook my head no, set down the suitcase in the hallway, and carried the photograph into the kitchen. I began to unwrap the package, but Mrs. Hamelin said, quite insistently, "No, don't! That photograph does not belong to me. Please don't open it. It would be a torment to see it here in my home, knowing it must be sent away."

This is not going to be good, I thought, this is going to be awful. Then I betrayed Martha's trust in absentia by saying, "Did Martha call you?"

"I have no idea what you're talking about, Jacob," Mrs. Hamelin said. "Please sit down."

"The director of the auction house in London called Esther," Mrs. Brevittmore said. "Also, the proper owner of the photograph, a Mr. Zellistar, telephoned."

I sat down and, without really knowing what I was doing, finished off Mrs. Hamelin's and Mrs. Brevittmore's espressos in quick succession, with two loud slurps, setting each small cup on the table. They just watched this in wonder.

"Naturally, you will no longer be employed by me," Mrs. Hamelin said. "This is effective immediately. Though you may stay in the cottage tonight. I wouldn't put such a dear and loyal friend out on the street, now, would I?"

When I didn't answer, Mrs. Brevittmore said, "No, you wouldn't, Esther." She began to clear the dishes, but Esther grabbed her hand, and Mrs. Brevittmore sat down again.

Now Mrs. Brevittmore lit into me. "For some thirty years, Esther Hamelin has built a reputation in the world of antiquarian photography that is unprecedented in its dignity. You have almost single-handedly put that reputation in the shadows. But only for the moment, Jacob. Only for the moment. Because Esther has already made her apologies to the appropriate persons. She has made her humble apologies, but she did not once place the blame on you, Jacob, but on herself."

"Would you care to know what has occurred over the past six or so hours, Jacob?" Mrs. Hamelin said.

"I owe that much to you," I said. "Of course."

"As Mrs. Brevittmore has already informed you, I received telephone calls from the director of the auction house, Mr. Michael Wedgewood, and, less than an hour later, from Mr. Peter Zellistar, who is the rightful owner of the Salzmann photograph. Both were painful calls to receive. Very painful. These two men explained what they were able to explain — in some detail, mind you.

"Yet those two telephone calls, I should tell you, were not without sympathy and understanding of a very impressive sort. For one thing, Mr. Hans Frisch — yes, I know all about him — Mr. Hans Frisch had been in Mr. Zellistar's employ for ages.

"In fact, the actual reason for the calls — the fact that Peter Zellistar paid twenty-two thousand pounds for the ownership of *Tombeau des Rois de Juda*—was scarcely mentioned. There would be no scandal allowed. No, each of these dignified men spent considerable time and effort to reassure me that our professional relationships, having the auction house in common, and therefore forged over many years, would remain completely intact. Still, I admit, I heard astonishment in their voices: 'How could such a thing happen? How could you employ someone so given to such disgraceful behavior?'"

"The thing unspoken often settles most bitterly in the heart," Mrs. Brevittmore added, chastising me harshly with that proverb, or whatever it was.

There was a long silence. Finally, Mrs. Brevittmore did clear the dishes, then repaired to her room. Mrs. Hamelin said, "Obviously, by what you said earlier, you've already informed Martha Crauchet of your actions. Am I correct?"

"Yes."

"I can only imagine the difficulties there, now. From everything you've told me, she seems such a fine person."

"I'll have to ask the people living in my mother's house to leave. I'll have to give them notice. Which I'll do first thing. I'll move back in there."

"That is entirely your business, Jacob. My business is to say to you how deep my disappointment is in you. And to also say, because it is true, that I will miss you. But you have to leave my employ."

"I understand."

"Well, perhaps you don't yet fully, but will."

I carried my suitcase out to the cottage and lay on the bed, staring at the ceiling. There was no way I could sleep. Impossible. At about three o'clock in the morning, I went back into the house and overheard Mrs. Brevittmore and Mrs. Hamelin talking in the kitchen.

"You simply had to look at it," Mrs. Brevittmore said. "I knew you would."

"How could I not?"

"It is a lovely thing to look at. I do confess it is a lovely thing to look at."

"And yet all the damage it's caused," Mrs. Hamelin said. "Some permanent, I fear."

A month later, I was enrolled in the library science program at Dalhousie University.

Library Science

MY MOTHER'S STALWART REPUTATION IN THE LIBRARY SYS-
tem didn't hurt. I was able to get strong letters of recommendation
from Jinx Faltenbourg and the other senior librarian at the Halifax
Free Library, Margaret Plumly. What is more, Mrs. Hamelin, when I
told her I was applying for the library science program, said, "I will
write you a letter on my private letterhead. Of course, only if you
want a letter from me. What happened in our professional relationship is over and done with. I can't say, on a personal level, it is water entirely under the bridge. But I can guarantee that a letter from
me on your behalf would betray absolutely no ambivalence. In fact,
I would enthuse and enthuse. Let me know."

In the end, I did request a letter from Esther Hamelin, though I
never read it. I couldn't tell if anyone in the academic office at Dalhousie knew about my mother's fall from grace, but if they did, not
a word was said about it. During my interview, the chair of the department, Dr. Deborah Margolin, said, "Well, part of your résumé
is your childhood, really. Being around libraries so much. But, Mr.

Rigolet, we do accept into our program people who didn't have a single book in their house growing up. We look for many qualities. Yet certainly we are pleased to accept you into our program. I take it all of your paperwork is completed. Technicalities, I'm afraid."

"Yes. I saw to that."

"I did notice that your cover letter had a certain . . . shall we say *anecdotal* element to it. Not tangential, mind you. More . . . subjective. Which is fine."

"Well, being raised by a librarian, I tend to think of the world of libraries with familiarity."

"Indeed. But without my curiosity running amok, may I inquire? You see, it was quite interesting to read that you were actually *born* in the Halifax Free Library. And quite interesting you felt the need to include this fact. Oh, well, none of my business. Besides, I myself had rather an emergency situation with my firstborn son — almost gave birth to him right in the ambulance, as a matter of fact. These things happen."

"I might have edited the letter a little more closely. It was my first cover letter."

"No, no, Mr. Rigolet, it's all fine. We will look happily toward working with you. Then, of course, there is the other extracurricular detail. About the graffiti. Do you recall?"

"I don't know why I included that, Dr. Margolin. My mistake."

"It's not that I need verification. It's not that at all. It was just that — and I didn't discuss this with the panel — that the drawing and caption you knew about, carved into the back of the old wooden card catalogue at the Halifax Free Library, is . . . unusual."

"I can only again say thank you for accepting me into the program."

I stood up to leave, and when I got to the door of Dr. Margolin's office, she said, "However, I would like to see the back of that card catalogue. If you might possibly arrange that, Mr. Rigolet."

I was not about to turn down a request from the chair of my new academic department. "We can go right now if you want. Do you have the time?"

She put on her coat and hat and followed me down the corridor, out to Gottingen Street. We walked the five blocks to the library. It was a beautiful day in Halifax. Jinx Faltenbourg was at the front desk and seemed pleased to see me. She immediately recognized Dr. Margolin, and they exchanged pleasantries in a formal sort of way. "How can we help you today, Dr. Margolin?" Jinx asked.

"Our new student, Mr. Rigolet —"

"I've known Jacob since he was five years old. This library was in effect his babysitter."

"Well, Jacob has agreed to show me something he apparently discovered when he was a little older than that — what would you say, Jacob, you were twelve or thirteen?"

I could not quite meet her eye. "Fourteen."

"Really, how interesting," Jinx said. "Mind if I tag along?"

"The more the merrier," Dr. Margolin said.

They both followed me into the part of the library containing the row of solid-oak card catalogues, with their drawers, metal handles, and alphabetized index cards. They were set against a wall. I went to the first catalogue on the left, and with a good deal of effort pulled it out far enough to be able to wedge myself a little between the cabinet and the wall, and then shouldered it at an angle so the back could be seen in its entirety. I was hoping the graffiti had miraculously been sanded away, but no such luck. I looked a quick moment at the etched drawing and caption: a naked woman was lying across a library table (it had a gooseneck lamp on it, the same sort of lamp as on my mother's desk in her former office); a man, naked from the waist down, wearing a police uniform shirt, badge visible, was holding her legs over his shoulders and was about to enter the woman; he was noticeably erect, and I don't mean his posture. Below the crudely etched desk was carved: *Special hours in the library — after closing time ORE.*

I stepped aside but didn't quite know what to do or where to wait, so I went into the children's room and stared out the window onto the street. When I turned to look at the card catalogues, I saw that both Jinx and Dr. Margolin were behind the one I had moved, leaning close, like archeologists scrutinizing hieroglyphs. I was horrified, but I had brought this on myself, having, in my letter of application, recklessly attempted, by mentioning my "secret" place, to suggest a more intimate (I actually used the word "familial") knowledge of libraries than the so-called average applicant. I wondered now why my application hadn't been tossed into the wastebasket. My fatal mistake had been not letting Martha read the letter before submitting it.

When I saw Mrs. Margolin and Jinx fit the cabinet back against the wall and begin to walk past the main information counter, I fell in directly behind them. Which is when I heard Mrs. Margolin say, "I wonder, Jinx, did you ever try that? I mean, with your husband. Or someone else. On a table like that?"

Their conversation continued to the front door, but I had stopped dead in my tracks.

We had dinner at Halloran's, Martha and I. We talked steadily, but somehow I felt that a certain unspoken thing lay in wait. After our meal we each ordered a whiskey and sipped them slowly. Martha seemed a little nervous and took my hands in hers. "Jake, about what you did with the French photograph," she said.

"I know you haven't forgiven me," I said. "I don't deserve to be."

"Forgiving, not forgiving — those words escape me just now," she said. "The thing I've been thinking about is that you dropped my trust. I trusted you to act differently than you did in London. What happened there muddled your intentions, and you became a kind of thief. But the flip side of that coin, Jacob, is that I dropped your trust too."

"How do you mean?"

"When I first studied your mother's file, the whole backlog of information, I saw that there was some sinister — I don't think that word is overblown — some sinister connection between Officer Robert Emil and Nora. Something that happened back in 1945. I felt it right here." She placed my hand against her stomach. "I felt it and I knew that something was wrong. Yet I stupidly tried to . . . I don't know what. *Protect* you, maybe. And that was treating you like a child. Your darling detective should've acted with more dignity toward her great love. But I didn't. And I dropped your trust. Even if you didn't know I had dropped it."

"Do you know the sinister thing yet, Martha? The facts of it?"

"No, not yet. But Tides and Hodgdon are on the scent of it, and so am I. In my own way. My way is different from their way. But the idea is that all three of us end up with the truth."

"You mean all *four* of us, don't you?"

"I only meant detective-wise."

We each ordered a second whiskey.

That night, after the episode of *Detective Levy Detects*, lying under the bedclothes with Martha, I told her everything that had happened at the library, not scrimping on details about the back of the card catalogue. She laughed and laughed. But then she was startled by a revelation. She sat up against the bedpost, took a few deep breaths, held my face in her hands, and said, "Jake, what did you say those initials were?"

"O-R-E," I said.

Martha slid out from under the covers and stood by the kitchen door. She looked so beautiful in that light, but her expression betrayed all composure.

"Jacob," she said. "Jacob — *think*."

"What are you talking about?"

She actually needed a drink of water to get through this. She went into the kitchen, poured a glass, and drank it right there at the sink. Standing in the doorway again, Martha said, enunciating each letter, each word, as if it was painful to speak, "O-R-E. Officer. Robert. Emil."

"You cannot mean —"

Martha sat on the end of the bed, took my hands in hers, pulled me close, and said, "What I *mean* is that it's *you* possibly being conceived on the back of a card catalogue."

I held her at arm's length. "I don't find that funny."

"Oh, me neither, Jacob. Believe me. Me neither. But I can't drop your trust again. I have to tell you that when I read in Nora's file that she socialized with Robert Emil, I realized that my cold case is most likely your father."

Look How Much Can
Happen of an Evening

AS IT TURNED OUT, THE COUPLE, JOHN AND PHILOMENA Teachout, who'd been living in my mother's house had decided to move to Regina, Saskatchewan, where they both had found work. Within a week they were packed up and gone, leaving the house, cupboard to tabletop, dusted and mopped to a shine. "To tell you the truth," Philomena said in a letter left on the kitchen table, "the photographs on the walls were oppressive. But we didn't feel we could take a single one down. Anyway, we felt fortunate to have your family house for the past year, and we thank you for that."

The first week of classes, beginning October 1 (the term began late due to delayed construction on campus) went well. Especially Introduction to Library Science, taught by Dr. Margolin, a seminar with only six students in it. She told us that Dalhousie had paid for the translation of the very book that had coined the phrase "library science": *Versuch eines vollständigen Lehrbuches der Bibliothek-Wissenschaft oder Anleitung zur vollkommenen Geschäftsführung eines Bibliothekärs* (1808), by Martin Schrettinger, the librarian at the Benedictine monastery in Weissenohe, Germany.

79

In fact, the first six weeks of Dr. Margolin's seminar consisted of reading and discussing Schrettinger's book, and two others, which, as she put it, were indispensable to understanding the origins of the field: *Advice on Establishing a Library*, which was written in 1627 by a French librarian and scholar named Gabriel Naudé, and the Indian librarian S. R. Ranganathan's *The Five Laws of Library Science*, published in 1931. I found all of this interesting and wrote the first of three required papers on *Advice on Establishing a Library*, because I thought that every single thing Gabriel Naudé said was intelligent; then again, when you know practically nothing, so much is a revelation. I received a B-minus on the paper, along with a bunch of questions and a strong sense of Dr. Margolin's disappointment in the margins. *You seem to have read Naudé thoroughly but without much discretion. Why not revisit your opinions with a more refined perspective for your next essay?* I soon learned that she had a reputation for being a tough grader. But beyond that, Martha said, "You just seem so much happier since you stopped working for Esther Hamelin." Privately, I had the notion that my studying library science might bring me closer to my mother. In fact, it had been Martha, during an Arts and Crafts session at Nova Scotia Rest Hospital, who told Nora that I had enrolled. "What did my mother say to that?" I asked Martha. "She was in a mood," Martha said. "Okay, but what was her response?" I asked. Martha said, "'My son Jacob, born in a library, please, dear Lord, don't let him die in one.'" "Whatever I expected, I didn't expect that," I said. "I told you she was in a mood," Martha said. "Making fifty Chinese finger traps in an hour put *me* in a mood too, come to think of it."

A month into my studies, on a Sunday at 7:15 p.m., Martha and I went to see *Days of Heaven* at the Cove Cinema on Gottingen Street. It was cold and rainy, and there was only a smattering of patrons. As we headed for our favored seats, three-quarters of the way back, Martha on the aisle, I suddenly heard "Jacob" whispered loudly. I turned to find Mrs. Hamelin and Mrs. Brevittmore sitting in the very last row. "Come sit with us," Mrs. Hamelin said. Martha said, "No, we have our special place." "All right, then," Mrs. Hamelin said, and she and Mrs. Brevittmore stood, followed us along the aisle, and sat next to us. Martha was on the far left of the quartet, and sent her box of popcorn down to Mrs. Brevittmore, on the far right.

The movie began, and none of us said a single word until it ended. This was a good thing, because you didn't want to be a person sitting near Martha and talking during a movie. Believe me, you just did not. When she heard someone talking, her temper flared like a running wild horse's nostrils; you felt she could rear up and kick a person. Otherwise such an even-tempered detective, Martha Crauchet. Otherwise so measured in her responses to most everything. "In a dark movie theater I'm like Jekyll and Hyde, aren't I?" she once said. "You don't have to say anything. I know I am."

When the film ended, the four of us decided to walk to the Wired Monk Café. A cold November rain fell. We each had an umbrella, which meant a shifting configuration depending on the width of the sidewalk at any given stretch of the way. When I walked next to Mrs. Brevittmore, she said, "Mentally, I was blowing kisses to Sam Shepard, the man who played the bachelor landowner who gets killed. I was blowing him kisses through the whole movie. Our little secret, okay?"

"Sure thing," I said.

"You just watch," she said. "When Esther talks about the movie, she'll extol the virtues of the cinematography, the beauty of the Montana landscape, the vistas, the panorama. And the more she does that, the more I'll know she was blowing kisses to Sam Shepard and to Brooke Adams, the woman who, though already married, marries the Sam Shepard character. They are both her type. Whereas Richard Gere seemed like a freshly scrubbed boy from an Ivy League college who didn't know his ass from a cricket out there in the Wild West."

The Wired Monk was crowded. But after folding our umbrellas and leaving them by the door, we found a corner table and sat down. "Coffee's on me," Martha announced. "A prostitute on Water Street paid me twenty dollars to service her. So I'm flush."

Both Mrs. Hamelin and Mrs. Brevittmore stared, aghast, at Martha a moment, and then the irony sank in, and Mrs. Brevittmore said, "Perhaps, Detective Crauchet, you might write down the exact location this took place. Esther and I often walk along Water Street, out past the docks, and when conversation stalls, we have little else to do, really." We were getting along well.

Coffees were ordered and served. "The cinematography was excellent," Mrs. Hamelin said about *Days of Heaven*. "Many scenes were like beautiful landscape paintings. And the whole story, of course, was an Old Testament allegory."

"The plague of locusts put a very fine point on that," Mrs. Brevittmore said.

There was a silence, we all sipped our coffee, and then I said, "Mrs. Hamelin —"

"Esther, please," she said.

"Esther, I was in the doghouse with you. And now we're sitting here together."

"Are you glad to be sitting here together?" Mrs. Hamelin asked.

"Yes," I said. "But I dropped your trust."

"And I promptly fired you," she said. "So not only have I burned the doghouse, I've given the dog away too."

"There, that's settled," Mrs. Brevittmore said.

"I should mention that I've hired a new assistant," Mrs. Hamelin said. "And now that I've done so, why not let's the four of us meet for a movie. I mean on purpose next time. Coffees afterward. That is, when it's convenient for all of us."

This was agreed upon with smiles and nods and the atmosphere relaxing even more. As we went our separate ways after the café,

Martha said, "Miracles never cease. Right, Jake? Who would have thunk it — you and Esther Hamelin double-dating, huh?"

"That thing you said. About the prostitute. *Servicing* . . ."

"Yeah, where did *that* come from? But it shook some recognition, or acknowledgment, loose at the table. You did know that they are lesbians? And guess what, Jacob? They may not find it all that easy to be out in public, given the conservative shithole Halifax can be. So, my goodness, there was trust there."

"Let's get married."

"Did you just propose? In the rain. In Halifax. On the way home from *Days of Heaven*. Not on your hands and knees. Though of course it's sopping wet out."

"I am proposing. Will you please marry me, Martha?"

"You already proposed a while ago."

"I'm proposing again."

"I'm just thinking, My goodness, look how much can happen of an evening."

"Yes or no."

"Yes, Jake, of course it's yes. I love you."

"Ad infinitum."

"Listen to that Latin vocabulary. I'm so happy. What with your library degree, you can soon start discreetly skimming off library overdue fines. Me, I can get involved in all sorts of graft and bribes. In no time we can take out a mortgage. House with a view of the harbor."

At the Kitchen Table

SO MANY OF MARTHA'S AND MY DECLARATIONS OF LOVE, bewilderment, moods, and, on rare occasions, doubt, all the human stuff orchestrated by intuition and desire to keep us honest with each other, took place at her kitchen table. Which brings me to the morning of December 3, 1977. It was snowing heavily, and when I looked out the window, I saw a woman trudging along the sidewalk, extending her umbrella straight out as if parting the snow blowing horizontally at her.

"More coffee, darling?" Martha said. It was a Saturday, there was no library science class for me, and Martha had the day off. "I've got something to tell you."

She poured me a second cup of coffee. She was dressed in just her cotton robe. I knew she would go running soon; the weather had to be much worse to stop her from that.

"I've been learning so much from Nora," Martha said. "At Arts and Crafts."

"Like what, for instance?"

Martha stood up, went into her bedroom, and changed into

jeans, a T-shirt and sweater, and thick woolen socks. She brushed her teeth, combed her hair, put her hair up in a ponytail held by a rubber band, then sat down at the kitchen table again. Me, I sat there in my bathrobe, no doubt looking a wreck, and said, "Want me to get dressed too? Would it help you to talk about this if I did?"

"For some reason, yes, I think it would, Jacob. There's no logic to it."

"Fine with me," I said. I went into the bathroom, showered, then got dressed in jeans and a sweater and thick socks, and put on my shoes. "Okay, all dressed up and nowhere to go," I said, sitting at the kitchen table.

Martha reached into her satchel and took out a piece of paper, which she set on the table amid the half-eaten toast, the coffeepot and cups, and the cloth napkins she preferred. "I'll just read down the list," she said. "This is some of the stuff I've learned during Arts and Crafts." She placed her pointer finger at the top of the list and said, "Number one. The name of the attending physician, jumped right out of the ambulance and ran into the Halifax Free Library, was Dr. Abraham Tone. Nora remembered him sliding his hand across the long desk in the main reading room and a lot of books flying every which way. Nora didn't suffer a very long labor, she said. Dr. Tone had a nurse along with him. When you were born they all got into the ambulance and went to the hospital. Nora said in 1945 the hospital was near the wharf, but eventually it was torn down and replaced by apartment buildings.

"Number two. Nora claims — reliably or not — that she remembers all ten of the songs on *Your Hit Parade* in April 1945 — I wrote them down. 'Sentimental Journey,' Les Brown with Doris Day. 'It's Been a Long, Long Time,' Harry James with Kitty Kallen. 'Rum and Coca-Cola,' the Andrews Sisters. 'On the Atchison, Topeka and the Santa Fe,' that was sung by Johnny Mercer. 'Till the End of Time,' Perry Como. 'Ac-cent-tchu-ate the Positive,' that's Johnny Mercer again. 'Don't Fence Me In,' Bing Crosby. 'Chickery Chick,' Sammy

Kaye. 'My Dreams Are Getting Better All the Time,' Les Brown with Doris Day again. 'I Can't Begin to Tell You,' Bing Crosby again.

"Naturally, I could have this list of songs checked out. I'm good at that. It's part of what I do for a living.

"Number three. And this is about the day you were born. Your mother said that while she was lying on the library table, she — and I quote — 'closed my eyes and pictured myself doing the Charleston. But for some reason I had a tall stack of books on top of my head like a circus act.'"

"Has she confessed that Robert Emil is my father?" I asked. "Has she confessed that Bernard Rigolet is not?"

"We haven't gotten that far yet."

My Father, Officer Robert Emil

Part One

A WEEK AFTER OUR TALK AT THE KITCHEN TABLE, MARTHA arrived at her apartment with Detectives Tides and Hodgdon. Hodgdon had brought takeout Chinese food from Mandarin Palace on Lower Water Street. When we were done eating, Martha said, "Jake, I brought the cold-case file on Robert Emil home with me."

Detective Tides cleared his throat and all attention turned to him. "Jacob, what I told your fiancée, Detective Crauchet — yeah, yeah, she told us you were getting married. So, anyway, Detective Hodgdon and myself went through the files with a fine-tooth comb before it went to Detective Crauchet. So I said to her, you know, right, that Jacob Rigolet's very own mother, Nora — and this is before she was hauled in for her outlandish fuckup at the auction, mind you — is mentioned in the Robert Emil file. Mentioned in *association* with Officer Robert Emil. Small world, eh? Small world, I mean it can fit on a pencil eraser, the world's so small here in Halifax, right Detective Hodgdon?"

"Right," Hodgdon said, eating the last piece of lemon chicken.

"I wanted that piece," Tides said.

Detective Hodgdon said, "So, we spoke directly to Martha here. And we asked what was the what of this. We asked if she knew much about your mother, Nora Rigolet, and she said no. And she was telling the truth because why wouldn't she? Our mutual trust is based on mutual trust, right? Pure and simple.

"But yesterday afternoon at work, Martha, out of mutual trust, called us to her desk and guess what she said, Jacob? She said this Robert Emil was probably. Most likely. Your actual old man. Jesus fucking Christ, Jacob, you want me to drive you over to the Angus L. Macdonald Bridge and take down your last will and testament and your fond farewell, or what? I mean, this must've been some news, Jakie. I mean, my own father was no saint. But this guy? Robert Emil? He was a sewer rat. No offense intended."

"Thanks for the offer to drive me to the bridge," I said. "It was nice of you."

"Look, Jake, sorry if my sense of irony might not be refined as yours," Detective Hodgdon said.

Martha lifted and dropped the thick file on the kitchen table, which stopped the conversation.

But then Detective Hodgdon said, "In my experience, when there's big family secrets, that's when police files can be very revealing. A lot of family history's in police files. Except, as often as not, the families themselves are ignorant of the files. My guess is that this is true here, am I correct?"

"Are you asking me," I said, "if I knew of any police files about my family, or if my mother knew about them?"

"I'm just saying, your fiancée, our colleague Detective Crauchet, is apparently going way out of her way," Detective Hodgdon said. "And it may or may not be proper police procedure, and me and Tides don't give a flying fuck either way. I'm saying that there's every possibility that Detective Crauchet, by reading these files, not to mention every little thing she's learning in Arts and Crafts — oh, yes, she told us about that too. Every little thing she is learning from Nora Rigolet in the loony bin. All of it put together is potentially making for a fuck of a family story you would not otherwise ever get to read, Jacob. Violating police procedure or not, Martha's giving you a gift, my friend. What can I say? She's smitten. What can I say?"

"Look at this kitchen," Detective Tides said. "There's a full pot of coffee. The radiators are working. There's a big fat cold-case file on the table. There's two lovebirds who actually like talking with each other. That's my description of paradise."

"I'm still hungry," Detective Tides said. "Let's go back to Mandarin Palace."

Then they were out the door.

My Father, Officer Robert Emil
Part Two

MARTHA TYPED OUT A KIND OF BIOGRAPHY OF MY FATHER'S
life:

He was born on October 24, 1913, in Halifax to Phyllis and Lester
Emil, who ran a leather goods shop. Phyllis was killed in the cat-
aclysmic nitroglycerin explosion of December 6, 1917 — a French
cargo ship, the SS *Mont-Blanc*, which was fully loaded with war-
time explosives, collided with a Norwegian vessel, the SS *Imo*,
in the Narrows, the strait connecting Upper Halifax Harbor to
Bedford Basin. Around 2,000 people were killed and over 9,000
injured. That day Phyllis Emil was in their shop but Lester had
stayed home with a bad cold and fever. The shop was obliter-
ated in the explosion and no trace was left of Phyllis Emil. Robert Emil was four years old. His father took him to stay with his
first cousin's family in Advocate Harbor, along the Bay of Fundy,
and he went to elementary school there. Lester failed to put the
leather goods business back together and committed suicide in

1920, when Robert Emil was seven. Robert lived with his aunt and uncle and cousins until he was sixteen, and he moved back on his own to Halifax, where he got a job as a night custodian at the courthouse.

At the age of twenty, he became police. That would be in 1933. So this means Robert Emil was Halifax police for twelve years before he became your father. He worked his way up the ladder. According to his official file, he was a dedicated policeman, yet he had "a short fuse" and "a definite intolerance to anyone outside the Christian faith, especially a hatred for Jews," more of which I'll get to soon.

Basically, Robert Emil had a decent but far from exemplary record as a police officer. His famous temper got him into hot water on a number of occasions. There were reprimands but no docks in pay or suspensions. The word "hothead" recurs often in the file. Now listen to this. In 1944, during a Passover Seder for servicemen at the Quinpool Road Hostel, Robert Emil drunkenly interrupted the dinner — he was wearing his police uniform — and shouted, "Dirty kikes." A number of Jewish servicemen threw him to the ground and took him in a car to the police station. In the end, he was merely reprimanded for "drunk and disorderly behavior due to the pressure of the job." The file also includes the fact that Emil said he "was angry that some of his friends died in Germany and France just in order to save a few Jews." Not a wonderfully insightful man.

But in regard to the cold case, which is focused on the death of Max Berall in the spring of 1945, Robert Emil's file is thick as a hassock. I'm sorry to tell you this, Jacob, but it is true. He was a real piece of work, your actual father. There is no possible way I can fully comprehend the relationship between what horrid things were happening in Europe and all the reported anti-Semitic incidents here in Halifax during World War II. Maybe a history professor at Dalhousie can set me straight on some things. But I can say that what seems to have particularly agitated Robert Emil was the visit of a Jewish radio personality named Edgar Roth, which took place in March and April of 1945. While Roth was in Halifax, he stayed with the family of Max Berall, who escorted Roth wherever he went. The file is full of newspaper articles about Edgar Roth's radio broadcasts.

Roth made his broadcasts on March 8, March 26, and April 5. These broadcasts were of varied content. But all of them took the United States and Canada to task for their anti-Semitism, for not being willing to comprehend and act on the news of the concentration camps early enough, and for continued anti-Semitic policies as they pertained to Jewish refugees. The transcripts of those broadcasts are in Robert Emil's file because he refers to them during his original interrogation, which took place as a result of the fatal anti-Semitic incident.

I'm trying to put this jigsaw puzzle together, Jacob. I have so far come up with four basic categories: 1. What happened in Robert Emil's life that led to him being so sick and screwed-up a person but someone who could also charm the pants off that statue of Evangeline in the park downtown — though of course she's wearing a dress, but you know what I mean. 2. What was the situation between Nora and Robert Emil — this is going to require a lot of stealth and patience in my conversations with your mother during Arts and Crafts, and my sense is, I won't get much of anywhere with this. To date I have not uttered the name Robert Emil to her. Too soon. 3. Did you know that Emil actually published, ten years ago, a detective novel called *Detective Emil Detects,* the title of which he obviously stole from my beloved radio program. What a plagiarist jerk! I'm going to track down a copy of that book. 4. Find out all of what happened in the terrible incident with Max Berall and all of what happened on the day you were born, April 18, 1945, which is also the day Emil was arrested under suspicion of murdering Max Berall. And suspicion of murdering Mrs. Yablon too.

Jesus, Mary, and Joseph, it's like a waking nightmare, this cold case. Which is warming up by the minute.

Your Father May Still Be
Right Here in Halifax

NEW YEAR'S EVE, MARTHA AND I WERE HAVING DINNER AT Mario's Pasta Joint on Lower Water Street. We'd been invited to a party, and to a dinner at Mrs. Hamelin's, but decided instead on a private night. To celebrate the end of my first semester in library science. To just be together alone. "I'm with people all day long," she said, "and I worked since six this morning, New Year's Eve. So this is very nice for me. Just us here at dinner. Happy New Year."

"*Detective Levy Detects* is on later, you know."

"How could I not know that?"

We ate our pasta and drank wine and talked, and then Martha said, "Do you mind a little shoptalk?"

"Whatever you want."

"Well, as far as I can tell, the violence perpetrated by Robert Emil was a case of small things leading to big damages."

"How do you mean?" I said.

"Reading the transcripts of Emil's interrogations, I discovered this one thing. He goes on and on about a 'Hebrew girl,' as he calls her. Her name was Flora Lipkus. They went to high school together.

According to Robert Emil, he proposed marriage to her about a million times, until finally Flora Lipkus's father, named Joseph Lipkus, had a serious talk with Robert Emil. That's how he put it in the interview, a 'serious talk.' Well, it seems that specific rejection sent Emil into a tailspin. And given his violation of that Passover dinner, and everything else, apparently he never did stop spinning. The weird thing is that there were so many anti-Semitic incidents during World War II. In fact, finally I did go over to talk to a history professor, Professor Kimbray, at Dalhousie, and he told me that in 1945 alone there were more anti-Semitic incidents in Halifax than in any previous year. I checked the police files, and Kimbray was right. Mostly there were eggs tossed and paper bags of horseshit thrown at synagogues, but there were some worse things. There was a bomb threat. Some older Jewish people got roughed up. Things like that. The city was pretty pent up after the war too, and there was the big riot a month after you were born, May of 1945, when the whole city went berserk. But by that time Officer Robert Emil had been exonerated for lack of evidence and had disappeared. And here's another thing, Jake. I can't find any death certificate or death notice for Emil."

"So you think he may still be alive?"

"Tides and Hodgdon think he may still be in Halifax. Tides found a copy of that stupid detective novel Emil wrote. He thought he might track him down through the publisher. No such luck. It was published by what's called a vanity press. Which basically means Emil paid for it out of his own pocket. The advantage we have is, while technically Emil's on the lam, he isn't aware that a cold case has been opened on him. He wouldn't necessarily have his guard up. On the more personal level, of course, him being your —"

"Technically my father."

"— him being your father complicates things, doesn't it."

The episode of *Detective Levy Detects* took place on New Year's Eve 1945. Martha and I drank champagne from water glasses as we listened. The episode was titled "Leah Diamond Fends Off 1946," and it consisted mainly of a party at the time-travel Devonshire Hotel, with the gangsters, gun molls, Leah, and Detective Levy dancing and drinking and celebrating and talking over the year's most interesting cases that everyone solved together on the streets of Toronto. But toward the end of the episode, Leah Diamond suddenly says, "Hey, who invited *him?*" Everyone turns to the hotel room door and the narrator says, "Right away, Goose Molito goes for his gun, but Leah Diamond says" — back to the actor's dialogue — "No, Goose, no, put that piece away. Let me take care of this." The narrator says, "Everyone saw that it was a man wearing a tuxedo with a banner wrapped around his chest that said HAPPY NEW YEAR 1946! But nobody wanted it to be 1946 yet, so they let Leah take care of the poor hapless fellow. She took him out into the hallway and used up a little lipstick on him and sent him half stumbling, half walking down the stairs and out to the street. Detective Levy and Leah Diamond watched through the window as the poor hapless fellow went bumbling along, probably looking for another party to crash. But nobody wanted it to be 1946 quite yet, and Leah Diamond did something about that. In the morning it could be 1946. But for now, dancing and whooping it up, all the boys and dames and Frederik and Leah were making time. Let the new year arrive somewhere else, some other hotel, not the Devonshire. Not yet . . ."

Radio Detective
Frederik Levy's Love Life

ON FEBRUARY 9, 1978, AFTER MY HISTORY OF LIBRARY Archives seminar in my second semester, I met Martha in the lobby of the police station on Gottingen Street. Apparently the desk sergeant, Fisk, a "charmless fathead," as Martha called him, had been informed that I was studying library science.

"Hello there, Jake," Fisk said. "Look, I may be out of line here, but let me ask you a question, eh? My wife, Thalia, she was cleaning out the attic the other day. Now, we have a house built in 1870. And while she's up there Thalia finds a tin box. And in the tin box is a book called *Butterflies We Tell Our Children*. It's got all sorts of illustrations of butterflies in it. Turns out it's part of a series of books written last century, each about different categories of nature — butterflies, birds, plants, mammals, all like that. Each and all of them in the *Tell Our Children* series. Now, the thing to know is, Thalia inherited the house from her parents, now deceased. They're over in Camp Hill Cemetery with Thalia's grandparents, who originally built the house. The important fact is, the book, *Butterflies We Tell Our Children* — get this — is one hundred and five years overdue. Taken out of a public library in Halifax in 1878. So Thalia sets this felony evidence on our kitchen table, and it's just sitting there."

Sergeant Fisk stopped there and looked at me inquiringly. Then he shrugged his shoulders and an outsize frown animated his face. He shrugged a second time.

"What's your question?" I said.

"Well, it's pretty obvious what I'm asking, Jake," he said.

"I'm thick," I said. "Humor me."

"This is a private family matter," he said. "Mind coming closer to the desk?"

I leaned up close against the desk, and Sergeant Fisk whispered, "Would you consider looking into this for me? Me being a colleague of Detective Crauchet's, looking into it for me."

"Looking into what, exactly?" I said. I was whispering too.

"Jesus, you are thick, aren't you? Looking *into* how much Thalia owes on *Butterflies We Tell Our Children,* what else? I mean, what were the fines back in the 1800s and whatnot. Because I consider by now that the book's stolen goods. Is how I look at it. And the way I see it, Thalia is directly responsible for it being a hundred years overdue, because she inherited the book and should own up to her responsibility. And me personally? I need to figure out, should Thalia not own up to her responsibility, should I turn her in. Because as a police, I cannot act as though I am not aware that a felony continues to be in progress each day the book is not returned to the library and the fine paid. I mean, Jake, I'm between a rock and hard place here, see what I mean? Thalia is my wife, but she's also a Canadian citizen."

"Why not let me take the book to the Halifax Free Library and tell my friend there, Jinx Faltenbourg, she's senior librarian, the whole story and speak on behalf of Thalia?"

"You would do that for Thalia? You never even met her."

"The wife of a colleague of Detective Crauchet's, of course I would."

"And here I thought Martha might be all romantically caught up with a queer, you know, library science and all, but here you turn out to be a regular guy man to man. Live and learn. Live and learn, and I can only shake your hand and say thanks and let me know how it turns out immediately."

Fisk reached into a drawer and removed a paper bag in which was the copy of *Butterflies We Tell Our Children*. He handed it to me. It was a beautifully bound book, with an inlaid depiction of a butterfly on the cover. He looked around as if worried that our exchange would be witnessed, which it wasn't. I put the book back in the paper bag. "On the down low, right?" Sergeant Fisk said.

"I'll take it over to the library in the morning," I said.

"Do your best," he said.

Martha came down the stairs, looked at the paper bag, nodded to Fisk, said "Good night, Sergeant Fisk," took my hand in hers, and we walked out to the street. On the way to her apartment I explained what had happened between Fisk and myself, which got her interested. I showed her the book.

"What if I just drove over to arrest Thalia Fisk right now?" she said. "I mean, handcuffs and everything. March her right past her husband at the front desk and get fingerprints taken and toss her into the holding pen. I could use the words 'She stays here pending investigation,' which I always love when I hear them on *Detective Levy Detects* but have never had the chance to use myself. What do you think?"

"I made a promise to Fisk, though," I said.

"Oh, right," Martha said. "There's that."

"I'm bringing the book to the library tomorrow morning, like I promised."

"Well, there goes my chance to say 'pending investigation,' but you are a good and honest man, so there's that too."

I thought: Maybe I have been forgiven for dropping her trust that one time, with *Tombeau des Rois*, in London.

In her apartment, Martha said, "Would you mind making potato leek soup? I've got all the ingredients. I need a bath and time to think, okay?"

"Think about what?" I asked.

"Today, all day, I was supposed to be concentrating on a forgery. A fellow who has an antique store on Bishop Street and sells autograph letters too. He sold someone a letter that was supposedly written and signed by Adèle Hugo, Victor Hugo's daughter, who lived for a while in Halifax. Turns out the letter's a forgery and the owner has skipped town, but just to Dartmouth, my sources tell me. I was supposed to be following up on this. But all day I didn't do it and didn't do it and it didn't get done. I'm sure this guy's going to be easily located tomorrow. But it was supposed to get done today."

"So why couldn't you concentrate on work today, Martha?"

"Let's talk about it after the radio, is that okay?"

I carefully prepared the soup, simmering it for about an hour, and Martha took a bath, and what with this, that, and the other thing, we didn't sit down at the kitchen table until *Detective Levy Detects* came on. The episode was called "Our Boy Confesses to Leah Diamond, and She Does It Right Back."

"Good title," Martha said. "Good for their relationship, huh?"

We ate the soup, listening raptly. The gang of hoodlums, Leah's mobster pals, as in every episode, help Detective Levy solve a case, a jewel thief and murderer is caught, and the gang has a big celebration in the Devonshire Hotel.

The party goes on until dawn, and when Detective Levy and Leah leave the hotel to catch a taxi to go out for breakfast, Levy confesses, "I love you."

"No kidding," Leah says. "I knew that since you first laid eyes on me."

"How about you?" Levy says. "When did you know you were in love with me?"

"For me, more gradually. Some ladies slip off their silk stockings more gradually than others. Maybe you never noticed."

"How long did it take, finally?"

"You want a date on the calendar?"

"Yeah. Yeah, a date on the calendar would be fine."

"Six weeks ago Thursday."

"Okay. So, six weeks ago Thursday, what happened?"

Screech of car tires. A shot rings out and Leah Diamond groans and says, "Oh, Freddy, I'm hit."

Sirens. In the back of the ambulance, Detective Levy tries to hold Leah's attention, to keep her conscious, but she keeps drifting off. "Stay with me, darling," he says. "I love you. Want to know something else? I love you."

Leah gets some traction and says, "I gotta confess something to you too."

"Yeah, what's that?" Detective Levy says.

"It wasn't six weeks ago Thursday. It was six weeks ago Tuesday."

"Why didn't you say so in the first place?"

"I didn't want to swell your head up, thinking I fell for you too early in the game."

The episode ends.

"Radio fiction, such as it is," Martha said. "Still, I'm very upset Leah's been shot. I happen to already be familiar with the next episode, so I know that Leah pulls through, but at this moment it feels like she might not. The power of radio, eh?"

"I've noticed one thing in particular about the criminals Levy goes after," I said.

"What's that?" Martha said.

"They all double up on crimes. Take this episode we just listened to. The guy's both a jewel thief and a murderer, right? No way would he just be one or the other."

"Sure, that's the end result," Martha said. "But you're missing something, Jake. It's always how one thing leads to another. The guy breaks into jewelry stores, correct. But the longer he doesn't get caught, the more confident he gets. And when he gets good and confident, he gets reckless, he gets careless, and when he gets careless, he makes a fatal mistake and gets cornered and has to shoot somebody, so now he's a murderer. It's one thing, it's the next thing, it's the next thing, and then the boys are called in — you also notice that Detective Levy has never, not once, solved a crime on his own. Because if he could do that, the boys and dames at the hotel — and who knows, maybe even Leah Diamond — wouldn't be needed, and they would disappear into the past. They aren't about to hang around where they're not needed, right?"

"I was just stating an observation," I said.

"Oh, come on, Jake. I'm no genius at figuring it all out. I've just heard it so often, I get the logic, that's all. Know what? It just now occurred to me we will never quarrel about the radio."

"Why's that?"

"Because when it comes to the radio, I'm always right."

That settled that, and we were kissing, leaning up against the kitchen wall and kissing. But Martha said, "I want to, but . . ."

"Don't tell me Leah Diamond going to the hospital has got you too distracted to go to bed with your fiancé."

Martha pushed me away in a dramatically huffy fashion, in the main playful, and then she looked all business. She walked to the front hall closet, took out a shoebox, and set it on the kitchen table.

"What's in the box?" I asked.

"Sit down, Jake, please," Martha said.

I sat down across from Martha. She opened the box and set the lid aside.

"Yesterday I was at Arts and Crafts with Nora. I told you I was going and I went. We were doing watercolors. My God, how many scenes of the harbor from those windows do the patients make every year? I can't imagine. Anyway, we sat at one end of the big table and each of us made a few watercolors, your mother and me. And she was telling me things, without me asking, about Bernard Rigolet."

"When I was growing up, he was always referred to as my father."

"Sitting there painting with her, I noticed this shoebox on the table. I thought it was filled with Arts and Crafts paraphernalia. But when I was about to leave, Nora said, 'Martha, you've been good to tell me so much. How you and Jacob met, and what you mean to each other. And I suspect you tell him about Arts and Crafts, as well you should. I'm happy for you both. I'm only sorry Jacob hasn't talked about such intimacies with me, but as you know, he doesn't come to visit. Now I have a favor to ask. It concerns Jacob directly.' She slid the shoebox over to me and said, 'Here's the four letters Bernard sent me from Europe. Would you kindly give them to Jacob for me?' The letters Nora's husband sent from the war are in this shoebox, my darling."

"Your detective work has taken a surprising turn."

"I feel lucky as far as that goes. I mean, when you think about it, how many women really ever get to know their husband's family? Let alone their husband."

We both laughed hesitantly.

"I'm torn," I said. "I want to read these letters and I don't"

"No, you must read them," Martha said. "Otherwise, you're a coward."

Letter from Bernard Rigolet

March 28, 1944

Darling Nora,

Night has fallen shipboard as we are out in the Atlantic, and it is fairly rough seas so far. I am lying in my bunk, all the other men in theirs, trying to sleep. I can't see a single one actually sleeping, though. Lots of seasickness whose consequences are not too pleasant to hear. So far so good in that department for me, but then again, we're only six hours out of Halifax, and no storms yet. There's two horses on ship. I went down to look at them. Just this little time out and so many unknowns up ahead, Nora, and I am both bucked up and a little afraid, back and forth, and I guess it's going to be like that. I am going over in my mind our last hours in the house together. I don't want to be driven crazy but then again you can't help where your mind goes, isn't that true? You seemed to be conveying yourself around room to room — what can I possibly mean by the use of the word "conveying"? Well, I mean that you seemed to be carrying yourself, physically, from room to room, like carrying a burden, or a weight. This was evident to me, and saddening, my love, because I knew the heaviness had to do with everything in life, our parting, the war, all of what we cannot predict. I noticed you signed on for all the extra hours possible at the library too. Part of this was, I'm sure, about having the income to get by, but remember, you'll be receiving my military paycheck directly too, every month. That was all worked out. My technical skill with radios is already in demand, even shipboard here, as I've been put on the technical core roster — that means I'll be going over every possible communications apparatus we'll have at the front. I won't bore you with the details except to say I already feel useful. Whoever thought that a childhood fascination with radios, and then being in the high school Radio Club and the Short-Wave Club that I attended regularly in Halifax right up until we got married — and I'll join right back up when I return home too! — who would have ever thought I'd be using my childhood radio skills in France and Germany during a war? Not me, that's for sure, not me.

The announcement — it's 4 a.m. — just came over the squawk box, what we've run into is called a Region of Delay — one fellow here says that's a term from ancient Greek, translated into English, that is, that applies to journeys, not always perilous ones, but journeys at sea especially — Region of Delay. I want to think about it more. I feel it might refer to both emotions and geography, not entirely sure yet. We're navigating a little south to avoid a storm — and speaking of Greek, there's a fellow I've met named Nick or Nicholas, last name Condaxis, who's of Greek ancestry himself, and who I overheard talking to three or four men about war in ancient Greece. I drew closer to listen and it was fascinating, I have to admit, and a good distraction too. "See, you have to have some perspective, some philosophy about what we're entering into," he said, "or else it's all going to seem useless and your hearts and brains and everything else will just be in a total state of confusion," is how he put it. Of course, a little bit, with Nicholas Condaxis, was a man trying to convince himself, is what I heard. But still he had me hooked, I admit. Maybe in the Halifax Free Library you have books about some of the figures that Nick Condaxis was talking about—the ones that come most directly to mind are King Leonides and Nick's favorite—well, the one he seemed to know most about anyway—fellow named Themistocles, who convinced all the people of Athens and all the politicians that Greece needed a navy to defeat the Persians at sea, because the Persian army was just too powerful. Stuff like that. Maybe because Nick is from Greek lineage he pronounces the ancient names so well, I don't know. He also speaks the Greek language. I think it will be good for me to stick close to him and maybe pick up some of his ways of thinking philosophically about what we are about to see and experience, Nora. Only some of the officers on board have really seen the war firsthand close-up, so there's not a lot of actual fighting to talk about amongst us tenderfeet. But I do like the way Nick Condaxis describes Greek warfare as if he was right there at the time. He's a scholar, really.

I'm feeling just now pretty bad we didn't have a chance to talk more specifically about my plans for a radio and radio repair shop in Halifax—I think it will eventually bring me a solid living, along with your librarian work of course, and I had scouted out several locales in Halifax, and the one I liked best was on Hollis near Water Street, but I'll just have to wait and see whether the building is even available by the time I get home, my darling, won't I.

There's a dentist aboard ship, and he's been very persistent, he wants to make sure that once we land nobody's got a bad toothache or any related thing. So this fellow, Dr. Aukland, he's pulling teeth like a madman and will be the whole voyage, I would imagine. That's hardly earthshaking news but it's the kind of news I have.

Tomorrow we get briefings and look at maps —

Nora, darling, I continue this days later and guess what? England has come into view. We God bless us have made it past German U-boats and even any air attacks, which I'm told is almost a miracle right there to begin with — and now out ahead of us is England. We will have only two days before we go to France. But longer term, Germany is definitely our destination point. We've all gotten two lessons in German so far — not much. I can definitely say I'm going to be happy to get off this ship, Nora — definitely yes I will, but today I had a case of nerves. I'm told it's only to be expected, like Nick said, "What kind of human being wouldn't get a case of nerves?" Not that I fully understood what he meant, only that I think he's right. I don't much feel in charge of my imagination, though, and it's been taking me to some pretty awful places — and soon enough, soon enough real life will replace imagination anyway, so I will need to be prepared for that as best I can. I'm here with solid good men and so many of them look ready and worried and every other kind of emotion a face can show. I'm certain I look that way too. What I want most to say is that I am happy we are married.

Love,
Your adoring Bernie

Straight-B Student

I WAS LEARNING A LOT IN LIBRARY SCIENCE, BUT MY GRADES were not tops. The first semester, in three classes I got straight B's; the second semester, which ended May 2, the same, except for a B-plus in History of Library Science — Second Part. I had met with Dr. Margolin two times to discuss my progress. In the second meeting, on May 4, she said, "My main concern is that your essays often lack your working out your thoughts along a clear enough line, Jacob. Would you consider a tutorial?"

"Do you think I need that?" I asked.

"Yes. I can make some recommendations as to whom you might work with over the summer. But in general you're doing just fine. Some are doing a lot worse, believe me."

"I'll take all of this as encouragement."

That evening in her apartment, I told Martha about this consultation, and she said, "Speaking of your mother — speaking of Nora —"

I took a second helping of meat loaf and mashed potatoes. "I didn't know I was speaking about her," I said.

"Not directly. But all through your curriculum so far, it's like you feel you have big shoes to fill, what with your mother being head librarian. Or *was* head librarian. So maybe there's some ambivalence at work here, know what I mean? Like, are you doing this because you couldn't come up with anything else to do? Or are you doing this because it's a way to stay close to Nora? Or are you doing this because you think you'll be good at it? Or all of the above?"

"It's like you want me to fill out a questionnaire."

"I guess I should say things more directly, huh? Okay. Why haven't you once visited your mother in the hospital, darling? It's your mother. What are you afraid of looking right at? What are you afraid of seeing?"

"When she first went in, I visited her all the time."

"You could join us during Arts and Crafts."

"I guess I could."

"She asks why you haven't been to see her, Jake. Every time, she asks."

"All right. I'll go next time you go."

"That would be a good thing. I have tremendously enjoyed visiting her."

"Practicing as you are to be her daughter-in-law."

"Well, maybe you should start practicing being her son again."

"I'm grateful she talks to you."

"It's obvious to me that Nora's relying on the fact that whatever she tells me, I'll tell you. I think part of the reason she's telling me so much is because she wants you to know everything too."

"How can you be so sure?"

"I'm a professional interlocutrix, remember?"

"This is the best meat loaf I've ever eaten."

"You don't have to say that. I already can't wait to get in bed with you."

"Okay, then. Both things are true."

"It's a slightly different recipe is all. My mother's recipe has oatmeal to hold everything together. But I did something different."

"What's troubling you, though, Martha? You have that look."

"The real reason I want you to start visiting Nora is so I can rest assured that should something happen to me — say, we're married for ten years and I'm shot during an investigation — how can I trust that you'll be there to take care of me? So far as it pertains to your own mother, you are flunking that particular test, Jacob. I know *wife* is different from *mother,* I get that. But surely you take my point. You can see what I'm concerned with here."

"Trustworthiness during the tough times ahead."

"Enough said about that. Just come with me to Arts and Crafts, please."

The Deeper Concerns of Martha

THE DEPTH AND URGENCY OF MARTHA'S CONCERNS ABOUT her line of work (she liked to call it "detectiving"), as she addressed them at dinner at Halloran's on June 9, put a lot of things in a new light for us. Of course, she had often talked about this or that investigation, as far as propriety allowed. But this was different.

"Detectives Tides and Hodgdon and I got assigned a flight risk," Martha said.

"What kind of flight risk?" I asked.

"First thing this morning, Jake, we were out on the street." Martha was dressed in her favorite black pantsuit, which she wore with black tennis shoes, for comfort. I started to pour wine for her, but she placed her hand flat over the glass and shook her head no. "Flight risk was a fellow named Torredon Stilgoe — what a name, huh? It sounds like a fjord. Anyway, this guy has a wife and — get this — six kids, all in an apartment on Queen Street. In fact, guess what? He's a groundskeeper at Holy Cross Cemetery, across the street from his apartment. You know how Holy Cross Cemetery and the military cemetery are contiguous, right? So anyway, Torredon Stilgoe has a thirty-second commute to work. There's the six kids, all under the age of fifteen, and his salary's what? His file says eighteen grand. He's at wit's end over finances. His wife, Justine Stilgoe, she's a part-time bookkeep at some place or other, I forget. Not regular employment by any means, and when she gets work, she's got to pay for someone to look after her kids, so there goes most of the income right there. Not a good situation, so being at wit's end, Torredon Stilgoe makes a decision. He decides to rob J. Nelson Imports at Commercial Wharf. He conscripts his cousin Rudolph to aid and abet. So now there's Torredon and Rudolph Stilgoe, one shitty little rusty revolver between them and stocking caps with holes cut out so they can see — I am *not* kidding — and they walk into J. Nelson's. Stupid stupid stupid, and they walk in and one of them, I think it was Torredon, waves the pistol around. The guy who oversees the payroll says, 'Are you here for the payroll?' And then Rudolph says — are you ready? Rudolph says, 'Well, what do you think, *Lewis*, you dumb fuck. Do you think we're here to play checkers? Of *course* we're here for the payroll!'"

"Rudolph knows the name Lewis?" I said.

"And why does he know the name? Because Rudolph works at J. Nelson Imports, that's why! So right away Lewis says, 'Hey, Rudolph, is that you? What are you doing?' At which point Rudolph turns to his cousin and says, 'Torrie, what should we do?' So now both robbers' names have been announced, and the robbers, I mean, what else could they do? They run out of J. Nelson Imports. Police pick up Rudolph, who went straight to a bar. And me and Tides and Hodgdon get assigned Torredon, who, as they say in the trade, was absent at his home address.

Our meal was served, and I said to Martha, "Torredon's still in Halifax, I take it?"

"We get a tip that he's snuck into his brother's apartment, which is on South Hollis near the Halifax Gas Company building — you know, you can look out and see the lighthouse on Georges Island.

Torredon's left his door wide open. The place stinks of booze. So we call in through the door. Torredon's clearly been drinking, because he's in some back room, or the bathroom, and he's shouting all sorts of nonsense, slurring his words, and we hear a bottle smash against a wall. 'Torredon, we have your cousin in custody. Come on out. There's three of us detectives here, Torredon!' So, being the intelligent, sensitive fellow that Torredon Stilgoe is — as sensitive as a fjord, right? — he fires his weapon. In Halifax how often does this sort of thing happen? Really now, how often?"

"So now, what, you had to shoot back?" I said.

"No, actually, Torredon walks out with his hands up. No weapon in sight. He'd dropped it into the toilet. We heard it flush — he'd tried to flush a revolver down a toilet. Oh boy, what fun."

"So both the notorious Stilgoe cousins are now in jail."

"Right, right," Martha said. "But Jake — Jacob, I have to show you something. I have to tell you something."

"What's going on here, Martha?"

Martha stood up, walked over to me, took my right hand, and placed it on her belt, to the left of the buckle. "Feel this," she said.

I ran my finger over the belt and felt where it had been gouged out. "The bullet whizzed right along my belt, Jacob. Thank God I was standing sideways and to the side of the door, because otherwise we might've been hit."

"So, Hodgdon and Tides were to the side of the door too?"

"That's not who I meant by 'we,'" Martha said. She lifted my hand to just above the belt buckle and pressed it firmly against her stomach. "That's why I didn't want any wine, Jacob."

I stood and held Martha and said, "I could not be happier."

"I think I'm only two months along, Jake, so let's not tell anyone else yet."

"Should we start thinking of names?"

"No, it's way too early." We sat down again. "Yes, two months ago, I think I know the night, Jake. I believe it was during or just after the episode titled 'Leah Diamond Solves a Case All By Her Lonesome.' You might not remember it, but it had a whole minute or two, as if the microphone was touching her clothes, remember? It was sort of like hearing a striptease in progress. Leah Diamond is talking to herself, figuring out the clues. All the while, as she's taking off her clothes, you can hear little oohs and aahs — and then into their hotel room walks Detective Levy. Well, I remember every minute of that, Jacob. And I really loved that. And I am totally convinced, right during or right after that episode, that's when our child was conceived."

Visiting Nora at Nova Scotia Rest Hospital

I'M NOT VERY GOOD AT PSYCHOLOGIZING, BUT THE FACT IS, I often dreamed of the auction at which my mother assaulted *Death on a Leipzig Balcony.* Also, Martha told me that now and then I'd cry out in my sleep, "No, it can't be you!" Which were the exact words I shouted when my mother had thrown the vial of ink against the photograph's glass. "You're still back in that moment," Martha would say. "That moment keeps coming back."

I think that's why I hadn't visited Nora yet. I couldn't let go of that incident. And if I went to see her, I'd have to let go of it. At least this was Martha's theory. She's far better at psychologizing. I mean, she had to study psychology to become a detective.

So after my morning tutorial at Dalhousie on June 27, I met Martha at the ferry dock, and we crossed the harbor to Dartmouth. It was a beautiful breezy day out on the water. I felt a little nervous. Why should this be when I was going to see my own mother?

On the ferry, Martha said, "In some ways, Jacob, the hospital is a dump. Not quite shameful but not up to what it should be. Far from a medieval insane asylum but certainly not state-of-the-art, not by any means. Funding problems and all of that. But Nora has a nice clean room overlooking the harbor. I brought her a handmade quilt. The attendants on her floor seem very kind, very professional, nothing like Nurse Ratched in *One Flew over the Cuckoo's Nest*. There are, however, some nasty rumors. And I've looked at complaints registered by families to the police department and some of those make me sick. I mean, how their loved ones are treated. You aren't going to like this, but I look closely at Nora for bruises or any signs of physical mistreatment. I know that isn't nice to hear. She always looks fine, though. She has so much pride in her appearance. She's so dignified and she always looks good. I don't think you need to worry."

"I should have been keeping close to this myself. I feel like shit about it."

"That's a start," Martha said. "Anyway, today's Arts and Crafts, and it's a hoot. In the historical literature on the hospital — Lord, what an education that is, which I've done some reading on. In one old book there's a section called 'Arts and Crafts for the Insane.' I took some notes. And the truth is, what they do in Arts and Crafts today is pretty much what they did in 1900. Jacob, I'm not calling Nora insane. She's not that at all. She's . . . she's . . . haunted."

"That goddamn photograph."

"Like Detective Tides always says, 'There's the symptom and there's the cause.' The photograph was the symptom, I think. But what's causing Nora such torment? It has to be more than one thing."

"You've been so great, seeing my mother like you have. Thank you. I love you so much for it."

The wind was up a little, and the ferry rocked slightly on swells, and we stayed at the aft rail. The Dartmouth docks were coming into view. We could see the hospital looming just inland. "So what we'll do is," Martha said, "we'll see what's doing in Arts and Crafts.

We'll sit with Nora at a separate table and see how she is. I did alert the Arts and Crafts leader you were coming for a visit."

We registered our names in the visitors' log at the front desk, and I followed Martha up the stairs to the third floor, then to a large room. Martha opened the door. There were about twenty patients, along with five attendants. Several patients shouted "Martha!" One of them, a woman in her early twenties, tall, her brown hair like a stringy wet mop, her eyeglasses so thick it seemed she could only see into them but not through them, dressed in pajamas and a robe and bedroom slippers, leapt up from her table and hugged Martha tightly, and an attendant had to pry her loose. "That's okay, Roberta," Martha said. This Roberta said, "You promised to arrest me one day, Martha, remember? You promised to arrest me and take me out on the ferry and push me into the harbor, remember? Is today the day, Martha, is it?"

"Not today," Martha said.

The attendant led Roberta back to her Arts and Crafts table. "A promise is a promise," she shouted back over her shoulder.

I saw my mother sitting at a corner table near a window. A male attendant sat with her, a large man, I'd guess around forty years old, wearing a white shirt, white trousers, and white tennis shoes. He had a large, friendly face, with an old-fashioned handlebar mustache and muttonchops, like he was from the previous century. He was cutting out ovals from a square of black felt. The scissors were tied to his right wrist with twine. My mother was placing the ovals of felt along the top margin of a large piece of white cardboard.

"Go on over," Martha said.

As I crossed the room, I took in my mother's appearance. Remember, I hadn't seen Nora since March 19, 1977, and it was now late June of 1978. A wave of shame rolled through me. But the truth was, just as Martha said, my mother had always taken great care in her appearance. And this was immediately apparent at her Arts and

Crafts table. When I was growing up, I never once saw her leave the house without, as she would say, "fixing herself up." She didn't have a deep closet, but she took great pride in her taste in clothes, and Jinx Faltenbourg liked to tease my mother: "Nora, for a chief librarian you always look like a night on the town, but for the fact that the Halifax Free Library doesn't keep such late hours." My mother was now fifty-nine years old, and when I sat at the table, she said, "Why, hello, Jacob. Your mother doesn't look a day over fifty-eight, does she? Mr. Peter Ashkouline, my attendant, and I are re-creating the biblical Noah's Ark on this piece of cardboard." Peter Ashkouline and I shook hands. My mother held up twenty or so pieces of paper. "I've made preliminary sketches — I've placed the ark right out the window, in Halifax Harbor. Ferries, steamships, and the ark, all the centuries at once, and it's quite entertaining, I think. For the past six months or so I've been specializing in the Old Testament. But how could you know that? My long-lost son. Perhaps Martha Crauchet mentioned it."

I leaned over and took my mother's hands in mine. "I'm very sorry I haven't been to visit you, Mom," I said. "It was stupid of me. It was very wrong."

"Never *once* visited," Peter Ashkouline said, cutting out more felt clouds. "And just think, we have people here who hallucinate visits from family more times than you visited. Which was none." He rose from the table and left the room.

"Guardian angel, that guy," I said.

"He likes to think of himself as that," my mother said.

I took Nora in fully now. Since the last time I had seen her, her hair seemed to have become more salt-and-pepper. It was cut fashionably short; Martha had arranged for a hairstylist to come in and paid for it out of pocket. Nora was wearing a dark green skirt with black tights, a white blouse under a black cardigan sweater, and black flats. She wore the same modest amount of makeup she always had worn. My mother looked quite sophisticated, and not just because she was against the backdrop of institutional pale green walls and the deprived light of the room, especially on such an overcast day. We could hear the steam horns of ferries out in the harbor.

Martha sat down at the table and started cutting out felt clouds, picking up where Peter Ashkouline had left off. "Your Martha's been my true guardian angel," my mother said, smiling at her. Nora set a small notebook in front of me. "Take a peek, Jacob," she said. "It's my register of visitors." I opened the notebook. At a glance I saw that Jinx Faltenbourg had visited at least once a week since March of 1977. Of course Martha's name was everywhere in the notebook. I recognized the names of other librarians and a few friends, such as Mildred Michaels, who was a bookbinder the Halifax Free Library kept on retainer. "You may write your own name in if you'd like," my mother said. "That's okay, Mother," I said. "Maybe next time." But as I was about to close the notebook, Martha kicked me under the table as she stared at Nora's notebook. It was then that I saw that on June 25, 1978, just three days earlier, was entered the name Robert Emil.

Martha's Seven-Month Plan

ON THE RETURN FERRY TO HALIFAX, GULLS KEENING JUST off the aft rail, Martha said, "Creepy, creepy, creepy. Robert Emil's actually been there. Why in hell would he visit her? How did he find out where she was? These are things I can't know — and I can't ask anyone about. I don't go to visit Nora as a detective, officially. I just sign her notebook like anyone else. Though the thought did occur to me that it was Nora herself who wrote in the name Robert Emil. You know, a moment of weakness and she scribbled his name. But I've voted against that. Jacob, we have to get Nora out of that place."

"But she's supposed to be there at least another year. That's what her doctors told me in a letter."

"I don't care. Nora will get worse the longer she stays. The thing that happened with *Death on a Leipzig Balcony* — it's all mixed up in Nora's mind with the fact that it was taken two days after you were born. Add to that emotional mix Bernard Rigolet getting killed. And after what she had done with Robert Emil? There isn't a woman alive who wouldn't be tormented by guilt. Married. Her husband away at war. It's the perfect recipe for merciless guilt, Jacob. But here's the thing: Nora's doctors don't know shit about any of this. Not in detail. I only know it because I've become Nora's interlocutrix. And let me tell you another thing. Today seemed a good day for Nora. She was clearheaded. But some days she's muddled. They've got her on an antianxiety medication, of course. But a very light dose."

"What are the options, do you think?"

"I spoke with Jinx Faltenbourg and she was direct with me. She said Nora couldn't get her old position back. But she also had no doubt that Nora could be on part-time salary at the library, as an assistant of some sort or other. Jinx said she would see to that. In time, Jinx said, there was the possibility of Nora becoming a licensed librarian again."

"I understand," I said.

"But where your mother finds employment is step two. Step one is to get her out of the hospital, Jake. Officially, she doesn't come up for review for six months. But, see, I've been thinking about this. And I've got a seven-month plan."

"You mean up to when the baby's going to be born. Right around then?"

"I've got it all figured out. In another month, I'll take a desk job. No way am I going to pound the pavement through my pregnancy. I've already told Tides and Hodgdon. I also told them not to gab about my situation at work. Probably they already have, though. I get a three-month maternity leave once the baby arrives. As for Nora, I'm going to find a private psychiatrist to visit her and talk to the doctors at the hospital. Let's start with that and see what happens. What do you think?"

"What I think is, my mother seems just like she always has, except in a foreign location. I love her dearly. She's the most remarkable person. But the more you find out, the less I feel I actually know who she is. Who she really has been all along. But when I saw her today, I thought, It's Nora, it's the same woman. Except she also threw ink at that photograph. I've got some confusions there, obviously."

"Seven months. To my way of thinking, in seven months everything will be moving like clockwork, Jake. Have a little faith."

"Don't do anything reckless in the meantime."

"Like Leah Diamond said on the radio, 'I might've done a foolish thing or two, but I ain't no fool,'" Martha said.

When the ferry was tied up, we stepped down the gangplank, walked to the Wired Monk, and sat down for coffee.

"It occurred to me," Martha said, "maybe Robert Emil read about the incident with the Robert Capa photograph. I mean, Jacob, the auction was reported in the newspaper. And Nora's name was mentioned. He might've waited for a while but then decided to take things from there somehow. I don't know. Unless we get him into interrogation, it's still guesswork."

"Maybe he's kept track of my mother all along. Maybe my mother and Emil have been in touch without me knowing it."

"One thing I've learned in detecting is that maybes don't always end up to be facts."

"But what about your cold case?"

"Yes, I have to tell Tides and Hodgdon about your mother's visitors' book, Robert Emil's name written there. I'm bound by law to tell them. And when I tell them, they'll go straight to the hospital and make inquiries. They'll try and trace an address for Emil. They'll certainly tell the attendants to contact them should Emil show up again."

"Why would he even visit in the first place?"

"He runs on perversities, is my guess."

Nora's Over the Moon

NIGHT OF JULY 15—I HAD A TUTORIAL THAT DAY, AND marked it on the calendar—the way Martha put it was, "Since getting pregnant, have you noticed, I want to . . . swoon into bed with you before dinner. And after. Morning sickness has been pretty light compared to what I've heard it can be. I'm keeping my fingers crossed."

"Swoon?" I said.

"Swoon where swooning is called for."

"I think you should move into my house with me, Martha."

"I've wondered about it. We could save money on my not paying rent. Anyway, my program's about to begin." Martha got up from bed, threw on her bathrobe, set the radio on the kitchen table. We sat down just as "The Case of Mara English" began.

In summary, Leah Diamond and her coterie of gangsters set out to help Detective Levy locate a woman who is cashing bad checks around Toronto under the name of Mara English. The gangsters send word out on the street, and in no time at all, Mara English is spotted in a hotel on Yonge Street. "The hotel where this gal's got a room makes our hotel look like the Ritz," Leah says to Detective Levy. "It's got rats for bellhops, the concierge is a cockroach, the breakfast cook's got one of those World War One mustard-gas coughs, and the dining room doubles as a funeral home."

When Detective Levy goes over to Mara English's hotel alone, jimmies the lock, and enters her darkened room, he finds a driver's license from Ontario province, plus licenses from Utah, California, and Florida, each under a different name. Then he hears a cough coming from under the bed. He aims his flashlight at her. "Okay, Mara," he says, "slide on out from under there."

"Say, how'd you find me?" she says.

"I looked under the bed," Detective Levy says.

Mara English stands up and covers her eyes against the flashlight's glare. "Hey, that moonlight's fake. You want to romance a girl, take her out on the veranda and look up at the real thing."

"Put on your coat, Miss English," Detective Levy says. "Gee, how original of you, hiding under the bed like that."

"Who says I was hiding?" Mara English says. "When you get to know me better, you'll see I always sleep under the bed."

Detective Levy delivers Mara English to the police station and then returns to the Devonshire Hotel and to Leah Diamond in their room. The gang is all there, and a celebration is going on. "Hey, what's all this? My invitation must've got lost in the mail or something."

"No, darling," Leah says. "I wanted you to be the first to know. But Trixie Beaumont, sitting on the end of the bed there, went to the doctor's with me, and then she blabbed her mouth."

"Wanted me to be the first to know what?" Detective Levy says.

"Darling, I need a big smackeroo." After the sound of Leah and Detective Levy having a loud kiss, she says, "I'm with child!"

The closing music came on, and Martha said, "How about that? Maybe me and Leah Diamond will deliver on the same day." She turned off the radio.

"That's a very strange thing for you to say," I said.

"Not at all. From the first episode, I felt some connection to Leah Diamond. It's hard to explain. I'm a detective. I work on facts and intuition. With Leah, my whole intuition's been electrified from the first. And now look, we're both with child. I love that way of putting it. *With child*. It's like we're already doing everything together, me and little what's-her-name."

"So you've decided it's a girl?"

"Well, your mother read it in the cards, so to speak."

"When did you tell my mother?"

"A week ago at Arts and Crafts."

"Was she pleased?"

"Very pleased. But my feeling is, she's still quite angry with you, Jacob. Still hurt you hadn't visited all those months. But believe me, she's over the moon about the baby. She can receive telephone calls, you know. Call your mother up. You'll hear she's over the moon."

Housewarming

SOME DAYS, LIFE FELT PRETTY WELL ORGANIZED. MY STUDIES were going all right. Martha and I had friends. *Detective Levy Detects,* much to Martha's delight, had been renewed for another year on radio, of course in reruns. We had enough money to live on. We could stretch our budget now and then. But other days felt . . . I'm hardly a poet, so how to say it? Like when an orchestra is warming up. All of the disparate sounds — oboe, violin, bassoon, French horn, tympani — you can't imagine how it will all turn into something beautiful.

One night in late August, when Martha was asleep and rain fell steadily past the windows, I sat at the kitchen table in her apartment and made a list: *1. Martha is pregnant. 2. My mother is still in the rest hospital. 3. The cold-case investigation trying to locate my real father Robert Emil is in progress — what happens if he's found, what next there? 4. Library science midprogram exams are in a couple months. 5. I haven't yet read all of the letters from Rigolet to Nora during the war — why so hesitant? 6. Figure some of this out!*

Martha and I agreed we should wait to be married until after our child was born. "I don't care at all about convention," she said. "My parents are gone. I don't have siblings. My aunts and uncles and cousins, distant as they've been, will be happy for me. They'll want to visit eventually. Nora's over the moon. So let's just wait. You'll have your degree and there will be a lot to celebrate. Usually in detecting, when too much makes good sense, that's when we dig deeper. But this all makes sense without having to dig deeper. I think we're making the right decision, Jacob, don't you?"

"Absolutely yes," I said.

Martha packed up her apartment and moved into my family house. With help from fellow students in the library science program, and a few policemen and policewomen, this took just two days. Sitting for our first dinner together in the house, Martha looked around and said, "Maybe we can take some of the photographs down. But otherwise, how nice."

On September 15, we had a kind of housewarming party. Morty Shaloom, from John W. Doull, and his wife, Maxine, stayed for hours. Michael Duvelle, Marcella Sylphide, and Deborah Chase, all students in the library science program, brought bottles of wine and some records for the turntable. The owner of the Wired Monk, Jennifer Holt, her husband, a wonderful watercolorist named Paul Amundson, the waitresses Bev Elliot and Trudy Page, and the waiter Thomas Finch all showed up. Jinx Faltenbourg and Margaret Plumly from the Halifax Free Library arrived early and stayed late. It was quite a feast, really. There was baked salmon with sesame seeds and dill, several rice salads, curried lamb stew (prepared by Margaret), baguettes, green salads, fruit salads, and Jennifer brought four cakes from the Wired Monk. Mrs. Hamelin and Mrs. Brevittmore brought champagne. ("Not a drop for you, Martha!") Since our first impromptu movie date, the four of us tended to meet weekly, for a movie, dinner, or just for coffee or tea at the Wired Monk. Mrs. Hamelin and Mrs. Brevittmore loved that café.

Detective Tides and Detective Hodgdon dropped by. They went

with Martha into the small study, where, she told me later, they caught up on the Robert Emil cold case. Then Tides spent the better part of an hour studying the photographs that still lined the living room and dining room walls, though Martha had removed all of the ones from the bedroom and hallways. Holding a glass of wine, he said, "I remember a few years back, the *Chronicle-Herald* printed the wrong photograph in connection with a murder, took place on Lower Water Street. Remember that, Martha?"

"How could I forget?" Martha said. "They accidentally — ha! — *accidentally* put a photograph of the wrong guy on the front page of the Sunday edition. The photograph was of a trade representative of some sort, who was in Hong Kong at the time."

"The wife of the actual deceased was incensed," Tides said. "The wife of the trade representative was incensed. Everybody was incensed."

"What brought that case to mind suddenly?" Martha said.

"Looking at all these photographs," Tides said. "I was just thinking how nice they are. This one and that one, the lovebirds here, the lovebirds there. Or the close-up there, of that fellow holding a royal flush during a poker game, look how smug and happy he looks, as if it's the first royal flush in history. But if you were to write the words 'wanted for homicide' — no offense meant, I'm just talking out loud here. If you printed that under the photograph, you'd assess the guy in a different way. I mean, you could have a photograph of a kid taking communion, but if the caption read 'Threw rocks from the bridge at a school bus window,' well, everything changes, doesn't it? The kid automatically looks guilty."

"So glad you can leave work behind when you come to a party," Martha said, laughing, which made Tides blush and laugh too.

But, really, everyone seemed to be having a good time.

Except for Mrs. Hamelin and Mrs. Brevittmore, all the guests left by 11:30. When Martha finally closed the front door, Mrs. Hamelin said, "Shall we get started on the walls, then?" Mrs. Brevittmore nodded in agreement, and they both began to take photographs down in the living room. Neither Martha nor I protested.

And Mrs. Hamelin and Mrs. Brevittmore set about things with such good cheer. The photographs had become oppressive, and I'd deal with Nora asking about them when the time came. In less than an hour, all the photographs had been taken down from the living room and dining room walls, placed in cardboard boxes, the boxes put in the attic. Afterward we sat at the kitchen table. Mrs. Brevittmore produced a bottle of sherry from her handbag and poured a small glass for herself, a glass for Mrs. Hamelin, and one for me. Mrs. Hamelin raised her glass and said, "Now you can start to put your own memories on the walls." Mrs. Brevittmore said, "Not that it's any of your business, Esther." We clinked glasses, Martha using her water glass, and sat and talked until nearly two o'clock in the morning. We made plans to see *The Spy Who Loved Me,* a James Bond movie starring Roger Moore. As she put on her coat to leave, Mrs. Hamelin said, "We've brought you a modest little housewarming gift." Mrs. Brevittmore, already wearing her coat, opened our front hall closet and took out a package. "I didn't even see you put that in there," Martha said. "And here I'm supposed to be a detective." Mrs. Brevittmore handed Martha the package.

"Now, remember," Mrs. Hamelin said, "you neither of you have to be a connoisseur to enjoy the subject matter at least."

The housewarming gift was a photograph depicting what appeared to be a grimy Victorian alley lit by gaslight, where three men, dressed in black suits with badges on their lapels, looked down at a figure wearing a wedding dress caked in mud. The figure's face was covered by a white handkerchief—two of the three men had handkerchiefs visible in their breast pockets. The dress and handkerchief almost glowed in the gauzy light.

We all stood studying the photograph, which was in a simple wooden frame. "This photograph is titled *Through a Detective's Eyes,*" Mrs. Hamelin said. "There's a story to it, Martha, that we thought would please you, and whose ironies and paradoxes would not only balance out the grim subject matter but also speak to the daily unpredictability of your chosen profession, which, by the way, Mrs. Brevittmore and I admire, and are more than a little mesmerized by, we admit. We read Agatha Christie aloud to each other."

"Never not by the fireplace," Mrs. Brevittmore said.

"Let's sit down again, please, and you can tell us about the picture," Martha said. She rubbed her hands together like an excited child. "This really tops off the housewarming, if you ask me."

We sat in the living room on the sofa and chairs and Mrs. Brevittmore started right in.

"Well, then, you can tell from the title that the men standing in the fog are all in detective work. The photograph was taken by Albert Mayer-Price in 1919. You may remember, Jacob, in my library, the photograph *Misanthrope Reading Newspaper?*"

"Yes, of course I remember it."

"That too was taken by Albert Mayer-Price. You see, Price was one of the first to contrive photographic set pieces. Like a scene on a theatrical stage or in early cinema."

"Oh, you mean this isn't an actual dead woman?" Martha said. Suddenly everyone laughed, because Martha had sounded so disappointed. "Do you mean the detectives and the woman are like actors?"

"Precisely," Mrs. Hamelin said. "Albert Mayer-Price hired people, or asked friends or acquaintances to pose. And that is what you see here."

"But that is hardly the whole story, is it?" Mrs. Brevittmore said.

"Not in the least," Mrs. Hamelin said. "You see, this photograph refers, if you will, to an actual incident. Quite ghastly, really. What happened was this. A young man named Brennan Map married a young woman named Ellen Lassitor. Both were twenty-eight and had all of a bowl of soup between them. They knew they could only manage a justice-of-the-peace wedding. But Ellen had always dreamed of wearing a real wedding dress. So Brennan stole one for her. Oh, yes, it's starkest poverty and desperate romance all jammed up, isn't it? It's all tabloid fodder. Not to mention the very worst way for newlyweds to begin a life together. But he'd do anything for her, and she'd let him. This Brennan broke into a wedding shop near Savile Row, slipped a dress right off a mannequin, for goodness' sake."

"Maybe practicing for his wedding night," Mrs. Brevittmore said.

"Anyway," Mrs. Hamelin said, "the mannequin's a detail you don't forget."

"I won't forget it," Martha said.

"Now, it's at this point that Brennan makes his fatal choice," Mrs. Hamelin went on. "Already he's broken into and entered the wedding shop, but you could imagine a judge being lenient if, say, he'd returned the dress, just boxed it up and sent it through the post, none's the harm. Yet the night proved more complicated. You see, Brennan looks around the shop and sees all manner of shoes and — how to say it without blushing — let's just call it nightwear."

"Silk stuff that would make a doubter bend in prayer, so to speak," Mrs. Brevittmore said.

"No doubt kept nearly under lock and key, given the era," Mrs. Hamelin said. "And so our Brennan fairly ransacks the place, loading up with nightgowns and such. Oh, my. But now he's filled a number of boxes, so how does he carry it all? It's a good fifty blocks to his shabby rooming house. So what does our genius do? He puts on the wedding dress. Lord as my witness, he puts on the wedding dress.

"A young man with his pedigree knows how to navigate exclusively by alleys to his destination. So he starts down the alleys, and when he's twenty or so blocks from home, fate steps from the shadows. Three pub crawlers stop him and probably say, 'Oy, oy, what's this, then?'— thinking to have their way with the fleeing bride. 'Just having some good fun,' as they later told the police. There was a four-column newspaper article on the murder. They all three eventually confessed."

Martha was astonished by this story, sad and gruesome as it was. "Well, I'm glad this photograph's not a *wedding* gift," she said. "For obvious reasons."

Much laughter.

"No, that hardly would've been appropriate," Mrs. Hamelin said. More laughter. "We'll be on our way now."

When Mrs. Brevittmore and Mrs. Hamelin left, Martha said, "Tomorrow, let's caulk all these nail holes, Jake. Then let's agree on the color for some new paint."

My Life in Library Science

LATE IN THE AFTERNOON OF OCTOBER 15, 1978, WEEKS into my third semester, I had a consultation with Dr. Margolin. I was hoping to be recommended for a yearlong paid internship after graduation.

"I see in your application that your first choice is the Halifax Free Library," Dr. Margolin said. "This potentially could be a problem, seeing as you may wish to be more independent of your mother's ... legacy."

"By legacy, you mean her mentally falling from grace? Because if you don't mean that, what could you mean? Because, as the chief librarian all those years, she had an impeccable reputation, so I'd be very pleased to be the *opposite* of independent of that."

"Sorry. Point well taken. I will write a letter recommending you for your first choice. Let me know how it works out."

"Thank you."

"You're welcome, Jacob. I studied your academic record this morning and must commend you for all sorts of improvements. You're not at the top of your class, yet your last two essays were more than competent. Your greatest strength at this point, as I see it, is your ability to write with such a personal tone. I would almost say poetic. Well, not quite. This can hardly be a surprise, seeing as you were actually born in a library. I'd say you have quite the personal connection to libraries."

I didn't detect any irony in what she said, so left it alone.

In the Waiting Room

MARTHA AND I WERE SITTING IN DR. CAROL HORN'S WAITING room, at her office at 201 Argyle Street, paging through magazines. Martha was there to have a routine examination. She looked up from her magazine and said, "I should tell you, darling, that Detective Tides has been tracing Robert Emil's pension, and guess what? Over the years his pension checks have been sent to no less than twenty-three addresses. All in Halifax. The man's been living like a ball in a pinball machine as far as addresses go."

"Not 'like father, like son,' because I've had only two addresses, counting my shabby apartment on Bennet Street for a short time. Boy oh boy, do I have a lot of catching up to do with my father."

"Lame attempt to be funny."

"I'd rather die than skip out on you, Martha. You know that."

"I couldn't imagine anything stupider, considering you're committed to marrying a detective. I'd track you down and not kiss you for a month, let alone anything in bed. I'd hide the bed."

"What's the most recent address for him? Isn't that where Tides and Hodgdon would go and break down the door?"

Martha reached into her handbag and took out a piece of paper on which were listed all twenty-three of the addresses at which Robert Emil had received pension checks, followed by the dates of residency at each place. "Last known address was Fifty-five Plover, apartment six."

"Can he be living on just his pension?"

"Have you been on Mars? Lots of people do."

"Twenty-three places . . ."

Martha decided to list them off, almost to believe it herself. "Some of the pension checks were never cashed — that's something. It means he knew the risk of being traced. Maybe it means that, maybe it doesn't. Anyway, there's One-fifteen Acadia Street, there's Five Fawson, there's Twenty-six Harvey Street, there's One-eighteen Lucknow, there's Sixteen Brenton Street, there's Twenty-eight Sackville, there's Sixty Bell Road, there's . . ." But then Martha's name was called by the nurse assistant, who told me Dr. Horn would summon me when the examination was finished, and we'd talk things over.

On the walk home, Martha said, "Dr. Horn said she's got a beautiful crib that her granddaughter used, and would like us to have it. She said to come by her house tomorrow after four, if possible, and pick it up. She's only two blocks from the house, Jake. We could carry it right on down the street."

"Everything sounds fine," I said, "with the baby."

"Do you want to know, boy or girl?" Martha said. "The doctor knows, but I didn't want to ask until I asked if you did."

"I'm of fifteen different minds about it. But fourteen say I want to know."

"I'm calling right now, then."

Martha walked into a pharmacy and went to the phone booth in the back. I was looking at her through the glass door as she dialed. After saying a few words, she was clearly put on hold. Then she closed her eyes and listened. Then she had a very wide grin.

She said something and hung up, slid open the door, and said, "My mother's name was Elizabeth, yours is Nora. How about Nora Elizabeth Crauchet Rigolet?"

"How about Elizabeth Nora—?"

"The music of that is clunky. I prefer Nora Elizabeth."

Letter from Bernard Rigolet

Darling Nora,

I have been with the First Army for three weeks now. Germany is cold as hell. It feels more like winter than spring. I wear double socks and still my toes hurt. I had a dream in which I put my bare feet in a cauldron of soup. My CO says a man experiences "like a blow to the heart the entire war during the first minute of combat, even if it's just a skirmish, but right after that, every minute feels like an entire life, and by the way, forget sleep." What he said turned out to be true, my dearest Nora. I hope to tell you all about this one day, at home in our house. I have your photograph with me of course. A few days ago a war photographer named Capa — Robert Capa — joined us. I heard mention he's working for Life magazine. He's a big deal that way. He's a handsome fellow, all right, and the first time he held forth about where he'd been and what he'd seen, a great sorrow filled his eyes. He referred to a woman, obviously his great love, named Gerda Taro. Also a photographer. The way he spoke of her, he called her his "wife," it felt like he'd be reunited with her any day now, except the truth came out: she was killed during the Spanish Civil War, run over by a tank, and she died in a hospital.

I can't really remember more. But he broke down then. You see, Nora, we really didn't know the man at all. But here is something: his Gerda Taro was raised in Leipzig! The very city we are marching to liberate. And it occurred to me, maybe that has something to do with why this Capa has joined us — not just for Life magazine, but maybe for more personal reasons too.

I am heartbroken with regret that we parted in Halifax on such a sour note, my darling sweetheart. It was all my fault, really it was. In part it was knowing that I was shipping out so soon and that there was some chance I would not be returning to you. Well, I could not stand being around that, and so I needed to quarrel and make it seem like it was somehow your fault that I was leaving, when of course it was anything but that. How could I do such a thing? Truly, I am sorry. Shakespeare may have said "parting is such sweet sorrow," but I did not and cannot feel any sweetness to it, not in these horrid times. Horrid what I have seen over here, what men are capable of doing, which I know is nothing new in the world, but being so close-up to so much death is new to me, Nora. I have been splattered by the entrails and blood of a man not two meters away from me — his name was Marco Fionella. He was from San Francisco. Had the German machine gun been pointed ten inches or so to the left, it would have been me. But I will spare you more of such scenes. There have been many.

I close my eyes and see you in the library, wearing your knee-length button-down sweater into the cold wind off the harbor, the time I showed up unexpectedly and without hesitation we went out for a coffee. Such a moment I can't imagine happening again, Nora. Then again, it is the only thing I wish to imagine happening again — tomorrow, please.

I have been "assigned" Robert Capa. That is, I'm to keep as close to him as possible as we move toward Leipzig. I'm to talk with him and talk about what is going on as it occurs, and provide whatever protection I may be able to provide, which in reality is probably very little, and he knows this and has said as much. He will take care of himself, he says. Still and all, I am assigned to Robert Capa. He has even given me a few tips on taking photographs. Maybe when I am back home I'll buy a camera, who knows? In three days, tops, we'll be in Leipzig.

Strange world where courage masquerades as duty, or vice versa, but what philosophy I can muster up sounds hollow, especially when drowned out by artillery. The crackle of the walkie-talkie near me as I write is enough philosophy for a day, I suppose, the disconnected voice telling us what we might expect just up the road. But no information over the walkie-talkie is ever what it turns out to be. We have stopped by all sorts of villages and seen all sorts of people, and all I can say is, if I never hear a word of German spoken again in this lifetime I will not feel anything but grateful. Tedium, waiting, marching, chocolate bars, no sleep no sleep no sleep, burst eardrums all down the line, so that many of my fellow soldiers shout for lack of being able to hear their own voices. But just now, what I hear is what we wrote ourselves for our wedding vows, "Until the end of the world and forever." I stick to that. That alone will get me through, if I get through. I close my eyes and can see you in the library. That time I mentioned, no excuses necessary to your colleagues, even though you were new to the job. You just stood up and off we went for that coffee.

Nora, it's damned hard to write you a spontaneous letter. I only mean because I know it might take weeks, even months to reach you, and what is happening here in Germany, day to day, can't be summed up, and it's difficult to actually know, let alone articulate, what I'm experiencing. I'm a jumble of half-thought-out thoughts in the face of things. I have only what's right in front of me. I was thinking this morning, in the minute or two I had to think, about how before I shipped out, when I stood at the Halifax wharf and stared out toward the Atlantic as far as I could see, that at the same time I was staring into myself equally as far, or something like that. But here in Germany I look only ten or twenty meters out ahead. My fear is that I will be so far away for so long, and not only that, but tasting death for so long, that I will begin to look at you — to look at us — as a figment of my imagination. I am terrified of this. This is all to say that a letter from you will help this in not happening. So I hope you have written me a letter and that I receive it.

Well, I've got to go find this Robert Capa fellow again. He's giving me a photography lesson.

I feel blessed in our marriage. All my love,

Your Bernie

Questioning Robert Emil

Part One

ON OCTOBER 17, DETECTIVE TIDES ARRESTED ROBERT EMIL at Deep Water Terminus on Halifax Harbor, where he was working as a forklift operator under the name of Vincent Rose. He owned up to being Robert Emil right away, and was taken into custody without protest. I was at home studying for an exam when the phone rang, and Martha said, "We've got your original father here" — the word "original" struck me as both comical and discerning — "and I got the okay from Tides and Hodgdon if you want to come down and have a look at him through the glass."

"I don't know," I said.

"First time is once in a lifetime."

"Okay, I'll come right down."

When I arrived it was about four o'clock in the afternoon. Martha and Detective Tides were standing in the viewing room. I stepped in. Tides pointed to a chair and I sat down in it. My whole life I had thought of Bernard Rigolet as my father. But here was Robert Emil.

Emil looked haggard. I think that's the right word for it, haggard. Yet when Martha came over and whispered, "You have his eyes, my darling," I could not disagree. Knowing Martha, she said it to make sure I was looking directly at the truth of things, not in any way to be hurtful, of course. Emil was sitting in a chair at a gray metal office desk. He was dressed in blue dungarees and a black sweatshirt, with a gray T-shirt showing at the neck. He had work boots on. His brown hair flecked with gray was unkempt, and he had a white-flecked growth of dark beard, maybe two or three days' worth. But I could see that, though he now exhibited a seedy look, he was basically a quite handsome fellow. I tried not to think of my mother's attraction to him, nor his to her, and just concentrate on what was being said in the interrogation room. And I mostly succeeded at that. Mostly.

Detective Tides dropped a thick file of papers on the desk with a loud thud. He picked it up and dropped it again for effect. "What a fucking stupid goddamn life you've had, ex-officer Robert Emil," he said. "Disgrace to the police department. Disgrace in the eyes of God. Why haven't you drowned yourself in Halifax Harbor by now?"

"Oh, I get it," Robert Emil said. "Good cop, bad cop. You're the bad cop."

"No, I'm the good cop," Detective Tides said, and Emil, just those few sentences in, winced as if in pain. "Let's you and me take a magical mystery ride back, ex-officer Emil, to April of 1945, the eighteenth of the month, to be exact."

"I can hardly remember yesterday," Emil said, tipping his thumb back like it was a bottle of whiskey, "let alone 1945."

Tides picked up the file again and let it drop to the desk. "This whole file will refresh your memory, ex-officer Emil."

"Stop with that *ex-* shit, will you? I served commendably in the Halifax police."

"You were *commended* for the fuckup sewer-rat citation. You disgraced the badge. You disgraced the uniform," Tides said. "It may have been before your time, but today we've got something called a cold case. Know what that is?"

"Not familiar," Emil said, staring at the desk.

"It's an old case, but everyone's suddenly got a brand-new interest in it," Tides said. "It's *your* worst nightmare — your *worst* nightmare, ex-officer Emil. Because me and my detectives are going to put you in prison for the rest of your days for the murder of Mr. Max Berall."

"Never heard of him."

At which point Detective Tides whacked Emil on the side of his head with a telephone book. I had seen this done once on television. "Lucky for Emil that's a twenty-year-old phone directory," Hodgdon said. "Not so many people in it as the one from this year. A little lighter, the old one."

"Jesus," Martha said. "Tides really likes doing that, doesn't he?"

Emil said, "Okay, you got me to remember Max Berall." He was rubbing the side of his head. "Hebrew piano player, right?"

"Person of the Jewish faith, very prominent in the Baron de Hirsch Synagogue. Person of the Jewish faith who had a wife and four children you half orphaned."

"I didn't murder anybody," Emil said. "But now that I think of it, I remember the murder. That was 1945, you say?"

"April 18, 1945, you shot him after midnight, so officially it's April 19. This is weighing on you thirty years, Emil. Just tell the truth. Some playwright or other said, Tell the truth, it's the easiest thing to remember. But I say, Tell the truth, 'cause when a sack of shit like you lies, everybody knows it."

"Get me a lawyer, you fucking idiot," Emil said, and Tides whacked him again with the phone book, even harder this time.

"All the attorneys in town are at the movies," Tides said. "But we left messages for them."

Tides put the phone book next to the file and left the room. Hodgdon went in with Robert Emil. Tides said to Martha, "You're up next."

Hodgdon reached out his hand and said, "Detective Hodgdon," and Robert Emil slapped his hand away and said, "Fuck you."

"Do you want to know something personal about me, Mr. Emil? I don't sleep. I do not sleep. I haven't slept since last Christmas. Want to know why?"

"I can't wait," Emil said.

"Because back then I heard a record. Right here in the station, Christmas party. Someone put on this record, it was a beautiful rendition of 'I Wish That I Could Hide Inside This Letter.' A sweet little fox-trot written by a fellow named Charlie Tobias, and this was a very special record. Only one copy of it in all the world. One copy. Imagine that. One copy, and you know why? Well, hell, I'm just going to play it for you. Why not?"

Hodgdon left the interrogation room, went to his desk, picked up a small record player, and started to walk back. During this brief interlude I looked at Robert Emil again. Martha stood next to me, her arm around my waist. "I know, I know," she said. "You can leave anytime, Jake." But I didn't want to leave. I was lost in it now.

Back in the interrogation room, Hodgdon set the record player on the desk and plugged it into a wall socket. The record, which was already on the turntable, spun. He set the needle down, and the musical prelude to "I Wish That I Could Hide Inside This Letter" began.

"I hate Lawrence Welk," Detective Tides grumbled, "but Hodgdon, there, this is one of his favorites. Me? It's fingernails across the blackboard."

Once the singer began, *My heart's in this letter I'm sending,* Hodgdon stood on his chair, held his right fist to his mouth like a microphone, and sang along like a crooner. The record was scratchy; Robert Emil stood and pressed himself to the wall and looked at Hodgdon like he was a madman.

"The song's already working its magic," Detective Tides said.

The bouncy Lawrence Welk accompaniment, the light, plaintive, sincere voice of the woman singer, not exactly belting it out, more a stylish lament: *I wish that I could hide inside this letter / And seal me up and send me out to you —*

Detective Hodgdon loosened his tie, threw his suit coat to the floor, jumped down from the chair, and moved within a few feet of Robert Emil. I thought Emil was going to cringe to the floor, especially when Hodgdon planted a kiss on Emil's forehead and quickly stepped back, still singing: *What a surprise in store / They'd bring me to your door / I'd pop right out and kiss you / Like you'd never been kissed before / We'd be so happy we could cry together / And then we'd love the way we used to do.* At the last second, quick as a cobra, Detective Hodgdon made a grab for Robert Emil's crotch, snapping his hand back. Emil crouched protectively like a child. Leaning against the desk, Hodgdon sang, *I wish that I could hide inside this letter / And seal me up and send it off to you.*

Music, and when the second verse began, Hodgdon took off his tie, whirled it around his head, and threw it at Robert Emil as he sang: *We'd be so happy we could cry together / And then we'd love the way we used to do / I wish that I could hide inside this letter / And seal me up and send me off to you.* Hodgdon got down on one knee, closed his eyes, and raised his voice an octave or two. *Special delivery / I'd V-mail this female to you-u-u-u-u.*

The record kept turning until Hodgdon pulled the plug. He looked at Robert Emil, who had now sat down in his chair again, and said, "Now that I've declared my love, ex-officer Emil, my partner Detective Tides is going to come in and demonstrate with that telephone book that he's a very jealous man. Give it some thought." Hodgdon left the interrogation room.

The four of us watched through the glass. I don't believe Robert Emil knew it was a one-way window. He seemed to be trying to regain some composure and fell short. He suddenly tore the cord from the record player and tied it around his neck, but the cord was far too short to throw over the heating pipe near the ceiling and hang himself, so he tried to twist it around his throat. Martha said, "Let's get in there," but Detective Tides said, "No, this is good, this is good."

"Yeah, he can't off himself that way. It just goes against instinct not to breathe," Hodgdon said. "Just watch." And then Emil gave up and threw the cord to the floor. "Jeez, what a half-assed attempt," Hodgdon said. "I've lost all respect."

Detective Tides went out to the main office and came back holding at least ten telephone books. Hodgdon opened the interrogation room door and in walked Tides, who set the phone books on the desk. He picked up the record player's cord, set it on the desk. Emil coughed up a little blood. "You can't do anything right," Tides said. "Ex-officer Emil, your whole life's a sack of shit."

Tides then started to sort through the telephone books, lifting each one as if testing it for heft and potential, setting one on the desk, tossing another to the floor. Robert Emil watched closely.

Tides sat down in the chair opposite Emil and said, "'I Wish That I Could Hide Inside This Letter' — what a song, eh? Recorded in 1945. Yeah, we've been listening through the one-way glass, there." Tides gestured over his shoulder. "Know where Detective Hodgdon got the phonograph record from? From the evidence box, police warehouse, just down the block. It belonged to one Mrs. Estelle Yablon, a very close friend of the deceased in question in our cold case, Max Berall. Let me be direct. Everything about these fine, upstanding *Jewish* Canadian citizens Max and Estelle was like having your own police badge shoved up your motherfucking Jew-hating ass —"

"You've got it all wrong. The night Max Berall was killed —"

"Oh, so *now* you remember it?"

"It came back to me. That night, I was security at Baron de

Hirsch, some Hebrew holiday of some sort. There'd been some threats. The war had got everyone twisted all around. There'd been some threats."

"Yeah, we know all about the *atmosphere*," Hodgdon said.

"How's that?" Robert Emil said.

"Because me and my partners are crack researchers, Emil. Crack. Researchers. We know all about incidents against Jews and synagogues in 1945 — the *atmosphere*. And you personally were part of the putrid air that year, ex-officer Emil. You personally. You were a putrescence in 1945, and you're a putrescence now."

"I was trying to protect those Jews."

"See, what we are looking at here is the murder of Max Berall and the disappearance of Mrs. Estelle Yablon, who identified you in a lineup as the man who ran from the alley where they found Max Berall, two bullets to the head. The back of the head, ex-officer Emil. You got rid of the weapon."

"They checked my police revolver —"

"But it wasn't your police revolver the two slugs came from."

"I never heard of Mrs. Yablon. I take it the name's Hebrew."

"She didn't show up for services the next Saturday at Baron de Hirsch. Which she never once missed in twenty years."

"Maybe she had a cold."

"Maybe she was deposited in Halifax Harbor. Like a savings account against you being in prison for the rest of your life."

"I was exonerated on all charges."

"No, you just weren't finally arrested. But guess what? There's all sorts of new forensic techniques since you were police, Emil. Since your putrid self was police. Since you were part of the *atmosphere* in 1945. Mrs. Yablon might not've surfaced in the harbor, but she's going to surface in this file on the table, here. You got two ghosts, Emil, and both are going to be screaming at you day and night until your putrescence of a soul shrivels up in prison. Why not just admit what you did."

"Fuck you."

Hodgdon slammed a phone book against Robert Emil's head. Emil spun backward to the floor. Hodgdon left the interrogation room. When he entered the viewing room, he said, "Martha, you're up."

Martha embraced me tightly and whispered, "You should leave now, Jake."

"Why's that?" I said.

"Because I don't want you to see me deliver the coup de grâce."

"You think you're going to get him to confess?"

"I meant the coup de grâce for today. The just-keep-him-shaken-up coup de grâce. Please, really, I don't want you to see this. Haven't you seen enough for one day?"

"What, are you going to hit him with a telephone book?"

"Darling, please."

Detective Tides said, "Jake, don't be a goddamn idiot. Detective Crauchet's got work to do. Go sit in the library, maybe."

I said all right, I'd leave. But when Martha went in to interrogate Robert Emil, I stood by the door of the viewing room. Tides and Hodgdon were focused on Martha and Robert Emil. Martha sat down at the desk. She folded her hands together. Then she slapped Emil across the face. "Oh, sorry," she said. "I don't know how that happened."

Emil looked furious but didn't say anything. Martha sighed deeply and said very slowly, "Did you know you had a son? Well, yes, you do have a son. His mother is Nora Rigolet. Your son is watching you right now, through that glass. He's seeing you for the first time. He's just learned what a useless piece of shit you are. He knows what you did."

With that, I finally left.

Detective Emil Detects

MARTHA CAME HOME THAT DAY AT ABOUT FIVE O'CLOCK. She was carrying takeout from Mandarin Palace, including my favorite, spicy fried pot stickers, which Martha called heart attack fodder. The kitchen table was filled with small boxes of food, plates, chopsticks, and napkins, and I'd set my notes for a required essay, "The Origin and History of Card Catalogues," on the counter. The radio played at low volume, classical music. *Detective Levy Detects* would come on at ten.

Looking at the stack of notes, Martha said, "That the essay on card catalogues?"

"I've got a lot of work to do on it still," I said.

"May I read it when you're finished?"

"I could really use some comments."

"Okay."

"How were you feeling today? Nora Elizabeth been announcing herself?" I reached over and stroked Martha's belly under her oversize trousers, cinched to fit.

"Kicking up a storm."

"How's the desk work going for you, Martha? Do you miss the gumshoe part of the job?"

"Less than I thought, though I'll want to get back to it. Besides, Tides and Hodgdon keep me up to speed. They like to flop down on the ratty sofa in my office and go into detail. You want to talk about Robert Emil or not?"

"I was worried. What if he got violent in there? What with the baby and all."

"I wouldn't step around the desk. I got my two cents in today, but no more Robert Emil up close for me. You are absolutely right. It might've been reckless. And I promised you I wouldn't be."

"You said you couldn't hold him, but you think he's a flight risk, so —"

"He's got to report in by phone three times a day. He's back working at Deep Water Terminus, the forklift. The company can't sack Emil until he's in the slammer. That might never happen, or it could take months. Plus a hearing. It's illegal for them to sack him just on the suspicion. Et cetera, et cetera."

"I've been thinking — I'd like to attend the next interrogation."

"I've already asked Tides and Hodgdon. They get it, that it's something important to me, having you there. So protocol's down the toilet, as Tides says."

"I've always found him a very articulate man."

"They're bringing Robert Emil in again in about two weeks. He's in deep shit, Jacob. Let me just say it. I read over Mrs. Yablon's testimony again, and I can't remember a better physical description, and she just outright says, 'Oh, it was Officer Robert Emil running out of the alley.' You hear her voice right there on the page, and there's nothing but conviction — I guess I mean that in two ways."

"I don't feel anything in particular when I look at Emil. I mean, I don't stand there and think, Wow, my real father, I really want to get to know him. Nothing like that. He's like seeing someone on a Wanted poster."

"But your feelings must get complicated, right?"

"It's more trying to imagine what Nora saw in this creep. But how can I know, really? During the war and all. Like Tides — or was it Hodgdon — said, the *atmosphere*."

"Yeah, the atmosphere nine months before April 1945. Just take care of yourself, Jacob. The pain of all of this may be, I don't know what, delayed."

"Still, when Robert Emil is next interrogated, I want to watch."

Martha and I ate and talked a little more, and then she said, "I've got to show you something." She walked into the bedroom, returning with her black satchel. She sat down again, held her stomach, and said, "Hey, feel this." I reached over and felt our daughter kicking. Really something, that. "Not to worry, Jake. It's all going along as it should."

Martha reached into the satchel and took out a book and handed it to me. It was a hardcover copy of *Detective Emil Detects*. The subtitle was *Adventures of a Halifax Policeman*. I turned to the back flap and saw a photograph of Robert Emil wearing his police uniform. Under that, the author's bio read: "Robert Emil was a policeman in Halifax, Nova Scotia, and received citations for bravery in the line of duty. This is his debut novel."

"*Novel* my sweet ass," Martha said. "Sure, call it anything you want, but there's so much in that book that squares with actual historical incidents and facts. Tricky in court to use so-called fiction as evidence of anything but the imagination, as a prosecuting attorney told me. But Tides, Hodgdon, and I can use this book in questioning Emil. You wait and see, Jake. We had a big confab about it, in fact. Laying out our strategy."

I handed the book back to Martha, who put it in the satchel. She got up, hung the satchel on the silent valet by the front door, and walked back to the kitchen. "I'm going to take a nap," she said, and went to lie down on our bed. I continued work on my essay.

Martha slept until almost ten o'clock. When she stepped yawning from the bedroom, she said, "I don't mind cold Chinese," and served herself a plateful. I turned on the radio. We had a few moments before the program started. "You missed the episode where Leah Diamond had her daughter," Martha said. "Big drama. She had the baby delivered right there in the hotel."

"You filled me in, though, remember?"

"Oh, right."

That night's episode was titled "The Kidnapping, the Murder." Martha got quite upset, as it was about Leah Diamond and Detective Levy's two-month-old daughter, Lily, getting kidnapped and held for ransom. Naturally, the gangsters and gun molls came to the rescue. Not only did they locate Lily, but they murdered the kidnapper, though that wasn't the end of it. Because as it turned out, three employees of the Devonshire Hotel — a concierge, a dishwasher, and a bellman — conspired in the kidnapping. It was the concierge, a guy named Miklos Noyes, who was found with Lily by Leah Diamond's pals in another hotel two blocks away. That's when one of the molls carried Lily out into the hallway, and the rest of the gang screwed on their silencers.

"I don't know," Martha said. "That was pretty rough to listen to all the way through, I admit. Still and all, Leah Diamond's my role model in all womanly things brave and true."

"Was it the kidnapping part especially?" I asked. I could see she was a little shaken.

"Yes, of course, that. But also, there it was again. Just like when that bullet creased my belt that time. I mean, what if, in the radio episode, there had been a shootout and baby Lily was right there?"

"Naw, wouldn't happen," I said. "Never would've happened."

"Why not?" Martha said.

"The scriptwriter would've got all sorts of hate mail, and nobody would want to listen anymore."

"Honey, I'm really zonked. I feel like, with my eyes open, I've already started tonight's dream."

"I guess that could happen."

"Figure of speech, but I'm going to bed. You want to lie down with me?"

We took off our clothes and lay in bed, and Martha said, "Don't forget tomorrow, Arts and Crafts. I'll meet you over in Dartmouth." Then she fell asleep. I lay pressed against her back, my hand on her belly. No kicking at first, then a little kicking. Then I looked through the open door and saw Martha's satchel on the silent valet. It hung there like a reproach, in the sense that suddenly it felt as if I should be keeping up with Martha's cold-case investigation to whatever extent I could. I admired how Martha looked at everything she'd learned about my mother's past as if it was some rare opportunity to deepen her understanding of me, of us. Sure, it was part of her detectiving. But it had gone beyond that months ago. She was bending the rules, allowing me to watch the interrogation of Robert Emil. It didn't seem to be causing difficulties with Detectives Tides and Hodgdon, but then again, maybe it was.

I got out of bed, threw on a robe, took the satchel from the silent valet, and carried it to the kitchen table. I took out *Detective Emil Detects*. I started reading it at around 11:30 p.m. and set it down, after reading the last page, at 5:15 the next morning. Jesus H. Christ, what a horrible writer, I thought—I mean, just the style of it, the way it reads sentence by sentence. So many clichés, and no policeman could perform so many heroic acts in a single week. The entire story took place between April 7 and April 19, 1945. Looking through a couple of folders in Martha's file in her study, I discovered that those dates coincided with a number of anti-Semitic incidents in Halifax, including a police tear-gas canister being thrown through a window at Baron de Hirsch Synagogue. The very week I was born in the Halifax Free Library.

When I got into bed, Martha groggily said, "Everything okay, darling?"

Blaming Ghosts

MARTHA AND I HAD DINNER AT MRS. HAMELIN'S ON SUNDAY, October 23, and that evening we met the fellow who had replaced me as her assistant and auction bidder. His name was Brice Falter. He was about thirty and had a degree in art history from McGill University, and was himself a painter. He used the smallest guest room as his studio, which was cleared out for tables and easels. "Brice is a good painter," Mrs. Brevittmore said at the table. "Quite enamored of Matisse, though not enough enamored of the Moroccan interiors, in my opinion."

Brice struck me as a little stodgy but very intelligent, and when he said that his sister, Rose, was seven months pregnant, Martha said, "Oh, my own due date is January 14," and talked with great animation. Brice obviously felt comfortable enough to share that not only was Rose a high school English teacher but also the coach of the fencing team, and fencing while that far along in a pregnancy presented all sorts of comical travails. "She would murder me if she knew I did an imitation, so just let your imagination suffice," Brice said. I could tell that Martha liked him.

At one point after dinner, Brice sat next to me on the sofa while everyone else remained at the dining room table. "You know," he said, "lately I've lost out on three consecutive photographs at auction. Mrs. Hamelin is none too pleased. With every other part of my job, I think she's pleased. But just last month, in London, I thought I'd locked into the cadence of the bidding perfectly, you know? I was in a kind of duel with an Australian, and it was going along, going along, and then the bid jumped. But it jumped only slightly above what my ceiling bid was supposed to be. Then the photograph was gone — and not to the Australian bidder, but to a Brit, someone who hadn't been heard from up to that point. Gone. Just like that. I really need this job, and I wondered if you had any advice."

"I can't offer much," I said. "I lost out often, and brought some back. Mrs. Hamelin is the world's greatest expert in showing disappointment. She might actually not *be* disappointed — she knows it's a tough world she's thrown you into, auctions. But that may be separate from how she's *implying* disappointment. Make any sense?"

"You know her much better than I do," Brice said.

Now everyone was sitting in the living room. "Jacob," Mrs. Brevittmore said, "I understand from Martha that you're to give a public lecture."

"Not exactly a lecture," I said. "Every degree candidate in library science is required to present a paper, an essay of some sort. You present it to the faculty and the other students in the program. And whoever else shows up."

"We'll be there," she said. "Won't we?"

"Most certainly," Mrs. Hamelin said.

"Please don't bother," I said.

"Nonsense," Mrs. Hamelin said. "What's your topic?"

"It's very . . . unconventional," Martha said.

"Really?" Mrs. Brevittmore said. "Jacob, we're already proud of you. Unconventional?"

"Maybe what Martha means is, I'm not very good at academic thinking," I said. "There's a whole lot I'm weak on, but I'm not weak on everything, and as I learned from my mother, the library science degree isn't everything. So much happens once you're actually working in a library. All kinds of practical knowledge."

"That has to be true," Mrs. Hamelin said. "But as for my question, what is the subject of your paper, Jacob?"

"Ghosts," I said.

"I see," Mrs. Brevittmore said, sipping her tea.

"More to the point, ghosts in Canadian libraries throughout history," I said.

"Interesting," Brice said.

"Not interesting yet," Mrs. Hamelin said. "Tell us more, Jacob."

"Okay — well, I ran across this personal reminiscence from a librarian from 1901, here in Halifax. She was a very poor woman who slept in the storeroom of the library. That particular library was demolished in 1926, but almost every night when this librarian slept in the storeroom, she was woken by a ghost. And according to her reminiscence, the ghost pretty much performed the same task every night."

"And what was that?" Mrs. Brevittmore said.

"Refile the A-to-C drawer of the card catalogue," I said.

"Only that drawer?" Mrs. Hamelin said.

"According to the reminiscence, yes."

"A mystery to be solved," said Mrs. Brevittmore. "And was it?"

"The librarian came to think that she was looking at herself."

"Herself in the past, or herself in the future?" said Mrs. Hamelin.

"Definitely the past. The library had been built almost eighty years before."

"And your essay is about her?" said Mrs. Brevittmore.

"I did more research, and it turns out there's quite a few reports of ghosts like that. These ghosts supposedly created all sorts of mischief, and some were destructive. So I'm trying to write a kind of brief history of ghosts in Canadian libraries. I might not have the glue yet, listening to myself here."

"Darling, I'm getting very tired," Martha said.

"Martha," said Mrs. Brevittmore, "clearly Jacob is at sixes and sevens with this essay. It's to be a public address. There's much at stake. Would you consider lying down in the guest room — top of the stairs immediately to your right — while we will work through the topic with Jacob? Then we'll wake you, and Brice will drive you both home."

Martha nodded in agreement and walked up the stairs. "Brice," Mrs. Brevittmore said, "be a dear and go fetch a bottle of Scotch, and a bottle of the lemon vodka too, please."

For half an hour Mrs. Brevittmore and Mrs. Hamelin were like interlocutrixes. They really raked me over the coals. They said that I had no real topic except some "generalized attraction to ghost stories," and there was a great possibility I'd fall flat on my face in public. "No doubt it won't affect your getting the degree, Jacob," Mrs. Hamelin said, "but if you can avoid embarrassment, that's best, don't you think?"

For the next few hours they helped me reach an understanding of what my real subject ought to be. Mrs. Brevittmore's advice was, "First, don't wear yourself out climbing a staircase of abstraction" — she may have been quoting some philosopher or poet there — "and try to grasp that your real subject is not whether anyone believes in ghosts, or if ghosts were actually seen in various libraries, as reported. You must instead try and think from the ghost's point of view: After death, why choose to remain in a library? What is the intrinsic and unique spirit of a particular library — or libraries in general — that would make it the perfect place to dwell in the afterlife, should one believe in the afterlife? Your thinking is too low. You need to lift your thinking up."

At nearly three o'clock in the morning, Mrs. Hamelin said, "Look, Jacob, go after something that may be slightly out of reach. Show some savvy. Show some braininess. Show some passionate thought. Anyone can just collate together ghost sightings and anecdotes. Good entertainment, perhaps, but is that useful scholarship?"

"I totally agree," said Martha, who had appeared on the stairs. I don't know how long she'd been listening in. "Let's go home now, Jake."

I worked hard over the following weeks, and when I gave the presentation, on December 1, it went well. Though the faculty and students were dressed in everyday street clothes, Mrs. Brevittmore and Mrs. Hamelin were dressed to the nines. Martha was too. After the mild applause and somewhat bewildered looks on the faces of my faculty, the four of us repaired to Halloran's for dinner, paid for by Mrs. Hamelin. Brice joined us for dessert.

Back at home, Martha said, "We missed *Detective Levy Detects*. But it was worth it. Some lecture you gave, Jacob. Like Esther Hamelin said, it didn't have a whole lot to do with libraries — unusual for a degree candidate in library science — but you gave us a few quite memorable phrases." Nice to fall into bed laughing.

Questioning Robert Emil

Part Two

THE SECOND INTERROGATION OF ROBERT EMIL TOOK PLACE
at 4 p.m. on November 3, 1978. Martha, feeling clumsy and uncomfortable, with an achy back to boot, sat in a chair in the viewing
room; Detective Hodgdon and I stood. Detective Tides was in with
Emil.

Of late, Martha had found the right distinction, and now referred
to Robert Emil as my "biological father," and certainly this was in
deference to the fact that my whole life I'd thought of Bernard Rigolet as my father. "You can't really blame Nora for that," Martha had
said to me one night in bed. "Bernard was the love of her life. Truly
he was. But he was gone so early in the marriage. Every bad part
of her story built from that. Looking through the glass at Robert
Emil, I can easily see it's awful for you, thinking of him with Nora.
Thinking of him as your father. Thinking of what was gouged into
the back of the card catalogue. All of it, all of it, all of it. But Nora's
only human — you have to forgive her. There were maybe, uh, *natu-
ral persuasions* at work. That's sort of from a Thomas Hardy novel,
but you get what I mean."

"Yes, you mean that Nora wanted to screw someone."

"Oh, *that* language, Jacob, is not out of Thomas Hardy. You want our daughter to hear that?"

For his second interrogation, Robert Emil wore a suit and tie and black shoes, recently shined. He was clean-shaven, his hair neatly combed. Clearly he'd attempted respectability. But Detective Tides took this on, first thing. "Ex-officer Emil," he said, "what corpse did you filch that suit off of, someone washed up by Deep Water Terminus or what? And what do I smell? *Perfume?*" Detective Tides leaned close to Emil and loudly inhaled, backed away, and said, "Oh, a dab behind each ear, huh? You smear some behind your knees too? A little rendezvous with a deckhand off the wharf or what? Maybe a French deckhand. Oh, Lord, don't tell me — not *Canadian?* Your perfume opens up so many options. Oh, well, that's not the treachery we brought you in on, is it? That's your *secret* life. What you did in April of 1945 isn't a secret, now, is it? Not any longer. Not with all the new forensics we have."

Tides set a briefcase down on the table. He snapped it open and took out a copy of *Detective Emil Detects*. It was festooned with bookmarks. With dramatic flair Tides squared the book front and center on the table. He sat across from Robert Emil.

"Now, ex-officer Emil," Tides said, "while your vast readership might consider this tome a work of fiction, you should understand that I consider it a confession. There are incidents, there are details of two murders, that were not available to the public. So on the docket today, my friend, is how can an esteemed author such as yourself have known about certain things? I have done my research, and you never requested the files on Max Berall and Mrs. Yablon."

"You ever consider that I have ESP" — Robert Emil pointed at the side of his head — "like that fellow Uri Geller? He's Canadian, you know."

"That charlatan — he's Israeli," Tides said. "His spoons were prebent. You got fooled by that jerk? Jesus, Emil, really? Know what the real test would've been? To take a spoon that's already bent and have Geller bend it back straight."

"Well, he lived in Canada awhile, then."

"You just can't take it he's an Israeli Jew."

"You should check your facts again, Detective. I think Uri Geller's Canadian."

"Maybe Geller personally told you about the murders in 1945."

"Yeah, maybe he did."

Detective Tides was clearly irritated with himself for allowing Emil to sidetrack him, so he opened the book and said, "This, on page one ninety-six, third paragraph: 'Surveying the scene, Detective Emil thought, "Maybe these Jewish people belonging to Baron de Hirsch Synagogue, on Oxford Street, are too cheap to pay their electric bill on time, maybe they think they're above paying a simple electric bill like anyone else has to, and here they are a very wealthy synagogue, rumor had it their Torah scroll was from Prague and cost ten thousand dollars." Anyway, the light at the back entrance was out. And when Detective Emil looked through the window, he saw the lights were out in the hallway too. "Cheap sons of bitches," he thought. "How much can an electric bill be, anyway?"'"

"My oh my, ex-officer Emil, such an eye for detail. Tolstoy's turning in his grave out of sheer envy. Jesus, how'd you craft such a paragraph? To the fifteen people who bought your book, you must be Nobel Prize material."

"By the way," Robert Emil said, "my suit was purchased at Gavelli's on Prince Street. I believe the word is 'haberdashery.' I believe I was fitted by a Hebrew tailor."

"What an act of generosity on your part, then," Tides said. "But let's get back to the lightbulb out in the alley. On page one ninety-six you're writing about the murder of a respectable citizen — that's your own term, 'respectable citizen,' named Max Brill — pretty close to Berall, don't you think? Your hero detective ends up solving this case, and he becomes — I can hardly read this out loud without puking, skipping ahead here to page two hundred fifteen — 'an honorary member of Baron de Hirsch Synagogue.'

"But what's additionally interesting to me in this two-hundred-thirty-six-page self-published confession of yours, ex-officer Emil, is the last paragraph: 'When he'd found the body of Max Brill and gave it a professional once-over before calling it in, he saw the number tattooed on Brill's forearm: 140456. Detective Emil jotted down the number in his notebook, tore out the page, and fitted it behind the driver's license in Brill's wallet. He didn't quite know why he had secreted it away like that. It was some instinct born of years of experience. Something told him to do it.'

"Now, the thing is, me and Detectives Hodgdon and Crauchet, we did considerable research, as I've mentioned. It's all in the file over there on the chair. And guess what we discovered? We discovered from the original investigation file that in his wallet — you left his wallet in Max Berall's pocket, didn't even think to make it look like a robbery — in his wallet was a folded-up piece of paper, and on this piece of paper was written the number 140456. God in heaven, do miracles never cease? But while you have your murder victim, Max *Brill,* a survivor of a concentration camp — of course your book takes place in 1948, not 1945, so sure, maybe a few survivors could have made it to Halifax by that time. But guess fucking what, Emil? Our research shows that Max Berall had a brother, Simon Berall, lives now in the country of Israel. And guess what? Simon Berall *did* survive Auschwitz concentration camp, and guess what number is on his forearm? So that is how Max Berall kept his brother close, see? Back in 1945, when Max didn't know if his brother had survived or not, that's how Max kept him close. He kept that number in his wallet.

"Said information about Mr. Simon Berall was not formerly available even in Max Berall's very detailed police file — forensics, photographs, autopsy included.

"You, you slimebag, are going to prison for writing that piece-of-shit so-called novel full of self-incriminating facts. So thank you for making life interesting for us. I speak here also for Detectives Crauchet and Hodgdon, of course."

My biological father, Robert Emil, could only half whisper, "A novel won't hold up in court. I've made some inquiries. A novel won't hold up at trial."

Detective Tides slammed *Detective Emil Detects* against the head of Robert Emil, who reeled backward to the floor. Tides then turned to the viewing window, held up the book, and said, "Should I get him to autograph this?"

Letter from Bernard Rigolet

THE EVENING FOLLOWING THE SECOND INTERROGATION OF Robert Emil, Martha had no appetite to speak of and went to bed at seven. "I'm fine, Jacob," she said. "It's just from carrying this extra weight — you know that my last checkup was perfect. Nothing to worry about. But I was at my desk at six this morning — you saw the paperwork today, right?"

"I'll whip you up an omelet if you wake up hungry, okay?"

"With what in it? Just in case."

"Goat cheese, mushrooms, just how you like it."

"I love you. I'm going to read a little Margaret Atwood. Want to read something in bed with me?"

"I'm going to reheat some lamb stew and listen to the radio in the kitchen. You relax."

"Arts and Crafts the day after tomorrow — don't forget. Do you want to write it on the wall calendar?"

"Good idea."

She shut the bedroom door halfway and turned on the lamp on her side of the bed. I decided against the radio for a while and took out the box of letters. Nora had kept them in chronological order, and now I picked up the next one. I think I wanted to return to Bernard's letters, at least in part, because I felt somehow I'd betrayed him by paying any attention at all to Robert Emil. I couldn't quite pinpoint my own reasoning here, but it felt like I needed Bernard as a kind of antidote to Emil — something like that. A therapist might've figured that out, but I didn't go to one. I didn't need one; I had Martha to talk with.

April 16, 1945

Dearest beloved Nora,

For two drear cold rainy days now we've been holed up about fifteen kilometers from the city of Leipzig. Rumor is we'll push on to Leipzig soon. We've got this guy with us, Corporal Oppen, and he's quite the historian. He gives us little lectures about the places Allied forces are laying to ruin. Like Dresden and like other places. He's trying to give us some appreciation of the architecture, the museums, and such, all before the Nazis, and he's very knowledgeable and when the boys actually let him get to talking, you can learn a lot. For instance, up ahead of us at Leipzig. There's all sorts of interesting buildings and museums. Also, it's where the Nazis destroyed the city's statue to Felix Mendelssohn, the classical composer you like a lot, Nora. Corporal Oppen made especially sure we knew that the Huns also destroyed the Leipzig Synagogue, a Moorish Revival building that he says was absolutely beautiful. Anyway, that's where we're heading.

Last night Robert Capa had a group of us in stitches. He was regaling us with stories about all sorts of famous people he's met, some of whom I'd heard of and some I hadn't, but either/or, it didn't matter, they were excellent stories. Who he really goes after most hilariously and cuttingly, in my opinion at least, is his great old comrade Ernest Hemingway. Five of us crammed into a tent, and Capa tells us, like he's describing a normal day, that he witnessed the surrender of General von Schlieben, who was the commander of Cherbourg, an important Allied victory, just so you know, Nora. Arrogant son of a bitch, this von Schlieben, is what Capa called him. See what I mean about learning about history in all sorts of ways? Let me see if I can get this right — oh, yes, Capa said that von Schlieben was so arrogant that he didn't allow his picture to be taken by the tedious American press. So Capa says to him, "I'm bored taking picture after picture of defeated German officers," and that's when von Schlieben got very nasty and Capa got a photograph of him in all his anger and all his humiliation and his piss-pants pissed-offedness — oops, there I go again with my army language.

But back to Ernest Hemingway. Capa had so many good stories about Hemingway, but the truth is, Nora, finally I couldn't tell if Robert actually liked Hemingway or mostly just admired him or maybe it was six of one, half dozen of the other. He didn't admire Hemingway's showing off and acting like he was an enlisted man, though Hemingway was not afraid of contact, Capa said. He just liked to lie a little about his exploits, as Capa put it: "He's a brave man at heart with a big imagination, him being such a great writer, a big imagination especially toward himself. But to listen to him it was as if he'd liberated Paris on his own, and then thousands of American troops followed in after. When really he mainly liberated the Ritz Hotel in Paris, is how I like to say it." If I had to pick one Hemingway story to remember, it wasn't about bravery under horrible shellings, or how he was a hero in this or that skirmish, or anything really to do with the front lines at all. The one I most enjoyed was the story about an accident Hemingway got into. I can't remember all the details, but basically what happened was that sometime in May of 1944, Hemingway met up with Capa in London and they had some high old times and had some big parties. And after one of those big parties, Hemingway was riding back to his hotel in a friend's car, and the friend was drunk and there were no lights due to the blackouts, and the car slammed into a water tank and Hemingway was thrown forward into the windshield, as Capa told it to us. Robert showed us the photograph he took of Hemingway, where Hemingway's in a hospital bed with his head all in bandages. Then Capa said, "But you should see the picture I took of him where my paramour Pinky was secretly lifting Hem's hospital gown and his bare ass was sending nurses screaming down the hallway." Please remember, Nora, that's Robert Capa's language, not mine.

Sergeant Binder, who has been fighting for two straight years, says once you've seen what he's seen, you might as well give up on sleep for the rest of your life, not because you won't get tired, but because you'll be afraid to close your eyes for what your dreams will contain. Had I heard that before getting to Germany, I might not've believed him, but now I'm beginning to. I feel very privately romantic toward you, my darling, but just cannot write romantic, not just now. Please understand. Those feelings get shoved aside by all the death here, all the marching, all the world being shelled to kingdom come, except two-three minutes when they come back and I can actually feel your hands, your shoulders, your back pressed to mine, and see you so clearly it's as if you just stepped out of a jeep right here in Leipzig. But God forbid that, Nora, God forbid you should ever see what I'm seeing. And yet I don't know how not to be a hypocrite in a way, because here I'm describing things as clearly as I can, and yet I hope you never see such things!

We haven't got any mail for two months, that's how it is. But I know you've sent letters and I know they are full of familiar things. Once we push past Leipzig, we may get the news that we can go home. That's on everyone's mind. That's what we all are thinking but most of us don't dare talk about it. Maybe shipboard to Halifax I'll get to read your letters. Maybe just before boarding ship, possibly from England, your letters will catch up with me. Mine are inadequate to the task past basic description, but you know how I feel. You know how deeply I love and miss you. They're collecting letters now — off this one goes. I will close my eyes and picture you opening it in our kitchen.

Love,
Your Bernie

Homage to Forest Potsholme

TWO POLICEWOMAN FRIENDS OF MARTHA'S, OFFICER KATRINE Oaks and Officer Edwina Ovid, organized a baby shower, November 11, at our house. It was a potluck, and I stayed long enough to see delicious food arriving on plates and platters and bowls, but was exiled for the evening, as well I should have been. I was so happy for Martha. In our bedroom before the guests arrived, she spun around in her maternity dress and said, "It's like wearing a colorful pup tent. Jacob, be honest, do you even want to take this dress off me later? It's okay if you say you don't. I know you love me."

"I'll leave the house," I said. "Then I'll climb in the bedroom window and take it off you while the policewomen are in the kitchen."

"That's a good enough answer for now," she said. Then the doorbell rang.

The Halifax Free Library was open until 9 p.m., so after stopping for a bowl of goulash at Halloran's, I went to the library, thinking that I would jot down notes for my final essay in library science. This essay meant a lot, because it was supposed to be philosophical. Actually, the assignment brought students back to their original application for the program, in that it asked for a "view of why you want a life in library science." No pun intended, but this final essay was designed to help us bookend our experiences in the program.

Sitting in a carrel in the biography section, I thought about how I'd come to any knowledge of myself via this curriculum, the lectures, the seminars, the discussions, the appointments with Mrs. Margolin, the conversations with Jinx Faltenbourg. My conclusion was that the most rewarding aspect of my studies, my life in library science to date, was in imagining my mother during all those years working in the library. It was as if her professional life had given me a model for my own, simple as that. I had no deeper theories here.

I couldn't know if I would stick with library science. Maybe I would, maybe I wouldn't. It wasn't a field of millionaires, that was for certain. Martha and I had already calculated probable budgets, though we understood that with the arrival of Nora Elizabeth, we would have to revise those calculations. I knew I'd be relying on Martha's practicality in so many things. She had already made arrangements for a small part of her salary to be set aside for a college fund, eighteen years in advance.

Why even get married? Because we could no longer imagine not being married to each other. "That was what we agreed on, and we'll feel stronger and stronger about that as we travel through time together" is how Martha put it. Right after she said that, she said, "Of course, I've been reading John Keats again. So I get such stalwartly romantic thoughts."

Back to the essay. I tried to find a person in history to identify with, some early figure associated with libraries. (History of Libraries was the course I did best in.) That's when I remembered the name Forest Potsholme, who became a cloistered monk in England in the 1600s, and who was quite the philosopher when it came to libraries. I remembered something he wrote that, when I'd come across it in a monograph, made so much sense: "When feeling alone, I think in séances; this gives me back people's lives whom I would otherwise have lost, and I feel less alone. When thinking harshly on the human condition, as I so often do, my antidote is to think gently on libraries, for if human beings are capable of preserving the history of our knowledge in the form of books, then there may still be hope." I adopted this philosophy of Forest Potsholme's as the sponsoring ethic of my essay, and wrote until closing time. In fact, I titled the essay "Homage to Forest Potsholme." Leaping ahead in time here, the essay received the grade of B. Apparently I was fated to be a B student. Martha said, "Not as good as an A, not as bad as a C. Since you have no choice in the matter, really, how else to look at it?"

The night of the baby shower, though, when I left the library I walked the streets for a while. I found myself down at the wharf. When I looked across to Dartmouth, I could see the hospital where Nora was interned. The whole episode of the auction, the years of my mother's suffering in the hospital, suffering no matter how much she tried keeping up her spirits, the disturbing strangeness of seeing Robert Emil's name in her guest book, and I felt a sudden, almost nauseating urgency to get her out of that place. I actually felt physically sick, and I mean I started to violently wretch up my guts, for lack of a better way to say it. It felt like I was turning inside out. I lost every ounce of strength and just lay down in my overcoat on the dock. The lights of the hospital swirled with the lights of the crossing ferries, the streetlamps, and even the moonlight, I don't know. Then I blacked out.

When I woke in a hospital bed, Martha was standing there with Officers Oaks and Ovid. "I think you're taking the fact that you weren't invited to the baby shower a little too personally, darling," Martha said.

Officer Oaks was less ironic. "We could've found you in the harbor, Jacob," she said. "Imagine what it would have been like for Martha to have to tell your daughter that you rolled into the harbor and drowned. You reckless jerk."

Officer Ovid said, "Most interesting baby shower I've ever been to — seeing that we got called out to revive the father. Of course, it's the first baby shower I'd been invited to. So there's that."

Officers Oak and Ovid left the hospital room. Martha sat down in a chair, which she had pulled close to the bed. She held my hands in hers. "You're a mess, Jake."

"I was looking across to the hospital in Dartmouth and that's the last thing I remember," I said. "I don't know what happened."

"Listen, I was going to wait to tell you this until we were in bed, having proved or disproved whether or not you'd want to take off this baggy dress I'm wearing. But I'm going to tell you right now. Nora's getting released from hospital, Jacob. December, January latest. I'm having her released into our custody — except I signed the paperwork, so technically she's being released into my custody. Legally, it's all on the up-and-up. They weren't going to turn down an officer of the law, now, were they? Plus, my name was on the visitors' list in such impressive numbers, right? So now Nora's going to live with us. At least till she can't stand it anymore, and then we'll figure things out from there. Jesus, me and Nora Elizabeth sharing a house with two librarians. How'd *that* happen?"

"I'm not nailing all those photographs of Bernard back up for her sake," I said.

Martha took out a piece of paper, looked at it a moment, and said, "The doctor here said you're suffering slight anemia and exhaustion. You just need some rest. They're pumping you up with something, maybe a few gallons of vitamins or something. He told me but I can't remember. It sounded good."

"I'm nodding off."

"Want me to take off this tent and get in there with you?"

"Sorry, this is a private room. Obviously you didn't notice that."

"Kidding aside, I'm kind of exhausted too. We had dance music on late. Officer Oaks bumped into the turntable and scratched the needle across Della Reese. It was one of my favorite ballads of hers, so I'm going to seek out a new copy. I love you, Jake, but I'm looking forward to just lying in our bed at home now. You try and have sweet dreams. I'll be here first thing in the morning."

Questioning Robert Emil

Part Three

MARTHA BEGGED OFF ATTENDING THE THIRD INTERROGA-
tion of Robert Emil, citing too much paperwork rather than exhaustion and discomfort late in her pregnancy. Tides and Hodgdon
got it right away; her not participating had to be put on the record.
Still, I went to the viewing room on November 17, but they didn't
give me much more than a tip of the hat. It wasn't exactly the place
to get friendly. Well, Tides did say, "Detective Crauchet informed
us her future mother-in-law — remember her, Hodgdon? Librarian
nut job threw the ink at the photograph of the American soldiers,
the heroes in Leipzig, Germany? Detective Crauchet said the future
mother-in-law's moving in with you eventually. Good luck there,
my friend." Both Hodgdon and Tides laughed, and then Tides went
into the interrogation room.

Robert Emil looked to have aged ten years since the previous interrogation. Martha told me he'd lost his job at Deep Water Terminus. He was now living in the Annex for Despairing Christians
— the name a little too melodramatic by my lights — which was attached to the Fort Massey United Church, corner of Queen and To-

bin Streets, which seven nights a week had a public soup kitchen and served breakfast to "the lost and indigent" on weekend mornings. Fort Massey United was Martha's church growing up.

Emil was wearing a rumpled trench coat over a fisherman's sweater and dark trousers, and was sockless under laceless black shoes. Talk about a fall from grace — though from what I'd learned of him, it wasn't a long fall. He was unshaven, his hair was matted, and he had dark pouches under his eyes, possibly from the ravages of insomnia, but who knows? I'm just describing here.

Detective Tides opened a file and took out a photograph, which he set on the table between them, turning it toward Robert Emil. "We think this is victim number three of your treacheries, ex-officer Emil, though this guy didn't die at your hand. True, he almost died at your hand, but he didn't technically die at your hand, and as much as we'd like to charge you for the fatal heart attack he had the day after Max Berall's murder, we can't. But our files tell us this man is all wrapped up in the disgusting piece-of-shit life you led back then, Emil, and so guess who's today's topic?" Tides tapped the photograph with his pointer finger. "Edgar Roth, Jewish radio personality. This picture was taken on March 5, 1945, a publicity shot for his appearance at Baron de Hirsch Synagogue, in the auditorium, separate from the area of worship.

"Now, when this Edgar Roth was in Halifax in April of 1945, he stayed in the home of Max Berall — upstanding Jewish citizen Max Berall. Whom you murdered."

"No proof, no proof, no proof," Robert Emil said.

"You know something, ex-officer Emil?" Tides said. "Me and Detective Hodgdon and Detective Crauchet, whose acquaintances you have already made, among us we have decades of experience. And our experience tells us that when a shitbag like yourself doesn't obtain a legal representative, when they don't weep for a lawyer, sob, cry boo-hoo, it means deep down in their putrescent rotting soul they want to confess to evil deeds, and they have just enough dignity — I don't really want to dignify the word 'dignity' — they have just a smidgen enough dignity to do that on their own, and not have a mouthpiece lawyer to intervene with legal gobble-dygook and bullshit. Somewhere deep down, it is offensive to such a person to be spoken for. Now, I wrote a bunch of letters to Sigmund Freud to ask him why this is, but he never wrote back. So I'm hard-pressed to explain it. One of life's little mysteries, I guess."

"Can I get a coffee?" Robert Emil said. Then he exaggeratedly whined, "Pleeeease?"

Hodgdon said to me in the viewing room, "Go get a black coffee, will you, Jakie? But bring it to me. You don't want to go in there with Tides. He might whack you with a telephone book, you'd spill hot coffee on your new corduroys, eh?"

I admit that as I carried the steaming coffee in a paper cup, I had a sudden urge to deliver it in person. To get a close-up look at my biological father. It seemed that Hodgdon intuited this, for when I returned to the viewing room, he said, "Don't even think of it, Jakie." He took the cup from my hand and held it. Soon Tides came out of the interrogation room and stayed a few moments, as if it was taking a little time for him to get the coffee himself. Then he went back in.

Tides set the cup down in front of Robert Emil and backed up a few steps, maybe cautious that Emil might fling the scalding coffee at him, which I thought possible too. But Emil sipped it and said, "You think you're getting a tip for delivering this coffee, you have your head up your ass."

"Boy oh boy," said Detective Tides, "no manners."

Tides perused a few pages in the file and said, "Emil — the thing is, we found the dartboard in the closet of that fleabag room of yours. Your place of residence before the Home for Degenerate Christians —"

"It's Annex for Despairing Christians," Emil said.

"Oh, sorry," Detective Tides said, a false note of contrition. "Oh, clearly you're a Christian, ex-officer Emil. But are you in despair? And if so, what are you in despair about, exactly? Might it be that your conscience is so guilty, and if it's tearing you all to pieces like that, your guilty conscience, how bad is it, really? What's it like? Is it like you raped a woman in the alley and found out it was your mother? What's it like, Emil?"

This set Robert Emil off, and he drank the whole cup of coffee in two or three great gulps, then clutched his throat and screamed, "Waterrrrrrrr!"

Detective Tides hustled from the interrogation room, poured a small cup of water from the dispenser near his work desk, and hurried back. He handed the cup to Emil, who stood and threw it back like a shot of whiskey. He was flushed and breathing hard. "'Contrition takes many forms,' said my priest once," Detective Tides said. "I don't think he was talking about scalding-hot coffee, though."

Robert Emil sat down, looking a little ill. He managed to say, "My mother was a good person."

"And I'm sure she would be very proud of you, Emil. I've never been so sure of anything. Very proud of her son's accomplishments in life."

Emil hunched down to the table, laid his head on his folded arms, and said, "Don't bring up my mother again or else I'll kill you."

Detective Tides said, "Being in my position is a real burden sometimes. Like the burden of Job. But as for your mother, yeah, okay — even Job was commanded by God not to lie with a fetching maid."

Robert Emil flung himself across the table, but Tides easily dodged him. They grabbed each other. With some sort of judo move, Tides swept Emil's feet out from under him, and Emil slammed to the floor. "Get up, motherfucker," Tides said, feigning toward Emil, who stood and went back to his chair.

"You have attempted to assault an officer of the law," Tides said. "Mom is beaming with pride, whichever place she's in. Anyway, I really can't tell if we're making progress toward your confession or not, ex-officer Emil. What do you think?"

In the viewing room, Detective Hodgdon said, "A real artist at work. He's very close now. You just watch, Jakie. Old Tides there, he's the master. I can't touch him. Once he gets the scent, I can't even get close. You just watch."

Detective Tides stretched back in his chair, sighed a few times, and said, "Jeez, Emil, my nighttime reading lately? A thousand pages at least, factoring in your stupid file and so-called fictional tome, *Detective Emil Detects*. Allow me to suggest your next title: *Detective Repents During a Life Sentence*. What do you think? But I actually don't give a shit what you think about literature. So here's what. About that dartboard we found in your fleabag closet, Emil. It had on it the same publicity shot of Edgar Roth here" — he again tapped the photograph on the table — "and his face was all punctured with dart holes. Now, that wasn't so nice of you, was it? And then we read in your file that you were spotted approaching the Baron de Hirsch Synagogue the evening of Edgar Roth's final Halifax radio broadcast — what was his title that night again? Let me look it up." Detective Tides found the right page in the file. "Oh, yes: 'How the Jews Have Been Good for Canada.' Very solid title, you ask me. And then here's what happened, Emil. What happened is, you were heading right into the synagogue — what were you going to do? That's when Officer Michael Palmer, five years on the job, intercepted you, as he was security that night, and asked you what was going on, and you must've panicked, because according to Officer Palmer, you got pale and said, 'Oh, nothing, just interested in all sorts of religious thought is all,' which didn't square, Palmer said, with what he'd heard about you."

"I was just going there to see a radio celebrity, Hebrew or not, just wanted to see what all the fuss was about," Robert Emil said.

"Sure, sure," Detective Tides said. "I understand."

He sat motionless, giving Emil a baleful look for a good two or three minutes. Emil didn't know what to do with this. He looked fidgety. Then Tides took from his file a few pieces of paper stapled together. When he did that, Detective Hodgdon, in the viewing room, handed me papers stapled together too. "You can read along if you like," he said. "After all, it's your Martha's handiwork."

"Now, ex-officer Emil," Tides said in a measured voice. "After many hard hours of research, our Detective Crauchet has provided us with a timeline as it applies to one Robert Emil. Say, whattaya know, that's *you*. Let's see here. Oh yes, it covers approximately eleven hours' time on April 18, 1945. You sure packed a lot into those eleven hours, didn't you? You were one busy bee, weren't you? Why don't you relax and let me read this to you — just relax and enjoy. Probably no one's paid this much attention to you in a long time."

Detective Tides took a sip of water and read:

3:15 p.m., April 18, 1945, Halifax, Nova Scotia. Officer O'Rourke and Officer Mezey serve notice to Robert Emil that he is to come to police headquarters to answer preliminary questions about the murder of Max Berall. Robert Emil claimed, at the crime scene, to have found Max Berall already deceased from gunshot wounds to the back and head. Robert Emil had called in the scene at approximately 1:15 a.m. on April 18.

However, officers did not find Robert Emil at home, which was 23 Bishop Street, apt. 5. Notice was slid under Emil's door. Officer O'Rourke and Officer Mezey then took up their search for Robert Emil in the city of Halifax.

4:30 p.m., April 18, 1945. Officer O'Rourke and Officer Mezey receive information that a Mrs. Byron Phase, next-door neighbor of a Mrs. Estelle Yablon (203 Green Street, Halifax), found Mrs. Yablon deceased in her kitchen. Ambulance and officers dispatched to scene. It is determined that Mrs. Yablon was shot at close range. Note: this is the same Mrs. Yablon who provided the police sketch artist with a likeness of Robert Emil. Mrs. Yablon had been working in the office of Baron de Hirsch Synagogue and claimed she saw Officer Robert Emil "plain as day" in an alley alongside the synagogue. Said Officer Emil was approaching Max Berall from behind. "Max was still very much alive." Mrs. Yablon taken to morgue.

5:50 p.m., April 18, 1945. At this point APB is sent to all officers for apprehension of Emil "for questioning only." At approx. 6:15 p.m., possible sighting of Emil leaving Oliver's Pub on Lower Water Street. Officers dispatched to Oliver's Pub. Bartenders and customers questioned by Officer O'Rourke and Officer Mezey. Sketch artist facsimile of Emil left at pub.

Approx. 7:35 p.m., April 18, 1945. Robert Emil identified by name as man participating in "loud skirmish" at Halifax Free Library. Call made by librarian Constance Lily. Lily questioned by radio dispatcher informs that Robert Emil has "gotten rough with Nora" — this refers to a junior librarian, Mrs. Nora Rigolet, wife of American military pfc Bernard Rigolet, presently in Germany. Officers dispatched to Halifax Free Library.

Approx. 7:50 p.m., April 18, 1945. Officers question Nora Rigolet at Halifax Free Library. Noted: bruises on wrist, nose possibly broken. Ambulance dispatched to scene. Noted: Mrs. Nora Rigolet is in ninth month of pregnancy. Medical personnel arrive. Officers O'Rourke and Mezey witness examination. Mrs. Nora Rigolet refuses to be taken to hospital. "I'm all right now. But Robert Emil said he was going to kill me." Officer Mezey stays at scene. Mrs. Nora Rigolet lies down on chaise in private office of chief librarian, insists that library stay open until its usual closing time, 9:00 p.m. Chief librarian informs Officer Mezey that Mrs. Nora Rigolet's personal physician is en route.

Approx. 8:50 p.m., April 18, 1945. Officer Mezey calls in, informs dispatcher that he is experiencing "acute pain in right side." He is driving to hospital. (Appendicitis attack is determined as cause. Officer has appendix removed that same night.)

When asked if Mrs. Nora Rigolet is secured, reply from Officer Mezey: "No. Send someone to replace me." Dispatcher offers to send another officer to drive Officer Mezey to hospital. Mezey refuses. Approx. 9:40 p.m. Officer Mezey reports from hospital; goes in for removal of appendix. Approx. 10:30 p.m. Officer Katherine Sorensen arrives Halifax Free Library. Finds Mrs. Nora Rigolet in stressful labor in office of chief librarian. Officer Sorensen calls for ambulance. Dispatcher hears shouting in background, shot fired. Officer Sorensen informs that Robert Emil attempted to enter library waving "police revolver." Officer Sorensen informs that she believes Emil was hit in leg but uncertain. Librarian Constance Lily locks front door of library, runs to back entrance, locks door there. Approx. 11:40 p.m., April 18, 1945. Officer Katherine Sorensen reports to dispatch that she has begun to assist in emergency birth. Ambulance personnel arrive. Male child is born to Mrs. Nora Rigolet at 11:43 p.m.

Approx. 11:50 p.m. Robert Emil seen in car, corner Sackville and Brunswick. Officers engage with megaphone. Emil responds by taking flight. Approx. 12:05 a.m., April 19, 1945. Robert Emil apprehended at ferry crossing, Upper Water Street. Approx. 1:15 a.m., April 19, 1945. Robert Emil questioned at police building by Detective Maurice Chalmer and Detective Sergeant Benjamin Humphries. During which Robert Emil exhibits heavy intoxication from liquor. Emil somewhat incoherent. Claims being distraught over relationship with Mrs. Nora Rigolet. Claims "gang of Jews have been in pursuit of him." Claims "every police officer is in danger from Jews in Halifax." Questioning ends approx. 2:35 a.m., April 19, 1945. Robert Emil incarcerated in police lockup.

"Your mother would be so proud," Detective Tides said, looking up from the timeline. "Running around the city like a rabid dog or something, maybe they should've tested you for rabies, huh? I don't see they tested you for rabies in the report. And I've read every page."

Robert Emil said, "Is my son hearing all this?"

When I telephoned Martha and told her what had happened during the interrogation, she sighed deeply and said, "There's enough now to lock him up. They'll lock him up."

Ours Is Not a Lending Library

THE CASE OF ROBERT EMIL WAS ON THE FRONT PAGE OF the *Chronicle-Herald* on November 19 — "1945 Murder Case Resurrected" — one column, lower right, continued on page 4. My mother's photograph from 1945 was included on page 4, fitted next to Emil's latest mug shot. Martha thought it best that I bring the article to my mother's attention before some attendant did. So on that cold, rainy day, Martha and I took the ferry over to Dartmouth and a short taxi ride to the hospital. We found Nora sitting alone at a corner table at Arts and Crafts, in the common room. We knew right away she'd found out about the article. When we sat down at her table, we saw that she had cut out the photographs of herself and Robert Emil and was gluing them onto some sort of collage. It was Martha who noticed that a photocopy of *Death on a Leipzig Balcony* was also part of the collage. "This is not good," Martha whispered to me. "It may be she's experiencing a relapse." My mother then crumpled up the collage, which had been about the size of a page of the *Chronicle-Herald*.

"My, my, look at you," my mother said, touching Martha's belly.

"You know, I'm really fine, Martha, dear. That collage was just a little ... well, let's call it a little fall from grace, shall we? No, let's not call it anything. I've scrunched it all up and now it's gone. Did you know that Jinx Faltenbourg was here, and she has offered me five hours a week. One hour per day at the registration desk, that is. The board has to approve, but Jinx is persuasive, you see. I could not be more pleased."

"Your room is ready and waiting for you, Nora," Martha said. "You know that when you leave the hospital, we have to bring you in for a monthly evaluation, right?"

"From now on, it's all about attitude and spirit," Nora said.

We stayed for about an hour and then met with one of Nora's psychiatrists, Dr. Kathe Radnoti.

"Medically — that is, psychotherapeutically — Nora has my complete confidence," Dr. Radnoti said. "When I took over her case, I want you to know that I reviewed it thoroughly. I studied it left to right, right to left. I've given a lot of thought to the precipitating episode — the attack on the photograph. Nora and I have discussed it at length. Perhaps she mentioned this."

"Not to us," Martha said.

"I can summarize my report. Basically, I feel that on March 19, 1977, at the Lord Nelson Hotel, Nora suffered — and I won't use clinical language here — a terrible episode. Notice of the auction of that particular photograph, where her husband can be faintly seen — but still he is seen, still he is recognizable — in *Death on a Leipzig Balcony.* My goodness, how could she not be filled with turbulent emotion toward it? This is all in my full report. Suffice it to say that radically disparate elements, individual and aggregate insistences, suddenly, at the Lord Nelson Hotel, overwhelmed Nora Rigolet. For months I have been presenting one thing and one thing only to my colleagues here — that a single episode, no matter its intensity, does not by definition portend relapse or relapses. In fact, every exhibit of Nora's person, since her initial episode a the Halifax

Free Library—poise, awareness, her insatiable appetite for books, the depth of comprehension of her present confinement—all and everything indicates a return to sanity. It remains my opinion that Nora has been done a great injustice. That immediately following the precipitating episode or incident at the Halifax Free Library, that perhaps six months of outpatient therapy, along with a leave of absence from work, would have been the appropriate course. I even suggest that, had such a course been taken, it may well have alleviated the preoccupation with the photograph leading to the dramatic incident at the auction. While I cannot say it was all shackles and leg irons, and I do feel there are some very fine qualities of care here at NSRH, along with vast amounts of room for improvement. Still and all, Nora's long inpatient stay was, to my mind, completely lacking in sound analytical procedure."

"When can she go home?" I said.

"There are more meetings, I'm afraid," Dr. Radnoti said. "Hospitals are bureaucracies, you see. But I am her advocate. I will push for the earliest date possible."

"We just want to get her home," Martha said.

"You already have the name of the therapist she's to see once a month, Dr. K. V. Mori, and she is excellent."

"Yes, I did my research, and she sounds great," Martha said.

"Did Nora mention *Jude the Obscure* today?" Dr. Radnoti asked.

"Novel by Thomas Hardy?" Martha said.

"Yes, that's the one," Dr. Radnoti said. "Nora's reading it—for the third time, she tells me. And I may be violating her confidence telling you this, but Nora has said emphatically that she hopes she doesn't leave Nova Scotia Rest Hospital until she completes it. 'Ours is not a lending library here, in case you haven't noticed,' she said to me. I tell you this because Nora's maintained her sense of irony. When there's no irony, a person's life goes a little gray. There's a flatness to the affect. Nora is far from that—'Ours is not a lending library.'"

I Couldn't Bear It If Something Terrible Should Befall Leah Diamond

AFTER STEPPING OFF THE RETURN FERRY, MARTHA SUG-gested that we get some takeout Italian food and have dinner at home. Serving it up at our kitchen table, Martha said, "Leah Diamond—did I tell you? Leah has a stalker. Creep named Dundee Alcove. You'll hear about it in tonight's episode, I'm sure. Does this guy have the slightest notion what's in store for him? Detective Levy's been alerted to it, also the whole cohort at the hotel. They are all out looking for Dundee Alcove. He's dead in the water, is my guess. I couldn't bear it if something terrible should befall Leah Diamond."

"Of course you couldn't."

"They'll have to do him in, Dundee Alcove."

"Maybe," I said. "But sometimes an episode doesn't end in murder. It ends sort of implying—you know, in the language, it's more *implied*."

Martha said, "'All their shadows carrying revolvers followed his shadow into the alley,' or 'Since we're in this love clutch, baby, it means that pistol is as close to my heart as it is to yours,' or 'Layla

House wept all the way to identify her husband at the morgue. Out of happiness.'"

"How do you remember all of that?" I asked.

We had eaten lightly, even for Italian, and when I was clearing the dishes, Martha said, "Maybe it was some spice, or maybe it's something happening to my body, or maybe it's something else — I don't know what — but Jake, you need to take me to bed. I need to go to our bed with you immediately. Leave the dishes."

This sort of imperative never required further explanation, only, to quote Martha's favorite author, Thomas Hardy, "obedience to the insistences of love." The first time I ever heard that phrase was in fact when Martha was reading a Hardy novel in bed, I forget which one, and she stopped reading, looked at me, and said, "Listen to this: *obedience to the insistences of love*." But she didn't want a response; more that she wanted me to hear the phrase. She really just wanted to get back to her book.

Let me put it this way: leaving the dishes was the least difficult thing I have ever done in my life. What Martha called the acrobatics of making love when she was so pregnant were tender and funny: "Let's get inventive with the pillows." Finally, when I lay pressed against her back and we were bathed in sweat, both of us desperately needing to sleep, Martha said, "Well, that problem got solved nicely."

Martha rallied awake for *Detective Levy Detects,* but it required a cup of coffee for me to get through the complete episode, which was titled "The Laughable Demise of Dundee Alcove." What happened was, this Dundee had an old beef with Leah Diamond, but at the same time was crazy in love with her. Now Dundee was threatening Leah's life. Leah had been completely honest with Detective Levy about the fact that there had never been anything romantic in her past with Dundee Alcove. "If you see his Quasimodo mug, you'll understand," she said as they were having coffee in a luncheonette somewhere in Toronto. During that same conversation, Leah uttered one of Martha's favorite lines: "I may eat a lot at breakfast, lunch, and dinner, honey, but deep down in my soul I'm really living on coffee." Given the combined brainstorming of all the gangsters and gun molls, add to that the deeply worried and protective instincts of Detective Levy, and add to *that* Leah Diamond's always being on high alert, not just for her own life but for that of their daughter, Dundee Alcove didn't have a snowball's chance in hell. And here, what was clearly a murder got detoured through radio language into euphemism: "Now, ladies and gentlemen," the narrator said, "at this point all you need to know is Detective Frederik Levy left the men's room of the Blue Sundays lounge, on Queen Street, with one less bullet than he arrived with, the loud construction-worker crowd at the bar acting as a silencer, and the world a better place absent one Mr. Dundee Alcove."

"Jeez," said Martha, turning off the radio, "I guess Dundee Alcove met a bad end. That was Detective Levy in a kind of jealous revenge killing. I didn't expect that."

"Seeing as he's been such a nice guy all along."

"Compared to the coterie of thugs wearing fedoras, sure."

"Are you happy Leah's out of danger now?" I asked.

"Danger is her middle name, though."

The telephone woke us at about 3 a.m. The phone was on Martha's side of the bed, so I got up and walked around the bed to pick it up. When I did, Detective Hodgdon didn't even wait to hear a hello before saying, "Shit has hit the fan — good morning, Detective Crauchet." I said, "It's Jake. Should I wake Martha?" "Well, Robert Emil's flown the coop. Some bureaucratic mix-up and an . . . *inexperienced* fellow at the station let Emil out. Dunderhead. That kind of thing happens now and then, but what's unusual — and listen carefully here, Jake — is that Emil has made threats of violence against all three of his interrogators, which means myself, Detective Tides, and of course it means Martha too. Do you understand what I'm telling you?"

"Yes, I definitely understand."

"Now, on the basis of Emil's written threat, we're out looking for him. Out looking for him *again,* I should say. In the meantime, we're sending an officer to your house. He'll stay parked out front with two-three thermoses of coffee."

"All right," I said. "How serious should we take this threat, do you think?"

"Emil's a nutcase. A nutcase with a knowledge of firearms."

Martha had woken and listened in. She deduced certain things from my side of the conversation. "Have they sent an unmarked car yet?" she asked. I looked out the bedroom window just as an unmarked police car pulled up to the curb. Then I detailed the phone conversation to Martha.

Deeply Communing with the So-Far Invisible World

NEXT MORNING, ABOUT 7:30, A KNOCK ON THE DOOR. IT WAS Officer Drew Sorensen, who, as it turned out, was the nephew of Officer Katherine Sorensen, who had shot and wounded Robert Emil in the Halifax Free Library on April 18, 1945. "Hello, sorry to bother you so early in the morning, but I need to use your bathroom," he said. I let him into the house, and by the time he had emerged from the bathroom, Martha, dressed in her outsize pajamas and robe, was putting on coffee. When I walked into the kitchen, she said, "I recognize Officer Sorensen, of course. But why is he in our house first thing in the morning like this?"

"Apparently, your people assigned him to look after us, Martha."

"Well, all right. This is our life just now. They'll find Robert Emil and then our life will return to normal. But Officer Sorensen — and I assume they'll send someone else to relieve him — he should stay inside the house. Sitting out in a car like that is a nightmare."

I carried a tray of coffee and coffee cake out and set it on the dining room table. "Sit down with us," Martha said to Sorensen.

"Thank you," he said. "Car's not all that good for the sacroiliac."

He bent backward and groaned, then sat down. "This looks great, thank you."

"You're Katherine's nephew, if I remember right," Martha said.

"That's correct, Detective Crauchet," Sorensen said. He was about thirty, tall, with a slight stubble of beard, a head of luxurious black hair kept at regulation length, and deep blue eyes. A very handsome young man with a slightly nervous bearing. "Actually, I'm hoping to make detective someday."

"I know about your aunt Katherine's heroic conduct back in April of 1945," Martha said. "I read about it in our present cold-case file."

Sipping his coffee, taking a forkful of the coffee cake, Sorensen said, "I can't walk or drive past the Halifax Free Library without thinking about my aunt Kathy, even though the incident occurred before I was born."

"She was tried and true that night," Martha said. "How is Katherine, anyway?"

"Fine. She lives near Peggy's Cove. She got remarried — my uncle Peter died five years ago. She married a boat mechanic, Tobin Pierpoint. Semiretired. Tobin, I mean. Aunt Katherine stays active in civic duties."

"Did they tell you much about why you're out at our house?" Martha asked. She was being the interlocutrix a little, and I could tell it was because she was anxious. She recognized her own tone and said, "It's just that" — she tapped her belly — "I'm thinking for two, you see."

"I certainly can see," Sorensen said. "Well, yes, I got the details, Detective Crauchet, and I know that's why you brought up my aunt's heroics, because all these years later, it's the same Robert Emil. I don't expect I'll have to discharge my weapon like she did at Emil, though. I'm confident we'll track him down long before he can carry out his threats."

"The Beelzebub Robert Emil raging through the streets again," Martha said.

"Seems like half the police force is out looking for him," Sorensen said.

"Were you shown his threats?" Martha said. "I mean, the physical evidence."

"Yes, ma'am," Sorensen said. "I did indeed read the piece of paper they were written on. He outright threatened to kill you, Detective Tides, and Detective Hodgdon. I hope you don't mind my putting it so bluntly. But it's true."

Martha poured Sorensen a second cup of coffee, smiling slightly. I could see Sorensen was worried he'd upset her. "I understand the policy is that you get three whole months maternity leave," he said. "My own wife, Patricia, she's not quite as far along as you, Detective, but when our baby arrives, I'm putting in for a week's leave myself, pay or no pay. But anyway, Detective, you'll be back on the job in no time. You have the most solid reputation I've ever heard of. And you know how people talk."

I could see Martha was surprised and pleased. "You keep sucking up like this, Officer Sorensen, I may have to write you a letter of recommendation when it's time for you to come up for detective."

"You know, my aunt Katherine, what happened with her and Robert Emil became kind of a family story. But I'm going to talk out of school here, because what everyone outside of our family doesn't know. When she discharged her weapon that night? It knocked my aunt off the rails. And she never got back on. Not really. That's why she asked for a transfer to a desk job. She figured if she got the desk job, she'd be able to sleep again."

"Did that work out for her?" I asked.

"As it turned out, yes," Sorensen said. "She could sleep again, and according to her, the rest of her tenure, which was twelve years, she was bored to tears."

"Can't win for losing," Martha said. She looked at me and said, "I'm going back to bed, Jake. I've got to call in sick to the office. No,

I won't say 'sick,' I'll say 'deeply communing with the so-far invisible world.'"

"Oh, can I listen in?" Sorensen said.

"I was just alluding to —" and Martha again patted her belly.

"No, no, I understood right away, Detective Crauchet," Sorensen said. "Your child. The invisible world. 'Communing with the so-far invisible world' — that was more poetry than I learned in high school."

"All right, then," Martha said. She walked to the telephone and dialed her office. "Yes, this is Detective Martha Crauchet calling on behalf of myself. I won't be in to work today." There was a pause. "Reason? I'm deeply communing with the so-far invisible world." Another pause, Martha listening. She then set the receiver down on the cradle. "That was the dispatcher, Anne Anderson. She said, 'Oh, I get it. I've been pregnant twice myself.'"

"Make yourself at home, Sorensen," Martha said, and went back to bed. But Sorensen looked stymied at where to sit, what to do, and finally said, "I think I'm just going back to my car for the rest of my shift." He went out the door.

Detective Hodgdon and Detective Tides showed up at about noon. When they entered the house, Tides said, "Sorensen's relief, that's Officer George Batch, he's out front now in the unmarked. He's got scones and coffee and wouldn't share, plus a few sandwiches."

Hodgdon looked at my work desk and said, "I guess Detective Crauchet's never going to have to fret about overdue book fines, eh? It's like I always say, everybody's putting in the fix on everything all the time. Just the way of the world. Just the way of the world."

"So, according to your logic," Detective Tides said, "Jakie, here, is going through this skyscraper of paperwork, racking his brains all these semesters at Dalhousie, inhaling book lice in the stacks, and leaving duplicates, triplicates, quadruplicates-times-a-thousand of his fingerprints on those typewriter keys, typing up his essays for months on end, just so Detective Crauchet can cheat the library system out of overdue fines?"

"Some people will do anything to save a few dollars," Hodgdon said.

"Where is Detective Crauchet, anyway?" Tides said to me. "By the way, I dropped a hint a moment or two ago about it being lunch hour. Or did you miss that, Jakie?"

"Martha says I'm good with omelets," I said.

"Eggs are breakfast food, but since we missed breakfast trying to chase down Robert Emil on the dank and dirty streets of our fair city, I'd be willing to call lunch breakfast, if you are, Detective Hodgdon."

"Let's try Jakie's omelets first, then see what we call it," Hodgdon said.

I set out making omelets with garlic, goat cheese, and mushrooms. I said, "These are going to be three-egg omelets."

"Why, Detective Tides," Hodgdon said, "I do believe that our host wants us to faint from hunger by midafternoon."

"I've only got six eggs," I said.

"Any potatoes?" Tides said.

"I'll fry some up," I said. "I didn't think of that."

Soon Martha came out of the bedroom, still dressed in her pajamas and robe. Taking in her appearance, Tides said, "Martha, the Miss Nova Scotia contest starts in twenty minutes. You don't even have your face on. What's going on here?"

"You two bazookas," Martha said, obviously delighted to see them. "Know how each contestant in Miss Nova Scotia has to have a special talent? Know what mine is?"

"Buttering toast for a candidate in library science," Tides said.

"Wrong," Martha said as I set the plates full of fried potatoes and omelets on the dining room table. Tides and Hodgdon sat down and started right in eating. I poured Martha a cup of coffee and handed it to her. "My special talent is recognizing how history repeats itself."

"Therefore my Miss Nova Scotia money's on the gal who wears a swimsuit that's more or less her birthday suit," Tides said, "sashays across the stage singing 'O Canada,' and the male judges have to cover their privates, because the stanza gets them so excited. *With glowing hearts we see thee rise / The True North strong and free!*"

"Your sense of humor goes unappreciated, Tides, as my daughter is listening," Martha said. "No, my special talent is recognizing how history repeats itself, at least in Halifax. Robert Emil has come back after thirty-some years, right? In 1945 he goes after Nora Rigolet at the Halifax Free Library. You both studied the files. Now he's making threats to upstanding citizens again. I'm a serious student of this, and I'm taking it very seriously, Detectives. And I don't mind telling you I'm frightened out of my wits. That's no bullshit, either."

Martha set her coffee cup on the table looking quite shaken. Tides got serious himself now. "Martha — Detective Crauchet. Look, all three of his intended victims are sitting here right now," he said. "You know us. You know why we're here. We're here because we know — or at least think we know — what this lowlife shitbag Robert Emil is capable of. You're all worked up not just because of having a child on the way, but because you've seen psychopaths at their trade, which is acting psychopathically, not to use too technical a term."

"I know," Martha said, and she looked like she was holding back tears. "I'm sorry. I am a little worked up, I suppose. But you guys are the best. Thanks for dropping by."

Detective Hodgdon pushed back from the table, stood up, and said, "Omelet first-rate, but needed salt. Potatoes first-rate. Coffee second-rate, but at least hot. Thank you."

"Ditto for me, except I rate the coffee lower," Tides said.

"Back to going after the bad guy," Hodgdon said. "Next stop is someone called in a possible sighting. So we're heading to the repairing slips, Chebucto Marine docks, over to Dartmouth."

"Really, we just wanted to check in on you, Martha," Tides said.

The detectives left the house. But in just a moment's time, Hodgdon opened the door again and said, "Martha, in case I don't see you again. That isn't going to happen, but just in case. I wanted you to know that in high school I had a girlfriend, Marcia Wherity. The only way she'd let me kiss her was if we lay down on a flat gravestone in Camp Hill Cemetery. It only lasted one summer between us. One time, I came home and my mother screamed, 'What happened to you?' I'd just stripped off my T-shirt and apparently had a whole epitaph — name and years and biblical quote — pressed into my back. You'd think, all the years we worked together, I would've told you this personal story. I'm sorry. I guess I was saving it."

Then he shut the door behind him.

Intuitive Prophecy

ROBERT EMIL REMAINED ELUSIVE. OVER THE NEXT SEVERAL weeks, neither Martha nor I grew accustomed to our lives at home under surveillance, or to Martha's police escort on her way to and from work every day.

Martha had decided to take the week before Christmas off, which would officially count as a week of her maternity leave in advance, and this caused no problem with her superiors. She'd brought home a radio that had the police frequency, so while making coffee, or after returning from my last exam, the grocery, or the pharmacy, or while rubbing Martha's feet or massaging her lower back as she read Thomas Hardy, Margaret Atwood, or Robertson Davies, I would hear through the static, "Detective Hodgdon and Detective Tides . . . proceed to West India Wharf. OTL [on the lam] Robert Emil attempting to cash check. Proceed with caution. Suspect considered armed and dangerous," or variations on that, as Emil was seen, or supposedly seen, in and around Halifax. We knew that Officers Sorensen and Batch, on their alternating shifts, were listening to the same frequency in an unmarked car out front of our house.

Then, at about eight o'clock on the evening of December 23, Martha and I were sitting with Mrs. Brevittmore and Mrs. Hamelin at our dining room table. They had come by earlier and cooked a pot roast, potatoes, and carrots, and brought a stack of records from the 1940s to play. They had brought such records before, and we all had a good time listening to them, talking, and watching as Mrs. Brevittmore and Mrs. Hamelin doted on Martha.

"Fuss all you want," Martha said. "It's nice for me. Besides, you've been the best friends I could ever have imagined. Jacob dropped your trust by doing something a bit on the shady side, and you had to fire him. Yet all along I thought that Jacob had other —"

"Potentials," Mrs. Hamelin cut in. "I could not agree more."

"Life has a way of working out," Mrs. Brevittmore said.

"Wowee, what wild breeze blew up your skirts just now?" Mrs. Hamelin said with a note of incredulousness. "Why, Evelyn Brevittmore, I do believe you just allowed yourself to say the nicest possible thing."

While I cleared the dishes, Mrs. Brevittmore, Mrs. Hamelin, and Martha repaired to the living room sofa and chairs. Sitting down with a groan, Martha said, "I appear to be large with child," which made everyone laugh. Mrs. Hamelin had put on an album by the Andrews Sisters.

"Jake, would you get me a glass of ice water?" Martha said. In the kitchen, the radio was tuned to the police frequency. I heard a burst of static, followed by "— ambulance dispatched to Marine Fisheries Department, Upper Water Street wharf — Detective Philip Hodgdon down — called in dispatch from, repeat, Marine Fisheries Department, Upper Water Street — all officers respond — ambulance immediately to Marine Fisheries Department —" Then static. I went in and lifted the needle off the record. Everyone looked up. "Martha," I said.

I brought in the radio and set it on the living room table between the sofa and chairs. Static, then: "All officers be on the alert for OTL Robert Emil — vicinity of Marine Fisheries Department — repeat, Marine Fisheries Department, Upper Water Street — Robert Emil attempted break-in of payroll, Marine Fisheries — ambulance dispatched — Detective Philip Hodgdon down — repeat, Detective Philip Hodgdon took three bullets —" More static.

"Jacob, please get Officer Sorensen to take me to the hospital now."

"I should go with you," I said.

"No," Martha said, and I understood right away that she needed to separate professional from family. "No."

At that moment, without knocking, in walked Officer Sorensen, who said, "Detective Hodgdon is en route to Victoria General. Detective Crauchet, if you're going, as I expect you'll want to, you have to drive with me. That's orders, ma'am."

Martha put on her coat and scarf and followed Sorensen to his car, and off they went. Mrs. Brevittmore and Mrs. Hamelin stayed in the house with me. We listened to the police frequency. I brought out some whiskey. We each had a small shot. Mainly we just sat there. "I've never liked the phrase 'things could be worse,'" Mrs. Brevittmore said. "It's never been particularly solacing to me. Martha looked so distraught."

Martha called from Victoria General to say that Detective Hodgdon was pronounced dead at approximately 9:15. Martha returned home with Officer Sorensen at about 10:30. Her face was streaked with tears, but she seemed quite calm, considering. "We're staying the night," Mrs. Hamelin said.

"That would be fine," Martha said.

Hodgdon had accompanied another officer, Michael Heller, to Marine Fisheries in response to a report of an alarm going off there and a night watchman's description of the burglar, which Hodgdon thought might be Robert Emil. As they approached the Marine

Fisheries office, Emil opened fire, striking Officer Heller once in the shoulder and Detective Hodgdon twice in the stomach and once in the neck. Officer Heller returned fire, but Emil ran from the scene. Several thousand dollars had been taken from a locked drawer. In the hospital, Officer Heller, about to go into surgery, had told Martha and Detective Tides, "Hodgdon was bleeding out, and he told me some things to say to his wife. He said — you know, kind of delirious, I guess, 'Don't forget to pick up English muffins,' then he was out."

The four of us sat in the living room. Martha was sobbing hard, and there was little I could do except hold her. Through her tears she said, "Intuitive prophecy."

Mrs. Brevittmore caught on right away and said, "*Far from the Madding Crowd,* is that it, Martha?"

"Yes," Martha said. "That's what Hodgdon had. You remember, Jake, when he popped back into the house and said, 'In case I don't see you again'? That was intuitive prophecy, all right. He had it. That's the exact moment Philip had it. He knew. Somehow he knew."

Silent Night

WE HAD A VERY QUIET CHRISTMAS EVE. IT WAS JUST ME AND Martha at dinner with Mrs. Hamelin and Mrs. Brevittmore. They had a big Christmas tree with lots of gifts under it; they were going to have friends over on Christmas Day. After dinner, we gave Mrs. Hamelin a rare book of photographs by the French painter René Magritte, which I had found at John W. Doull. We gave Mrs. Brevittmore a signed copy of *Murder on the Orient Express*, by Agatha Christie, ordered from London by Morty Shaloom. They both seemed pleased. Of course, considering Detective Hodgdon's death, it was difficult to feel festive. But Mrs. Brevittmore's eggnog helped a little (Martha had a sip), as did all of us going to the special midnight preview showing of *All That Jazz*, at City Center, which was directed by Bob Fosse. Officer Sorensen sat directly behind us. After the credits rolled, Mrs. Brevittmore pronounced about the movie, "Wonderful choreography, and a great character study of obsession and passion."

"Drugs and booze too," said Mrs. Hamelin. "Melodramatic sacrifices of art and all of that."

Anyway, each in our own way and for our own reasons, we all liked the movie very much. On the sidewalk, bundled up in coats, scarves, and gloves, we said our goodbyes. Ever honest and to the point, Mrs. Brevittmore said, "Sacrilege or not, this evening I've thought a lot more about the death of your friend and colleague Detective Hodgdon than of Christ the Savior."

"In church, next time we go," Mrs. Hamelin said, "we can say a prayer for both."

Martha, Nora, and I spent New Year's Eve at home. Sorensen and another policeman, Charlie Hinton, took turns in the unmarked car. My mother was allowed to be with us just for that one night, and that meant we could show her how we'd fixed up a bedroom for her, and how everything was neat, clean, and in its own place. "It's all perfect," Nora said. "Not to worry about a thing. I have all of this to look forward to. The house looks wonderful. And I get to sleep in my own bed at last! Thank you for putting it in the smaller bedroom. That was the most thoughtful thing."

Jinx Faltenbourg and her husband, Toby, came by at about nine o'clock. Jinx and my mother spent time in the kitchen together over a cup of coffee, but Jinx and Toby had to be somewhere else by ten-thirty, so they left before ten. "I'm big as a house," Martha said, sitting on the overstuffed chair in the living room. "I bet the always svelte Leah Diamond, this far along, was only as big as a hotel room, not a house, and probably was out dancing her sweet ass off on New Year's Eve. I can't keep up with her, can I?"

"Who's Leah Diamond?" my mother asked.

"Wife of an old-time radio detective, Mom," I said. "She's part of a program Martha and I are devoted to called *Detective Levy Detects.*"

"I've heard of it, I think," my mother said.

"I don't think you'd like it much," I said.

"Wait, wait, wait, Jacob," Martha said. "Don't keep your own mother out like that." She looked at the clock on the kitchen wall and said, "Five minutes, the New Year's broadcast is on. Go get the radio and we can all listen. How about that, Nora?"

"It takes place just after the war ended, Mom," I said. "That atmosphere going to be okay with you?"

"Jacob, dear, I was as happy as anyone when the war ended. You were a baby, and I went to all sorts of celebrations. We had one at the library, I recall. You had a little flag in your push carriage: 'Happy Days Are Here Again,' it said. That carriage and that little flag are still in the basement. No, no, I love a radio program where you get to go back in time. You're sweet to worry. But I highly doubt any episode takes place in Leipzig."

"No, all in Toronto," Martha said.

"Thinking about it," Nora said, "after the war the radio meant a lot more than it does now. It brought people together. It struck people's imaginations in a different way. I remember asking my great-aunt Joyce what it was like to see television for the first time, and she said, 'Well, I thought Jack Benny was far more handsome on the radio.'"

The New Year's episode, "Silent Night," sounded more like a Christmas title to me, but soon I found out what it meant. During the first few minutes, all the gangsters and dames are whooping it up in Leah and Detective Levy's hotel room. But their little daughter is crying in the bedroom. A doctor arrives to examine her, and declares that the baby has an ear infection, and the loud noise is going to keep her awake. "Well, that's that," Leah says. "Everybody skedaddle!" So everyone but Leah Diamond and Detective Levy — and of course the baby — rumbles out of the hotel room, trying to keep their voices down. "Happy New Year! Happy New Year!" they say all down the hallway. "Let's go to Billie Blackburn's room!" And then all is quiet. Leah starts to narrate her every move, whispering, "Tiptoe, tiptoe, over to the fridge." In the background we can hear Detective Levy softly laughing. "Sshhhh," Leah says. "Open up the fridge, take out the champagne, will the cork wake our little darling or won't it?" *Pop!* "Oh, we're in luck, Freddy. Our little angel is snoozing away in dreamland. Remind me to send the good doctor a new stethoscope or something, will you?" We hear champagne being poured into two glasses. Then Leah Diamond and Detective Levy say, in a duet, "Happy New Year," and we hear glasses clink, then sipping.

At this point, it sounds as if Leah and Detective Levy have settled onto a sofa, and they begin, in whispers, to go over the highlights of the past year. "Just think of all the near misses we had," Levy says. "There was that close call with the jewel thief Bix Maddock, close call with Phyllis Wodwoe, remember? At the wharf. Boy, was she ever gun-crazy, that one." "Oh, let's stop there, please," Leah says. "If we talk about near misses, they might come back and seem nearer than ever." "That's fine, Leah," Levy says. "Besides," Leah says, "here we are, aren't we, a fire in the fireplace, our hearts beating, not like so many of our men and woman over in Europe." "No, not like them," Levy says, "but all those ships brought so many of them home, right, my darling?" "So many of them, yes," Leah says. "Happy New Year to them, then," Leah and Levy say, and the episode ends there.

Martha and I kept looking at Nora to see the effect on her, but she had seemed as rapt as we were with the episode and now looked just fine. "Turned out nicely, it seems to me," Nora said. "The baby's on the mend, no doubt. The happy couple gets part of a hotel room — of course not the bedroom — all to themselves. Why, that's practically a second honeymoon right there! Their rowdy friends get to dance the night away. The war's over for everybody, living or not living. I think I'd enjoy listening to more episodes."

"Oh, you don't have to say that," Martha said. "But you should know, your son's not — how to say it? — he's not as *emotionally* attached to the program as I am. But he stays closely apprised of it because of my being attached. And his being attached to me."

I took my mother back to Nova Scotia Rest Hospital on New Year's Day 1979.

Eleven *Very* Crowded Hours

THREE DAYS LATER—THAT IS, JANUARY 4—THE PUBLIC memorial service for Detective Hodgdon was held at 1 p.m. at Cathedral Church of All Saints. (There had been a private funeral for immediate family on the day before Christmas.) We sat in a middle pew, with Martha on the aisle, "for the legroom," as she put it. She surveyed the room and said, "This would've been the perfect moment to fulfill my lifelong desire to shoplift a blouse at Carel's department store, because every Halifax police and detective is here in the church right now." But she wept with varying intensity throughout the musical selections and eulogies. Standing at the back of the church following the service, Detective Tides, dressed in a beautiful dark suit, said, "They asked me to speak, but I could come up with only a sentence or two that would've been proper language for church. But Philip and I saw some things, didn't we? We saw a lot together. And we could communicate with each other. But had I tried to tell the truth up there at the pulpit, the language would've been . . . a desecration. I ran some ideas past my wife last night, what I might say, and that's the word she used."

Now it was about 3 p.m. Officer Sorensen drove Martha and me from Cathedral Church of All Saints to the wharf, where we caught the ferry to Dartmouth. This was the day my mother was to be released into our care and taken home.

We arrived at the hospital at 4:15. I knew the time because the sign-in register required our names and time of arrival. Martha had arranged for a hairstylist to do something "modern within reason" for my mother, and when Martha saw what the stylist had done, including a henna rinse, she declared it "perfect for your new life, Nora." My mother said, "Now that my rather long convalescence is over. Thank you, dear."

My mother had on a black woolen suit and dark green blouse, heavy knee socks, and galoshes. She must have heard the weather report, which said that Halifax was slated for sleet and high winds. She put on her overcoat and wrapped a wool scarf around her head. "I've made all the necessary goodbyes," she said. "I've tossed out dozens of Chinese finger traps. I'm so happy to be leaving here, I can't begin to tell you."

Martha carried one of Nora's suitcases and I carried another. Nora held a big cloth handbag with a floral pattern on it. The three of us walked down the stairs and out to the waiting taxi. There I introduced my mother to Officer Sorensen, and Nora said, "Am I still a prisoner until he sees me all the way to the house?"

Martha said, "It's a different kind of formality, Nora. We'll explain it later, okay?" I could see that my mother did not like Martha's answer.

We unloaded the suitcases near the ferry kiosk, paid the driver, and went inside. Glass walls had been fitted to the kiosk, and there were electric heaters near the benches. I purchased cups of hot chocolate, carried them over on a cardboard tray, and handed them around to Sorensen, Martha, and Nora, and kept one for myself. There were perhaps ten other waiting passengers. We could see that the ferry, out from Halifax, had reached the halfway point in the harbor. By now it was windy, and the sleet looked to be almost as horizontal as venetian blinds. Sorensen was surveying the other passengers, and when Nora noticed this, she said, "He's quite the nervous Nellie, our Officer Sorensen."

We finished our hot chocolates. When the debarking passengers were cleared, we walked up the gangplank onto the ferry and found places together on the wooden bench that ran the length of the lower deck. The engines rumbled under our feet. The water was slightly rough, but not too bad, really. Nora said, "Years ago, with the ferry heading in the opposite direction, it honestly felt like the river Styx."

"Is that a river in Nova Scotia?" Officer Sorensen asked. "I'm a fisherman."

"I've never quite known where it is," Nora said. "I doubt the fishing is very good, though."

"Newfoundland for trout is my preference," Sorensen said. "Did you know I once went out on a fishing boat on a fjord in ancestral Norway? I mean where my parents are from. That's how they always referred to it, ancestral Norway. The wild waters in that fjord made Halifax Harbor seem like a puddle after a summer rain."

We were close to docking when Martha went into the ladies'. In a few minutes, a perfect stranger, a woman about age fifty, walked out of the ladies' and over to Nora, leaned down, and whispered something. My mother gave me her handbag and said, "Wait here." Nora hurried into the bathroom. Nora and Martha stayed in there until the ferry docked. The other passengers debarked, and Sorensen and I waited on our bench. Eventually the cleanup crew began their work. We waited with the suitcases for another half hour. One of the ferry pilots walked down the metal stairs, saw us, and said, "You fellows don't look like you'd need help with those suitcases. But do you?" Sorensen reached into his back pocket, took out his wallet, snapped it open with one hand, and showed his badge. The pilot just nodded and went back up the stairs. "First day on the job,

I was instructed to use utmost discretion when I did that. But I used to partner with Officer Canti Chaffen — Canti being short for Cantilever — who'd name a kid that? And Canti would whip out his badge just at a ticket taker at the movies, say, and look like something was hush-hush. What a cheapskate, eh?"

"They've been in there a long time," I said.

"If Detective Crauchet needed more help, she'd ask for it," Sorensen said.

When Nora and Martha finally emerged from the ladies', Martha was leaning against my mother. "False alarm," Martha said. "Nothing to worry about."

"Are you all right, Martha?" I said, holding her opposite Nora.

"A little weak in the knees," Martha said.

We navigated slowly to Sorensen's car. Inside, Martha said, "I'm feeling much better now. Dizziness completely disappeared. Whew! I'm just fine now. Nora would like it if we stopped at the Halifax Free Library. There's a small welcome party for her there. Forgot to mention this, Jake, but it won't take but fifteen or twenty minutes. It'll be very nice for your mother."

"You look fit as a fiddle," my mother said. "But tell me, are you sure?"

"I can't wait to see the look on everyone's face," Martha said.

Officer Sorensen said, "I have to call this change of plans in, Detective Crauchet."

"Do that, then," Martha said.

Once Sorensen reported our destination (he noted to the dispatcher that it was 6:40 p.m.), it was less than a fifteen-minute ride to the library. When we stepped inside, there to greet us was the entire library staff, including two people neither my mother nor I had met before. They were introduced as Corine Edwards and Melissa Axelrod. Then Jinx Faltenbourg made sure that everyone had a glass of spiked punch, and she made a toast: "Welcome back to our dear Nora. As you know, Nora was chief librarian for —"

Just then, Sorensen's walkie-talkie crackled and we heard, "— Sorensen, Halifax Free Library. Officer Sorensen, Halifax Free Library."

This stopped the proceedings. Sorensen did not apologize, nor did he leave the main room where everyone had gathered. He held the receiver to his ear, said, "Sorensen here," and almost instantly looked alarmed. He got Martha's attention and waved her over. We all could hear the static and a crackling voice, but had no idea yet what was going on. Everyone stood there silently waiting. Sorensen spoke softly to Martha, who sat down on a swivel chair, closed her eyes, and shook her head back and forth.

Martha took the walkie-talkie from Sorensen's hand and spoke into it: "This is Detective Martha Crauchet — what the hell is going on? I need details. Now!" She fit the receiver to her ear and listened for a good thirty seconds, spoke briefly and quietly to the dispatcher, then handed the walkie-talkie back to Sorensen.

Martha stood up with some difficulty from the swivel chair. "Everyone listen up, please," she said. "We've got a situation. Officer Sorensen here is going to see that every single one of you leaves the library immediately. I'm sorry, but when I say immediately, I mean *immediately*. No questions asked. Just go." She turned and nodded to Sorensen, who walked to the front door and looked out at the street. He nodded back in the affirmative to Martha, who said, "All right now, everyone — everyone, be careful now, single file, single file, please." The entire staff threw on their coats, hats, and scarves, slipped on gloves or mittens, and left the library. There was just myself, Martha, Sorensen, and my mother left.

"Martha —" I began.

"Robert Emil was identified a few blocks away," she said. "I let the others go because I didn't want a hostage situation. I mean the other librarians. I had to take that possibility seriously. Judgment call, but dispatch agreed. Emil's not interested in them anyway." She looked at Sorensen, who, without a word, went out the front door, surveyed the street, then came back inside. "Everybody's away safe and sound, Detective," he said. "I'm going out to my car. I have a shotgun in the trunk." He hurried out, returning within two minutes carrying a shotgun and a box of shells.

"Oh, my Lord in heaven," Nora said. "What can he possibly want after so many years? I just don't understand."

"Nora, leave this discussion for later, please. Just try and stay calm. This is serious stuff," Martha said. "Jake, maybe we should try and get your mother home."

"No," my mother said. "Don't you see? This is why my release date was today. So I could be with you no matter what."

"Jake, you and Sorensen please move those heavy card catalogues up against the front door," Martha said. Sorensen and I set to that. Martha picked up the walkie-talkie and said, "Detective Crauchet, Halifax Free Library. The following people are here. Officer Sorensen, Jacob Rigolet, Nora Rigolet. Please advise."

Martha listened to the receiver. Then she bent over with a groan. Nora took the walkie-talkie from her and handed it to Sorensen, who said into it, "Officer Sorenson now — continue." Nora walked with Martha to the bathroom, which was down a short hallway. I ran over, but my mother pushed me away. "Wait out here, just for a moment," she said.

I walked back to the main room. Sorensen said, "Not good."

"What's going on?" I said. "Martha is in some sort of distress. I think we should call an ambulance."

"They may not want to risk that just now, Mr. Rigolet."

"What the hell are you talking about?"

"Robert Emil is armed and dangerous."

"Where the fuck is he? Is he *here*, at the library, or what? Because I think Martha needs an ambulance."

"Please try to calm down."

"What?"

"Please — just try to calm down, Mr. Rigolet," Sorensen said.

"Since you asked, Robert Emil was on the front steps. Now he's not. He's armed. More squad cars are on their way."

I hurried to the bathroom and went in. Martha was sitting on the tile floor, propped up against a wall. Nora had covered her with her overcoat. "Her water broke," my mother said. "She's fine — it's just —"

"I think I'm in labor, Jake. Go get Sorensen. Now, please."

I ran back out and yelled, "Sorensen, Martha needs to talk with you!"

Sorensen said "Eight-ten" into the walkie-talkie and followed me into the bathroom.

"Officer Sorensen, what is your medical training? Tell me this minute," Martha said. "What is your medical training?"

"Basic," Sorensen said.

"Are you capable of delivering a baby?"

Sorensen's jaw tightened and he looked doubtful.

"— situation, please, Officer Sorensen," the walkie-talkie crackled, "situation, please."

Martha waved for Sorensen to hand her the walkie-talkie. She said, "This is Detective Crauchet. I'm having contractions — I'm having a child, read me? Advise, please."

Martha listened a moment, then said to Sorensen, "An ambulance is being sent. Back entrance. Two squad cars will receive and protect."

Sorensen looked relieved and said, "I would have tried."

"I know you would have," Martha said. "And you would have done just fine. But this is best, right?"

"I'll go back to the main room now," Sorensen said.

"You do that," Martha said. But Sorensen didn't leave the bathroom. "Jake, take off your watch and give it to Nora. Nora, I'm having contractions. Help me time them, please. My watch reads eight-thirty."

Martha locked eyes with mine, and I could almost read her mind: *Same place you were born, Jacob. What in the world?* And God knows what Nora must have been thinking.

I sat with Martha. We held hands, and she began to take deep breaths. "This helps," she said. "Don't forget, I work with very competent people. If they say they'll send an ambulance, they'll send an ambulance. But it may take them a little time to figure out how to do it just right. This daughter of ours feels in a hurry, though. But how would I know? I've never done this before." She laughed and shook her head and said, "Don't you dare think, Jacob, don't you dare think this means Nora Elizabeth is fated to be a librarian!" This made everyone laugh, but then Martha grimaced and braved through a contraction. Her squeezing of my hand had more strength behind it than I could've imagined. "Did you note the time, Jake? Note the time, note the time. Write it down somewhere. Use the inside of a book if you have to."

The first siren we heard was not the ambulance. Sorensen's walkie-talkie informed us that "Robert Emil has discharged his weapon," but the rest was swallowed by static. Sorensen pressed the walkie-talkie to his ear and spoke into it, but my mother and I were paying attention to Martha, who was doing deep-breathing exercises, taught at three sessions of a birthing class we'd taken, sponsored by her police union. The truth was, Martha seemed to remember everything she was taught, and I seemed to have forgotten everything. I said, "You're doing great, Martha, you're doing great, you're amazing," and she said, "I love this child so much already and I want so much for things to be okay, but this isn't what I had in mind, Jacob. Not exactly—" A contraction seemed to ripple through her entire body. She closed her eyes until it passed.

My mother had remembered that blankets and pillows and washcloths were kept in a small utility room, and she now appeared clutching some of each. We fitted a pillow behind Martha and tucked another pillow under her legs, and she said, "Oh, that's so much better." Then she let out a long, low groan.

Sorensen listened to the walkie-talkie, then said, "The ambulance is out back. They're just waiting for another squad car — that won't be long, Detective. Just a moment longer."

Martha wrapped her arms around my neck and pulled my face next to hers and held it there, tightly, as she felt another contraction. "Oh, my Lord, that one was really — Jake, Jake, Jake, listen to me. Know what's actually helping me? Thinking about Leah Diamond. Don't ask me why. And don't you dare tell a living soul I said that, either. I'm not supposed to be making sense right now."

"Our little secret," I said. Martha let go and fell back against the pillow. "Where the fuck are those —"

We heard gunshots, and Nora said, "Oh no, oh no." Then there was pounding on the rear entrance door, which was down a short hallway off the children's book room. Officer Sorensen went down the hall, revolver in hand, and unlocked the door. In rushed three medical personnel, a male nurse, a woman doctor, and a fireman whom Martha recognized, and she said, "Pete Gossining, aren't you a sight for sore eyes."

Fireman Gossining unfolded a gurney, set the wheels, and he and I lifted Martha onto it. "I'm Dr. Kestral," the physician said. "Let's see what's going on, shall we?" She pushed me back from the cot. "Give us lots of room, please," she said.

Dr. Kestral listened to Martha with her stethoscope and then turned and glared at me. "Maybe you could just . . ." she said, and began to help the male nurse, named Ridgeway, according to his nameplate, slip off Martha's clothes. Once they had done that, they covered her with blankets. Fireman Gossining hurried back outside, and when he returned he said, "We're ready for her in the ambulance." But Dr. Kestral said firmly, "No, she's having her child right here, *right now.*"

There was no argument, and with an excruciatingly strong contraction, Martha called out what must have sounded like nonsense to everyone but Nora and me: "My husband was born in this library too!" Dr. Kestral's warm smile and nod of her head was meant to comfort Martha and us: *Not to worry, at such moments I've heard just about everything imaginable.*

My mother and I were instructed to wait in the main room. We looked on as best we could. Another nurse had arrived to assist. I never got her name. Sterilized instruments and a deep plastic container of steaming water were brought in. And that was all we could see. We heard Martha both crying and laughing wildly, and we heard the encouraging words of Dr. Kestral and the newly arrived nurse. Then we heard Nora Elizabeth crying. "Now, let's cut the umbilical cord ... There we go." From Nora Elizabeth came a little sneezing cough, then more crying. Dr. Kestral looked at her watch and said, "Time of birth, ten-eighteen p.m.," and Martha said with the last of her strength, "She's so beautiful." I now was allowed to come over. Our daughter was swaddled in white, and Martha held her. "She's so beautiful," Martha said again. I leaned over to kiss Martha and then Nora Elizabeth, but as soon as I did, Dr. Kestral said, "Take a few more minutes. But we need to get them to the hospital. Everything's fine. It's just this library is not the place for your wife and child right now, is it?"

Martha and I were left alone with Nora Elizabeth for a short while. Then fireman Gossining and nurse Ridgeway lifted the gurney and wheeled Martha and Nora Elizabeth out the back entrance. It was snowing. I could see squad cars, their lights flashing, on either side of the alley where the ambulance was parked. I said to my mother, "Have Officer Sorensen take you home. Tell him to stay with you until I get there." In the ambulance with Martha, Nora Elizabeth, and me were Dr. Kestral and nurse Ridgeway. Just as Victoria General came into sight, I heard static crackle on the ambulance's radio, then, "All units, all units, Robert Emil DOA Mercy

General, eleven-oh-four p.m." Old-time radio was not real life, but still, I had heard enough episodes of *Detective Levy Detects* to know what those initials stood for.

Martha and Nora Elizabeth were in room 51. Dr. Kestral was the attending, and I could see that this pleased Martha no end. "As you can see, they took me off emergency," Dr. Kestral said. "Because I asked them to, so they did. Because I wanted to follow up properly here." Sitting in a chair in the corner, I could now get a closer look at the doctor as she checked Martha's and Nora Elizabeth's vital signs and wrote on the chart, which hung at the end of the bed. Dr. Kestral appeared to be about forty-five years old. She was quite "willowy," as Martha would later note, and had a rather thin face, with high cheekbones and dark brown eyes. She struck me as intense and kind.

"Everything looks fine," Dr. Kestral said. "Your daughter might have a little jaundice. But that's common, not a bit of concern. We'll put her under a special lamp in the nursery. Presto-chango, jaundice is gone in most cases. By the way, you'll want to start nursing her as soon as possible. Someone will be in soon to help with that."

In walked a nurse. "Hello, my name is Ruthie," she said. "I'll be on until seven a.m. See that red button there at the end of the cord? You need anything, just press the button." She fluffed up Martha's pillow, put a thermometer in her mouth, and waited for Martha's temperature to register. She read the thermometer, said "Peachy," jotted a few things down on the chart, and handed Martha a cup full of ice chips. "These will help the dryness," she said. "Nurse Marcia Heller will be in soon, help with swaddling and nursing, all sorts of good stuff, okay?"

"Thank you," Martha said. Her hair was wet from all the exertion, strands stuck to her forehead. When she looked over at me, she said, "I must look a fright."

"I've never seen anything so beautiful," I said, "the two of you."

"You better have said that," Martha said. Nora Elizabeth was sleeping.

Dr. Kestral left the room. "I feel like nursing her," Martha said. "But look at her sleeping. Just look at her, Jake."

"Just start right in trying," Dr. Kestral said, having overheard Martha as she returned to the room. "Perfect timing, here's Marcia now."

Marcia Heller was all smiles. She walked over and gently arranged Nora Elizabeth at Martha's breast, and Nora Elizabeth moved her mouth in a funny way, opened her eyes, cried a few seconds, then latched on to Martha's nipple. Martha said, "Oh," and Marcia showed her the proper way to support the baby while nursing. "That's perfect," she said. Marcia sat on the end of the bed for a few minutes, observing. "No more need for me here," she said, and left the room.

"Thank you, Marcia," Dr. Kestral called after her. Then to Martha and me, "Enjoy your privacy for about another hour. Then I'm afraid there's a detective needing to ask a few questions. His last name is Tides, if I heard it right."

"He's someone I work with," Martha said.

"I've already spoken with him," Dr. Kestral said. "I told him he could only stay a short time. And believe me, I'll see to that."

Dr. Kestral left the room again.

Martha and I had an hour with Nora Elizabeth, who, after nursing, was fast asleep. Martha dozed on and off. Once, when she woke, she said, "Jake, we missed *Detective Levy Detects*," which seemed, given the circumstances, a comical non sequitur. But Marcia, the nurse, heard it, and said, "Why, that's *my* program too!"

Martha sat more upright. "Did you by any chance hear tonight's episode?"

"I live two blocks from the hospital," Marcia said, "so when I took my break, I went home, listened, and came back."

"Pray tell," Martha said.

"Let's see, well, I suppose the big news is, Leah is pregnant again," Marcia said.

"Wait a minute," I interjected. "How can that be? Their kid is only a few months old."

The answer was so obvious to both Martha and Marcia Heller that they could only stare at me. Finally Martha said, "Jake, it's a new year of episodes. The station's simply decided to skip ahead a year or so. Get it?"

"*Tsk-tsk-tsk*," Marcia Heller said, looking at me. She turned her attention back to Martha. "And Frederik Levy, what a doll. He's in heaven with the news. There's a little problem brewing with stormy-tempered Dutch Ponsot, at the hotel. I don't know what the problem is yet. Always a storm brewing, right? But as for Freddy — I call him that — as for Freddy, he's a dreamboat. The perfect husband. Want to know what I mean by perfect? I'm a person likes to spend a lot of time alone. So my idea of perfect is being married to Freddy, the next best thing to living alone."

Martha laughed so hard at this, Nora Elizabeth startled awake, but in a moment fell right back asleep.

"Sorry to break up the party," Detective Tides said from the doorway. "Can I come in?"

Marcia Heller took Martha's temperature, recorded it on the chart, and left the room. Detective Tides came in, took a peek at Nora Elizabeth, and said, "Beautiful kid born in the library, eh? Well, you, me, and Hodgdon have seen all sorts of things, haven't we, Detective Crauchet?"

"We certainly have," Martha said. "I cannot believe Philip is gone. I still can't believe it."

"Yeah, hasn't sunk in for me, either," Tides said. "I don't want to interrupt your family time here, both of you — all three of you, I mean. But I have to ask some questions. For the report, sorry."

"They said you were in the waiting room," Martha said. "Let's attend to business."

Detective Tides was brief and perfunctory, which seemed best, really. Martha was looking exhausted and needed to sleep, and Tides saw that. But he had these questions. In the main, Martha and I substantiated what Detective Tides already knew, having to do with everything around Robert Emil's threats. "Right," he said, checking off each question. "Right, good. Got it."

Then Tides said, "Well, that about does it, then. I'll check in on you at home, okay?" He hesitated a moment, then said, "There's just one thing. Kind of confusing, actually. The extremely personal nature of this lowlife Emil's vendetta against — against Nora Rigolet in particular. Against your mother, Jake. I mean, the incident in April 1945, and it boomerangs back around, you might say. Right back around to the events of tonight. Now, let me say — at the risk of this making you uncomfortable, it being about your own mother, Jake — let me just say that I saw photographs of Nora Rigolet in 1945, and forgive me for saying it this way, but she was a real looker. And real lookers in my experience have always drawn creeps like a magnet — not that women who aren't real lookers don't as well. Women, just by being women, draw creeps like a magnet, but let's leave it at that. I seldom say things in just the right way, but I mean well and you get my drift. Martha, you've learned over the years how to accurately get my drift. Anyway, so I'm perfectly satisfied to believe that the pathological deal here with Robert Emil is, he got fixated on Nora Rigolet and never, all these years, let up on his fixatedness. Every sort of behavior happens, and we write it down in the report. I've studied his file very, very closely, Emil's. I mean, I should get a college diploma just for studying his file. And yet there's something I'm not quite understanding here. But now he's all shot up dead and gone, isn't Robert Emil? So I'll shut up now and file my report. Unless there's something you two can tell me that in your best judgment you think I should know." He sighed heavily and hesitated a long minute. "Besides the fact that both times, 1945 and tonight, a child was born to the Rigolet family in the Halifax Free Library and

Robert Emil was in close proximity. But you know what? I am not averse to recognizing it as a remarkable coincidence. Not me. Besides, we've seen all sorts of that, haven't we, Detective Crauchet? Over the years working together."

"Yes we have," Martha said. "Thanks for doing your job so well."

"Quite a night, eh?"

"Feels like we've all lived a lifetime since —"

"Yeah," Tides said, "right, right. Since what? Since the funeral service, which was one p.m. Life's been flying by since one p.m." He looked at his watch. "Just past twelve midnight now — about eleven hours. Some of us made it out alive, some of us didn't. Eleven *very* crowded hours."

Detective Tides shut the door quietly behind him.

The Tahiti Portfolio

MARTHA, NORA, AND I SPENT THE NEXT WEEK BASICALLY AT home. Like any new parents, we were exhausted, and didn't know if we were doing things right with our daughter, and Nora said, "There is no right or wrong, there's just paying close attention and taking turns with everything, figuring it out. Nora Elizabeth's strong and beautiful and perfect in every way that's important. That's what you build on."

"You sound like Reverend Peck, from church when I was a kid."

"Reverend Peck? I thought he was a jerk," Nora said. "If I ever sound as sanctimonious as him again, send me back to the hospital in Dartmouth immediately."

We could see that my mother wanted to be present every moment for us. To help with everything. She wanted to keep assuring us that the living situation was fine, that she didn't feel like a guest in her own house. And we were assured. "The time will come when I'll find a small apartment," she said. "I'm going to legally sign the house over to you. That'll be easy. That'll just take a moment."

We got Nora Elizabeth's crib set up in the dining room. We

brought her in for her one-week checkup. Things were fine. People dropped by to have a look at the baby. You have a child, life completely changes overnight. We'd been told that, and we believed it, and now it was true. My mother began working again at the Halifax Free Library. Just those few hours a week.

On January 14, we had a visit from Mrs. Hamelin and Mrs. Brevittmore. They brought a pot roast with potatoes and carrots, and a peach pie. Favorites of ours. They took over the house, which greatly amused my mother. The three women hadn't spent time together, and after dinner Mrs. Hamelin said to Martha and me, "You two go in and fuss over your baby. We want to get to know Nora better." And we could hear from Nora Elizabeth's room that they were asking my mother all sorts of questions about her time in Nova Scotia Rest Hospital, her years as chief librarian, and so on. Interlocutrixes in a familial style, and Nora sounded pleased to be engaged as such. They were all drinking sherry and having a good time.

When we put Nora Elizabeth down for the night, and I went in to make Martha a cup of tea, Mrs. Hamelin said, "Jacob, I have something to ask you. Something of some importance. Do you mind terribly?"

Martha came in and joined us in the living room. I set her tea on the table in front of her. Mrs. Hamelin said, "Jacob, quite obviously you have an entirely new life. How wonderful for you how things have turned out. Through all the adversities, how things have blossomed. But I must ask you something."

"Please ask," I said. "I can't really imagine."

"Here goes, then," Mrs. Hamelin said. "I want you to bid at one last auction for me. Now wait, wait — just wait before you say no. You've met Brice Falter, of course. Brice has been doing a good job for me. He's a pleasant young man. His mind's a little lacking in originality. He's got all that education. He's been about average at auctions. I'll keep him on, and he seems to want to stay on."

"He most certainly does," Mrs. Brevittmore said.

"What I have to ask is this, Jacob," Mrs. Hamelin said. "New child, new family arrangement, almost newly minted in library science — quite enough for one life. But would you consider putting your *older* talents to use for your old employer — for *me?* Not entirely putting this on your shoulders, either. No, what I have in mind is you accompanying Brice Falter to the auction. Assisting him, one might say. And you'd only have to walk there, because the auction" — and at this point Mrs. Hamelin looked at my mother — "is at the Lord Nelson Hotel, as a matter of fact. In a couple of weeks."

"I won't go near the hotel," my mother said, placing her hand on Mrs. Hamelin's wrist and laughing a little, "not to worry. Besides, even if *Death on a Leipzig Balcony* — because I know what you're all thinking — my fatal mishap. Even if *Death on a Leipzig Balcony* were up for auction, I would stay here at home with my granddaughter. So let's all be out front, shall we, and not worry about it? I had lots of time to think things through at the hospital, didn't I."

"I'm sorry I even have to refer to the Lord Nelson," Mrs. Hamelin said, "especially in regard to an auction. But I'm afraid that's where the auction is to be held."

"Tell Jacob which photograph you're interested in," Mrs. Brevitt-more said.

"Yes, back to my request, of course," Mrs. Hamelin said. "Actually, it's not a single photograph I so desire. It's a whole portfolio. Quite rare. Quite unusual. The photographer is Eugenio Courret, French born, who arrived in Peru in 1860 and, with his brother, formed a studio there in 1863. Brice did quite well with the research, by the way.

"The portfolio contains some of the earliest photographs of Tahiti — well, there was this fellow, Gustav Viaud, who'd arrived there a year earlier and who took wonderful photographs too."

"Usually I wouldn't ask," I said. "When I was working for you, I'd know from the research anyway, and from talking with you. But why do you like this Courret's work so much?"

"Do you miss it even a little?" Mrs. Hamelin said. "Of course I only refer to auctions."

"I miss doing well at them, a little," I said. "But when I screwed up, or when I lost out, for any reason, I don't really miss that. But you gave me an education."

"As to your question," Mrs. Hamelin said, "I'm simply mad for this portfolio. It contains mid-nineteenth-century views of Papeete, which is the capital of Tahiti. There are government buildings, a small dock with dugout canoes, children in the forecourt of a church, wonderful views of the harbor with sailing vessels, street scenes —"

"*Ahem,* perhaps that's enough detail," Mrs. Brevittmore said.

"Oh, quite right, sorry," Mrs. Hamelin said. "I suppose I was overtaken by the nostalgia of working so closely with you, my dear Jacob."

"I think that's nice," Martha said. "Jake, what do you think? I know what I think."

"Your two cents is worth a million dollars to me," Mrs. Hamelin said.

"Your last semester's off to a solid start," Martha said. "Nora is with us, helping out every day." She looked at Mrs. Hamelin. "And we could not have better friends."

"I'll come by tomorrow and look at the research," I said.

"And I'll see to it that Brice is present," Mrs. Hamelin said.

The next day at around 2 p.m., just as Martha and Nora Elizabeth began their naps, I walked over to Mrs. Hamelin's house at 112 Spring Garden Road. Mrs. Brevittmore answered the front door wearing her coat and hat, and said, "There's cookies and tea set out in the library. Everyone's waiting for you, Jacob. I'm off for my daily constitutional."

I went into the library. "Oh, Jacob, there you are," Mrs. Hamelin said, looking up from a book on the long table. "You of course know Brice." Brice and I shook hands. I sat down across the table from him. "Now, then," Mrs. Hamelin said, "have some cookies and tea, but let's start right in, shall we?"

We spent close to four hours with the research. During that time, with her usual meticulous attention, Mrs. Hamelin had us examine, through magnifying glasses, reproductions of several photographs in the portfolio: *Palais Pomare, Papeete; Large Tahitian choir seated on a picket-fenced lawn; View of a native shoreline settlement; View across the rooftops of Faaa; View of three European men standing in front of a portico of a house on a tree-lined street; Architectural study of a government building.* Mrs. Hamelin provided exacting commentary on each photograph, and it was impossible not to feel her acquisition fever — that phrase of hers again — rising with each photograph.

When Mrs. Hamelin went upstairs for her before-dinner rest, Brice and I spoke a short while longer. "Jake, I've lost out at two of the last three auctions. London, Rotterdam, Boston," he said. "It'd be great if I could win out with this Tahitian portfolio."

"I can see that," I said. "But I don't know how I can be of specific help. But since Esther wants me at the auction — which is surely no reflection on your skill — let's look at her list of who else is going to be bidding, and I'll see if I can remember anything about them. Other than that, I'll be right there next to you. What's Esther's ceiling bid?"

"Twenty-five thousand, Canadian," Brice said.

"She must want this portfolio badly," I said.

"When you worked for Mrs. Hamelin," Brice said, "did you ever have the feeling you disappointed her, even when you brought back the photograph she wanted? Because I do. I feel there's higher and lower grades of disappointment, but disappointment nonetheless."

"Yeah, you mentioned that once before," I said. "I felt it all the time. Maybe not quite as much as you."

During the intervening time between our meeting with Mrs. Hamelin and the auction itself, I kept studying the Tahiti photographs. But only for an hour or so a day. I was mainly paying attention to life at home and my final essay deadline for library science. One afternoon, Detective Tides dropped off a few case files and said, "Nobody's expecting you to look at these, Martha, but if you feel like it, here's what I'm working on just now." He stayed for dinner.

The auction was held on February 5 at 7:30 p.m. in the street-level drawing room of the Lord Nelson Hotel. I suppose I shouldn't have been surprised that the auctioneer was the same one, Reginald Avery. He looked even more the worse for wear than the last time I'd seen him, which was on March 19, 1977. The room was crowded, and people stood along the walls as well as sat in the rows of folding chairs. Brice looked like he was attending a funeral (maybe he thought he was, in effect, attending his own funeral, if he didn't win the day), in his dark pinstripe suit, black shoes, white shirt, and black tie. I tried to loosen him up a little, saying, "You interviewing for the undertaker job I saw listed in the paper, or what?" as I glanced up and down his somber suit and tie.

"For some reason, the more formal I dress, the more serious I feel about the auction," he said.

"Got it," I said.

The Tahiti Portfolio, as Reginald Avery called it, was fourth up on the docket. It was placed upright on a table, not on an easel, and was opened to exhibit two different photographs on two pages. "Now, ladies and gentlemen, if you would refer to item number four in your programs. A very rare opportunity, ladies and gentlemen," Avery said in that sonorous voice of his, "very rare indeed. From the exotic French Polynesian territories — the island of Tahiti — *The Tahiti Portfolio.* Presently in the ownership of Mr. Ezekiel and Mrs. Sandra Bitters of Vancouver, British Columbia, a family perhaps best known for its collection of the works of Eugène Cuvelier. But this evening, the pièce de résistance of their fifty years of collecting and curating, *The Tahiti Portfolio* by Eugenio Courret, French born. The photographs were taken between 1863 and 1864. The only known edition. Near to perfect condition. The portfolio holds sixteen different albumen prints of Tahiti, and each image is 4¾ by 6¼ inches, mounted on a 9½-by-12½-inch sheet. Each print bears a blind stamp on the mat: 'Courret Hermanos Fotografos Calle Mercaderes 197 Lima.' Ladies and gentlemen, I am instructed by the family of Mr. Ezekiel and Mrs. Sandra Bitters to begin this evening's bidding at five thousand dollars. Do I hear five thousand, ladies and gentlemen? Five thousand dollars for the rare *Tahiti Portfolio*." Right away an auction paddle was held up, three rows ahead of us on the aisle. "The woman in row five, on the aisle, thank you," Reginald Avery said. "Do I hear seventy-five hundred? Seventy-five hundred dollars, *The Tahiti Portfolio*?"

I must say, the bidding was fast and furious; at eighteen thousand, Brice still had not raised his paddle. I studied his face in profile. He was rapidly blinking his eyes, not a good sign, I thought. But I didn't say anything. Suddenly I sensed a — what? Something off to my left, coming up the aisle. Later, when I reported this incident to Martha, she called it "your mother's ghost of an auction past." Whatever it really was — hallucination, reenactment, déjà vu, or some psychological term I had no earthly idea of — it was over with quickly. I turned my attention back to Avery. "Nineteen thousand, we have a bid of nineteen thousand. Do I hear twenty? Do I hear twenty thousand dollars, *The Tahiti Portfolio*." At which point Brice jumped the gun, and not only held up his paddle, but actually called out, "Twenty-two thousand," a completely unnecessary escalation, of course, because Reginald Avery had asked for only twenty thousand. I reached over and, more roughly than I intended, pulled Brice's head close to mine and whispered, "Brice, be careful here," and then Avery pointed at Brice and said, "Gentleman in the sixth row, center, twenty-two thousand dollars. Do I hear twenty-three. Twenty-three thousand? The bid is at twenty-two, do I hear twenty-three?" Avery now pointed to his left as he said, "Lady in the maroon dress, second row, third in from the aisle, bids twenty-three thousand. Thank you, madam. Do I hear twenty-four, twenty-four thousand? *The Tahiti Portfolio.*"

This was the moment I determined that Brice should turn his previous mistake into a strategy (was I possibly thinking of Hans Frisch in London?), so I leaned toward him and whispered, "Go for twenty-five — do it. Now."

Brice raised his paddle and said, "Twenty-five thousand!" And before Avery could even repeat Brice's bid, a man in the second row, center, shouted, "Thirty thousand!" The bidding for *The Tahiti Portfolio* was over and done with.

I told Brice that I would walk to Mrs. Hamelin's with him and take full responsibility for not winning the bid. Brice said he appreciated that, but that he was the one who had listened to me. We went back and forth about this all the way to 112 Spring Garden Road. Brice unlocked the front door and we went inside, where Mrs. Brevittmore and Mrs. Hamelin were sitting together on the living room sofa. Mrs. Hamelin was just hanging up the telephone. "Open the champagne!" she said, and Mrs. Brevittmore popped the cork of a bottle of champagne. They had set out four glasses, and Mrs. Brevittmore filled all of them. "Come celebrate with us," Mrs. Hamelin said.

Confused, Brice and I sat down on the opposite sofa, took up glasses, and held them in midair as Mrs. Hamelin made a toast: "To the most shameless collector on earth — Esther Hamelin!" We all clinked glasses and sipped the champagne.

We sat in silence for a moment, and then Mrs. Brevittmore said, "Enough suspense, right, Esther? Relax, relax, the deed is done, and *The Tahiti Portfolio* is now Esther's."

"I'm sorry to tell you this," Brice said, "but I was outbid, Mrs. Hamelin."

"Oh, I know that," Mrs. Hamelin said. "I received a call right away."

"Then I don't understand at all," Brice said, taking quite a gulp of champagne.

"The man who bid thirty thousand, I know him very well," Mrs. Hamelin said. "Mr. Leonard Calendar, who has a very good eye for photographs, but for him it's all in the bidding. He doesn't really collect. Not on the worldly level, like some of us, though he does have some fine items. He just likes to win. I've followed his habits for decades now, you see. He's a type, you might say. A certain type you find in the world of auctions. And when I received the call and heard who had won *The Tahiti Portfolio,* I simply telephoned Leonard — he always stays at the Lord Nelson. We spoke only moments ago, in fact. I offered him thirty-five thousand. And he was pleased as punch. I knew he would be. And he was. Let's refill our glasses, shall we?"

"Am I forgiven, then?" Brice said.

"I'm sure you bid what I said was my ceiling price — what more could you do?" Mrs. Hamelin said.

The way I read her expression was that she was not so very pleased with Brice, yet still pleased with the outcome. There it was. A grade of disappointment.

Letter from Bernard Rigolet

April 19, 1945

Darling Nora,

We are in the city of Leipzig. You should see the looks we get from the locals. One woman ran out of her house and spat at us, threw rotten apples and yelled, "See because of you what we have to eat!" Because of us? What about who started this war, her beloved Führer, her beloved Hitler! Blind cow. I looked in her house and saw the fire burning in her fireplace and I think of men we've buried in the frozen ground and God forgive me but there have been times I've been very close to firing a round into one of those houses, I swear I have. You won't like to hear this about your Bernie, but it is true nonetheless, my darling.

These past eleven hours have been the most crowded hours possible for a man to experience. Crowded in horrible ways. Hours I would give anything to erase out of my mind. But I'll probably never be able to. Forgive me for telling you but I have to tell someone, I have to write it down, or else I don't know what. Or else I'll explode with the sheer crowdedness of it maybe.

You have to understand that by this time — the 15th of this month — the British army liberated the concentration camp at Belsen. The world's going to see pictures of suffering like it's never seen. Robert Capa said he could've photographed the camps but decided to leave that to others. But somehow he kept getting information — he actually got information from Martha Gellhorn, who ran in the same crowd with Hemingway, and we even heard a radio broadcast by Edward Murrow — I wondered right away if you heard it at home, Nora. All I know for certain is those camps were pure evil. There are a lot of them, and all of them are pure evil. We're not that well informed with it, but we all know that much. Sam Marcus has family in Germany, and he is going insane with each little snippet of news. He hasn't slept in weeks, he says, he's out of his mind and can't do a thing about it, except go nuts.

Anyway, for a couple of days there were three smaller shows and we took a lot of casualties. Our battery faced skirmishes and by the grace of God we got through them, but with casualties. Darling Nora, I write this at noon on April 19, in Leipzig, which we have now occupied. Yesterday there was a big show here.

We were fighting our way across the Zeppelin Bridge over the Weisse Elster Canal, moving toward the center of the city. We got pinned down by rifle fire, stopped, moved on, it seemed inch by inch — when the first platoon crossed the bridge, when they were right out on the bridge, I think every single one of us thought it might get blown up, but it didn't happen, but when some men started across, they couldn't make it because of gunfire, and nobody could make out where it was coming from. So we backed away from the bridge. I didn't actually see anyone point to an apartment building off to our left, but suddenly that's where some of the platoon all went toward. It was a four-story apartment building that overlooked the bridge. Some guys were shooting along the upper windows, just in case any snipers might've been there, we didn't know who was up there. I went along on toward the apartment building and we all finally got to it. We needed to get some height, we needed to look out and see where the rest of our sector went and all of that. Troops went every which way in that apartment building. Me, I followed this sergeant named Rodney Ekhert and a young clean-cut pfc named Ray Bowman up the stairs, along with a few others, and Robert Capa close behind holding his camera. I mean, here everyone had been hearing that the war was over but it sure wasn't over for us!

We got to this one apartment which had a balcony and Ekhert and Bowman set up a machine gun and started blasting away. The rest of us were crouched back, but every once in a while stood up and shot out the window, not really sighting anything in particular, just support fire more or less. But mainly we were crouched back, and that's when Ekhert went to get more ammunition and Bowman was left alone at the machine gun, sweeping bullets across his sightline, blasting away — and suddenly his body went slack and he fell back and onto his side. I could see his young face, and he had a single hole in his forehead, and blood was starting to pool. Robert Capa was just behind me to my right and snapping pictures — I think he'd already caught Ekhert and Bowman side by side at the machine gun and then Bowman alone, and after Bowman fell, some other soldier, I think it was Richard Barrical, pushed forward and took over the machine gun and started blasting away, and he was half sitting right on Bowman, but he really had to be, to get to the machine gun. Two of us pulled Bowman back along the floor, sliding him along in his own blood, and everything was very loud. I heard Barrical cursing and shouting at the German troops, and Nora, I'd be loath to repeat what he was saying, but you can imagine.

Barrical was still firing away when some of us, including Robert Capa, hurried out of that apartment building and went looking for the sniper, and we found a bunch of fascist soldiers cowering inside a streetcar. Soon a pretty big group had surrounded the streetcar, and a few warning shots got fired, and the scumbag coward fascists walked out with their hands up. One was shouting "Kamerad! Kamerad!" You have no earthly idea, Nora, how fuming angry we all were and I half expected somebody to shoot these Nazis on the spot, and the world might not have felt a better place but it certainly wouldn't have felt a worse place, either, for all of that. I wanted to shoot them myself. I admit that is who I was at that moment. I saw Robert Capa come up then and start snapping pictures while some of my battery were kicking the fascists along, swift kicks to their rears, and slamming rifle butts into their ribs, one fell and got back up, some hard blows across the face, too, hard blows with rifle butts across the face. They were led off into a building and what I heard later was, one fascist gave up the sniper, and the sniper was shot while trying to escape out back of the building, is how I heard it. What's true there is fact, and what's not true is hopeful fact. I felt nothing for the Nazi, I feel nothing for him as I write this. I feel everything for pfc Bowman and his family.

This evening we walked around Leipzig a short while, then set up makeshift tables in one of the apartments in the same building as the one where Bowman was killed, a nice apartment with nice things in it, and we set up there and ate rations. Some of our platoon were in other apartments too, eating rations. Capa came in to announce that Ernie Pyle, the famous war reporter, had been killed on Iejima, Okinawa, shot in the head by a Japanese machine gunner, and Capa was very shaken and pale over this, all his contagious bravado, all his spirit gone all of a sudden, leached out, and he just slumped in the corner.

A little while ago, too, we heard that Ernest Lisso, deputy mayor of Leipzig, committed suicide along with his wife and daughter. Sweeping through and clearing out buildings and houses, we found a lot of suicides. More than you can possibly imagine.

The things that have happened here, darling Nora, the things I've seen, the things I've written to you about, I've become them. But I know I've become them just for now. I know that when I get home to you I won't be them anymore. Maybe for a while but not for long. This is knowledge and conviction well thought out and I want so very much for you to understand this and believe it. I believe it and you will see for yourself once I get home to you. When might that be — on the calendar, I mean. (Because I never really left you, not in my heart.) Well, on the calendar — this is what I've been told — it might not be for three more months at the least, possibly as much as four or five more months, depending to what extent the war is actually over, in reality, not just the rumors. But believe me the war isn't over quite yet, my darling. I'm here in it. It isn't quite over.

Here's something I need to write to you. If somehow we could be at breakfast together a world away from this war, Nora, if only. I would quietly and calmly try to tell you what happened this afternoon here in Leipzig, a city much in ruins now. Here is what I would tell you in the calmest way possible. I was patrolling through the streets with two of my infantry mates — pfc Paul Langdon and medic Ken Kelly — and down a small street I saw a library. The roof had been blown away by artillery fire no doubt, and one wall was crumpled to pieces, and I could see right into the library. I told pfc Langdon and medic Kelly that I wanted to go take a look, and they said sure, let's go, and so we walked over to the library. They both stood outside having smokes and surveying the wreckage. "I don't read German — nothing in there for me," medic Kelly said, and pfc Langdon laughed, and I laughed too. But I made my way over the piles of brick and such and on into the library. As far as I could tell, it had three rooms — two small rooms and one large one. Shelves of books were exposed to the weather now, and many books were charred and almost unrecognizable as books, but there were also quite a few that seemed to have survived the onslaught of artillery and such. A long solid beautiful desk was right out in the open, and it somehow looked almost completely unscathed — there was even a book lying there on it. I picked my way into one of the smaller rooms. The outside wall of this room had a gaping jagged hole in it and the card catalogue was on its side, the drawers open and cards scattered every which way on the floor, and I had the strange impulse to get down on my hands and knees and return them to their drawers. Don't you think that's odd? Maybe just to put the world a little back in order. I don't know what.

The long strain is telling. I wish I hadn't written you about such ghastly things. But here is the rest of what happened. There lying against the wall behind the card catalogue was a woman. She was dead and had one arm completely blown off and other parts of her mangled, but she was wearing . . . I guess you might say a formal dress. It wasn't a housecoat or anything like that. No, it was a get-dressed-up-for-an-evening kind of dress, which was ripped to shreds. Dried blood was splotched on her face and forehead, her eyes were staring open (I reached down and closed them), and she had a blood-splattered book in the hand that was still intact. I sat there next to her. Pfc Langdon called and I called back, saying I was going to stay on there awhile, and he called back saying they were walking on, which was just fine with me. Pretty much I just sat there and might've even dozed off a minute or two, believe it or not, because that's how sleep comes in our circumstances. Then I reached down and looked at the book she was holding. I couldn't read the title but saw the name Rilke. That must be, I thought, the same writer you so love, Nora, my darling. I opened the book and saw it was a collection of poems. That has to be the same Rilke, right? And that is when our worlds were connected all of a sudden — libraries, that book, our hearts traveled such great distances. And because this war is definitely not over, my darling, there are going to be bad things to come yet, I can just feel it. I can just feel bad things yet to come. I don't know if you will even get this letter, but awkwardly put, if death befalls me, I am holding your hands in mine. You may eventually read this in your library, surrounded by such articulate writers of books, and here I'm just trying to use words. But I was today connected to you in a way most men God willing will never be connected to their beloveds, and I am, for all the pain and sorrow and mystery of it, so very grateful.

Love,
Your Bernie

This fourth and final letter was paper-clipped to a folded-up article from a May 1945 issue of *Life* titled "End of War — an Episode," and in smaller print, "Americans Still Died." This article included Robert Capa's photograph of two American soldiers at the machine gun on the balcony of the apartment building in Leipzig, their eyes redacted by solid squares of gray, and also Capa's triptych that showed the sequence of moments immediately after pfc Raymond Bowman was shot and killed; time is marked by the spreading pool of his blood. My mother had written in pencil: *One day before Bernard was shot and killed.*

Family Life

MRS. HAMELIN AND MRS. BREVITTMORE CAME FOR DINNER
on March 1. Martha had been back at work for two days. My mother
apologized for the food. "This is a simple meat loaf and mashed potatoes and salad," she said. "I'm a touch out of practice." But we all
thought it was a grand meal. Nora Elizabeth was in her crib in the
dining room and slept through much of dinner. Afterward, Mrs.
Hamelin presented her with a gift that almost made us fall apart
with surprise and gratitude. It was a specially printed promise to
send her, all expenses paid, to Paris for a month upon her graduation from high school. "I won't be around to see that wonderful day,
I'm quite sure," Mrs. Hamelin said. "But you can rest assured, Nora
Elizabeth is now mentioned in my last will and testament."

"Knowing Esther as we all do," Mrs. Brevittmore said, "you won't
be surprised it's more *will* than testament."

"I *have* lived a very willful life, haven't I?" Mrs. Hamelin said.

Nora Elizabeth woke up then, gurgled and cried a little, formed
a crooked smile, and waved her arms about. Martha nursed her
while the rest of us cleared the dishes, and I carried out the platter

of tiramisu that Mrs. Brevittmore had prepared. Martha propped Nora Elizabeth against a pillow and held her hand across her body to keep balance, and we all had the baby in view while we talked. But soon enough, Martha said, "She's nodded off, I'll be right back." Martha took our daughter into her bedroom, came back, and served herself a helping of dessert.

"I've brought my own gift," Mrs. Brevittmore said. She handed a wrapped package to Martha, who opened it excitedly. "A friend of mine took up knitting a year ago, which is the closest thing to me taking it up as I'll ever get." The gift was a hat, mittens with sleeve clips attached, and a pair of pajamas that looked like a tuxedo, which made everyone laugh. "I want one of these!" Martha said.

"I'm sure a commission can be arranged," Mrs. Brevittmore said.

"These are terrific, thank you so much — these are so thoughtful," Martha said.

"As you can see," Mrs. Brevittmore said, "they're for a couple months from now."

Mrs. Hamelin and Mrs. Brevittmore stayed until about 8:30. The moment they left the house, my mother said, "I need to speak with you both." We sat back down on the sofa. "I don't really want to change the mood," my mother said, "on such a lovely evening. But I'm not sure there's any perfect time. Simply put, I want you to know I'm really all right. I know you know I am. But I need to say it in my own way to you."

"Nora," Martha said. She sat next to my mother and held her hands.

My mother shook Martha's hands up and down quickly, but then folded her own hands on her lap, as if to begin a rehearsed, if not formal, speech. "It has not been easy for you both," my mother said. "I would have given anything to have been *available* all along. Through your courtship, I mean. And before that, of course, for you, Jacob. And it seems that my whole early life — I'm not proud of so many things I did as a young woman. Like the television courtroom dramas say, 'Let the record show, she was unfaithful to her husband while he was at war.'" She took a moment to regain her composure. "But here we all are. Here we all are together, and what is done is done. I cannot forgive myself for certain things, and won't. But if you forgive me, Jacob, then I can continue. I'm hardly a sentimentalist, as you know. I carved out a dignified life as a librarian, a life I lost and now will never have fully back. My years of experience apparently are still needed a few hours a week. But I don't feel that I'm charity at the library. I don't feel I'm seen that way in the least. I have some savings. You will tell me when it's time for me to find an apartment of my own. Or I will know when the time is right. But I cannot continue in the house without telling you what happened. What happened to me at the auction. At the Lord Nelson Hotel."

"Mother, I understand maybe more than you think I do," I said.

"Martha kept me apprised in the hospital, Jacob," my mother said. "The police files, everything. I knew your entire view of things had to be changing. I felt as this was occurring it was the reason you didn't come visit me. Because you weren't sure, given all the new information, whom exactly you would be visiting. I was afraid you now thought I was not the mother you thought you knew all your life. Which to some extent had to be true."

"To some extent," I said. "But that's no excuse for not visiting."

"To me it's a very good excuse. But let's leave it at that, shall we, for now?" my mother said. "As for the photograph, the photograph by Robert Capa. You both simply must have questions. The therapist assigned to me in the hospital had questions. And I'll try and tell you what my understanding of what happened to me is."

"This isn't necessary, Mother. We can move on."

"No, Jacob, I'm afraid that's not true. I think we can't move on, as you put it, unless I tell you what I need to tell you. As to the photograph, I mean. You see, in Bernard's last letter — and I saw it open on the kitchen table two evenings ago. In his last letter, as you know, he described the incident captured by Robert Capa in *Death on a Leipzig Balcony.* And I remember like it was yesterday seeing the very article in *Life.* It was delivered to the library, you see.

"And I looked at that magazine long hours. In fact, I took it from the library. Me, a librarian, I took it from the library and hid it away, and I kept finding new places in the house to hide it, because I thought that if I hid it in enough different places, eventually I'd forget where I'd put it. As if *Life* wasn't published in the hundreds of thousands, after all. But you see, that's what I attempted anyway. I was under that delusion. But I could always find it. And I'd stare at it, wondering what Bernie felt at that very moment. Because I'd had his letter, you see.

"And I won't reprise all the sessions with the doctors in the hospital. But if there was one thing that came from those sessions, something I firmly believe, it was that somewhere deep in my heart and mind, unlocatable places, perhaps, or I thought they were — like that issue of *Life* I kept trying to hide — what was always on my mind was that apartment balcony in Leipzig. And Bernard's last letter. The letter I received from the War Department. That Bernard was killed on April 20, 1945, the day after his letter was dated. And it was all there. There all along in my mind. All those years.

"So that when, God forbid — but He didn't forbid it, did He? — God forbid the cruel happenstance arrived one day. The cruel happenstance: notice of the auction. The list of works on auction. Just a ferry ride away.

"In my . . . my *state.* In my . . ." My mother broke down a little here, and sobbed out some words. "Robert Emil was my punishment." Then she sobbed heavily for quite a while. "And my punishment might have stopped Nora Elizabeth from even being born. If Robert Emil had somehow managed to get into the library. If somehow . . ."

"That is not true at all," Martha said, embracing Nora. But my mother gently pushed her away and said, "No, the truth is the truth. It *is* true."

My mother blew her nose in a tissue and continued. "That day in March 1977, it was so easy to slip from the hospital. I knew the routines so well. Oh, just another goddamn day of making Chinese finger traps. I'd cut out the notice of the auction and taped it on the back of the mirror in my room. And for days before the auction I could scarcely breathe. Still, it was so easy to slip away. I knew the hospital staff was always distracted during tea. I stole money from the tin box and walked free as a bird right out the food service door, just as you please. I made my way easily to the ferry. And once in Halifax I made my way easily to the Lord Nelson Hotel.

"I had my jar of ink from Arts and Crafts. But I wasn't quite prepared for seeing the actual photograph. Once I did see it, even from a distance, I was pulled forward by it. It felt like a rope was attached to my chest pulling me forward. There it was, the thing itself. What this says about my mind, I don't know. As I got closer and closer, it came alive, like a scene from a movie, I suppose. But not that, exactly. But I did *hear* it. I did hear the photograph. It had shouting voices and gunfire, and I was going deaf from it. And really that's the last thing I remember, except for our beautiful young interlocutrix in the stifling room, now my beautiful daughter-in-law who's given me a beautiful granddaughter. What C. S. Lewis—I read a little of him in the hospital. Just enough, I suppose, though hardly transfixed by his ideas, just enough. Somewhere or other he used the phrase "miracle trajectory," and I'm letting it apply to what's happened to me. And here I sit, unforgiven by myself but healthy of mind and a librarian again. I love you very much."

My mother sat for a cup of tea and then went to her bedroom. I heard her radio. But it wasn't tuned to *Detective Levy Detects,* as the radio next to Martha's and my bed was. It was more than halfway into the episode titled "The Apology." Martha and I took off our clothes, Martha all but a T-shirt, and got into bed and listened. There was a gunshot and then a body fell to the floor. A woman said, "I'm so sorry, baby." The narrator said, "It was the first time in the marriage of Maggie King and Orlando Wisteria that Maggie had apologized for anything. But then again, she had just murdered her husband."

That effectively ended the episode. Martha switched off the radio. "Not to worry, darling," she said. "I'll never be like that."

"Me neither," I said.

With those assurances shared, our love and humor intact, with our legs entwined and our bodies pressed together, we closed our eyes. Yet as Martha told me later — and she thought this occurred around 3 a.m. — my mother called out in great alarm in her sleep, "Do not go up to that balcony! Turn back! Do not go up there!" Three, four, five times, which finally woke the baby, who began to softly cry, at which point Martha woke me and we went to Nora Elizabeth's crib. Martha lifted her up, and by the time the three of us were under our bedclothes, Nora Elizabeth's crying had stopped. So had my mother's alarmed cries, but how could we know how the battle for Leipzig turned out in her dream?

And thus our normal family life continued.

Acknowledgments

Thanks go to Melanie, Tom, and Alexandra for reading drafts along the way.